Angel Blade

Carrie Merrill

SOUL FIRE
PRESS

an imprint of
Christopher Matthews Publishing

Boston, Massachusetts

Angel Blade

Editors: Jeremy Soldevilla, Stefanie Hotaling
Cover design: Neil Noah

ISBN 978-1938985-94-2
ebook ISBN 978-1-938985-96-6

Published by
Soul Fire Press

SOUL FIRE
PRESS
an imprint of
CHRISTOPHER MATTHEWS PUBLISHING

http://christopher matthewspub.com
Boston

Printed in the United States of America

To my mom and dad,
who said that everything I
ever wrote was amazing

Acknowledgments

This book would not be possible without the help of so many individuals.

First and foremost, my entire writing life would not be possible without my parents Lynn and Linda Merrill. Their completely biased opinion that my work is the best out there gave me encouragement to keep going and to finally get this book published. My brothers Cody, Morgan and Jordan and my sister Donna also provided much love and support throughout the years and they were great sounding boards for all my ideas.

The work of excellent editors makes everything better, so I want to thank Jeremy Soldevilla and StefanieHotaling. Also, special thanks for the excellent cover design by Neil Noah. The staff at Soul Fire Press has done such a wonderful job in realizing my dreams with this novel.

And my beta readers deserve special mention: Honey Newton (you are such a good friend and inspiration), Sunny Katseanes (BFF's since high school), Natalie Weeks Larson and Shanien Singley (buds since grade school), and Heather Burnham (best reader I've ever known).

PART I

"The two most important days in your life are the day you
are born and the day you find out why."
— Mark Twain

To Walter -
Fight your Demons!.
Carrie Murrie

CHAPTER 1

SHE WAS NO LONGER AFRAID OF DEATH.

There was a time when she wouldn't have thought that, but things had changed so much, and now, she was here.

She couldn't move; that made the pain so much worse. Only small, quick respirations would do for now since taking in a deeper breath caused a piercing pain through her ribs. Because the pain affected her ability to breathe, the nurse had affixed an oxygen mask to her face with a flimsy elastic band that wrapped around her neck. The air drifted across her nose and lips in a continuous breeze that dried every bit of moisture in her mouth.

And these were just the few minutes of consciousness she remembered today.

It was too difficult to keep her eyes open anymore; not with all the morphine running through her veins. Nikka let them drift closed, but she could still hear the low whispers in the room. It was her mother's voice speaking to another woman, probably the nurse, but it was too difficult to tell.

"The oxygen is there to keep her comfortable," the nurse spoke, barely loud enough to hear over the flow of the air. "But if she has another episode, we will have to talk seriously about your other options."

"Options?" It was her mother's voice. "You mean a ventilator?"

"I'm afraid so."

"But Dr. Taylor said that if she was put on a ventilator, then she may never get off of it," her mother said with a slight crack in her voice.

Silence. Nikka could envision the nurse nodding her head.

"I . . . I can't do this right now. I need to speak with my husband first. He'll be back soon. He just ran home to take a shower and he said he would be right back."

"Of course. I'll call Dr. Taylor," the nurse said.

Nikka forced her eyes open when she sensed her mother approaching the bedside and settle into a chair. Mom grasped her hand; the flesh of her palm so warm against her skin. Nikka turned her head and gazed at her over the oxygen mask. There were tears sparkling in her eyes, illuminated by the gray shaft of light that shone through the window.

The daylight seemed unnecessarily harsh, and it was times like these that she missed her eyelashes. Something as simple as eyelashes could make such a difference in light like this.

Her mother placed a hand on top of her head and forced a smile. Nikka could feel her skin against her smooth, bald scalp. Normally she would have a bandana or a stocking cap on her head to help maintain her body temperature, but the nurse had removed it when placing the oxygen mask on her. It must have been interfering with the elastic band, or she had forgotten to replace it.

It wasn't long ago that she would have taken these things for granted. Even a year before, she would never have thought she would be in this situation.

She was seventeen years old when she first got the diagnosis of leukemia. Everything had been going well up until that point. Senior year had just started and she was looking forward to the prom when one day she just didn't feel well. Two weeks later, what she and her parents thought was mono became much worse. A year of doctor visits, chemotherapy and radiation therapy turned into hair loss and plenty of vomiting. After several setbacks, the doctors recommended a bone marrow transplant, but even that didn't seem to work.

And now, a year later, she withered away, a mere 82 pounds of atrophic muscle and thin skin stretched over bones, trying her best to breathe and to stay conscious, and even that was becoming quite difficult.

All those chemotherapy sessions and the nausea that ensued, her mother would often cry to her father about how difficult this was for all of them. They didn't realize it, but she could hear them through the walls of her bedroom.

"Why did this have to happen?" her mother would say to him.

It doesn't matter why, Nikka remembered thinking. It happened. That's all. You can't go back and change it.

People always seemed to wonder about the why of everything. You will never really know why something happens to you. She now realized that, in the end, it is how you deal with it. Sure, everyone will have their struggles, fighting against the inevitable. Heaven knows that she was frustrated with the vomiting, the pain, and the fatigue. But the course was set all along. She understood that now.

Her eyelids grew too heavy to keep open any longer, and she let them drift closed once again. This time she would sleep; she knew it. The combination of the painkillers and the other injectable medications into her IV line were too powerful to fight against. No matter how much she fought to stay awake, there was no winning against the pharmaceuticals.

But there was the problem of the dreams that seemed to plague her sleep now. She didn't know if it was a side effect of the medication or progression of the cancer, but the images in her mind grew more terrifying each time she slept. Sometimes she saw fire that burned the flesh off her bones. At other times she found herself in a vast, cold, empty darkness where she could sense a thousand eyes staring at her as if they were waiting in anticipation. And with each dream, she was naked— not the kind of naked where you think you forgot to wear clothes to school. No. It was the kind where you are cold and helpless and shivering. And she still had no hair; not a single strand anywhere on her body. Naked and hairless, standing in the dark while something sinister watched from the shadows.

This time she could see a chilling fog that surrounded her in a gray blanket. The moisture adhered to her skin. Something moved in the dense cloud, slithering and creeping over the uneven ground. Every time she attempted to move, the fog would thicken, wrapping around her legs and arms to hold her in place.

The thing continued to circle her, its body scraping against rocks or twigs in the soil. A low growl rumbled through the fog. She could feel it in the center of her abdomen as it reverberated back into the haze.

A faint, orange-red glow began to show through the fog. Was the cloud thinning? She wasn't sure, but the hold it had on her seemed to slip. The glow became stronger, and she realized it was a pair of eyes gazing at her. The growl came again, and this time she could smell its rancid breath, like the decay of an animal on the roadside in the summer heat.

Then its voice rumbled toward her. "I will find you."

When she awoke, she felt her father's hands against her arms as he called her name.

"Nikka," he said, a hint of fear in his voice. "Honey, you're okay."

She had tried to scream in her dream , but now she realized that she had merely grunted and thrashed around on the bed. This was enough to startle her parents and the nursing staff to try to intervene.

The nurse lifted Nikka's eyelids and shone a bright light into her pupils. Then she checked the monitor.

Nikka opened her eyes again and saw the wave of relief pass over the nurse's face.

"It . . . was . . . just a dream," she spoke, but her tongue felt so dry.

The nurse nodded. "Well, your oxygen saturation is stabilizing for now. We need to keep an eye on that blood pressure. It's still a bit low."

Why was she telling her this? There was nothing she could do about it anyway. But then, Nikka realized the nurse really didn't know what else to say. *Honestly, what could anybody say in that moment that would make this any better? Wow, you about died there. Good thing you didn't. Well, keep trucking on.*

She caught a glimpse of her mother's face, still lit by the gray light in the window. There was deep worry etched into the lines above her eyes and around her mouth. And it was because of this look that she didn't tell her mother about the dreams.

"Hey, kiddo," her father said and planted a kiss on her forehead. He was the only one that didn't always treat her like she was about to break in two. "I picked up the next issue of *X-men* for you."

Graphic novels and comic books: her guilty pleasure. Even her closest friends didn't know that she was such a freak over these simple books. It was something that she had shared with her father ever since she could remember. When she was little and still couldn't read, she sat on his lap while he read through each panel of *The Amazing Spiderman* or *The Hulk*.

While her friends were all talking about which guy was cuter or where they wanted to go to college, she could only think of being a graphic novel artist. And she had been serious about it. Serious enough that she had been accepted into the Art Institute of Chicago. But then the cancer struck, and she was lying here instead of attending her first semester. Just another of so many things that she had to let go, and she always knew she would never get them back.

He withdrew the latest *X-men* issue from his bag and slipped off the clear sleeve. With his chair sidled up next to her bed, he opened the book and started to read. She could barely see the panels, but it didn't matter. Just hearing him speak in Dr. Xavier's voice was enough.

Wolverine had just come across the source of a powerful evil when another voice echoed from the doorway of her ICU room. Her father stopped reading, and she could hear him rise from his chair.

"Mr. Connors," the voice said. It was Dr. Taylor. He shook her dad's hand and turned to her mother. "Mrs. Connors. How are we doing today?"

We? He had nothing to do with them in that sense. The doctor was not involved in the *we* of this situation.

"Things are about the same," her mother spoke in almost a whisper.

"Blood pressure has been unstable," the nurse said, "but O2 sats in the 80's as long as we keep the face mask on her."

There was a moment of silence between the four of them as the doctor reviewed the graph of her vital signs. Nikka forced her eyes open again to see him escorting her parents out of the room and to the hallway, where she could still see them through the window. *Great. More adult talk that we can't let the child hear.* But they didn't know that she could hear some of the conversation from where they stood in the hall.

"Well, I think it is time to discuss some difficult options," Dr. Taylor started. "Her blood work is—well, frankly, it's not good. Her numbers keep decreasing. Her body is just shutting down."

Her mother took in a small breath. "But what about another round of chemo . . ."

"That would only suppress her numbers further. It could kill her outright."

Her shoulders slumped. "What else can we do?"

There was a pause that seemed to last longer than it should have. "Well, it's time to start thinking of comfort measures."

"Comfort measures?" her father's voice echoed into the room.

Ah, there it was. That phrase. Comfort measures. The two words that are at the end of every brochure and book you read about having cancer. The thing you talk about when there is nothing left to talk about. She figured it was coming, especially the way the nurse had been behaving over the last several days, always looking away when Nikka tried to speak to her.

"Yes. You need to decide soon how aggressive you would like to be with her care from this point on. If we place her on a ventilator again, she may never come off of it. We can supply her with morphine for the pain, but she's not able to eat much anymore. There is always the possibility of a feeding tube, but . . ."

"But, you're saying that we need to think about how long we want to prolong her suffering," her father whispered, but she could hear every word.

Dr. Taylor slowly nodded his head. "Morphine and oxygen can keep her comfortable throughout this stage. Have you looked into hospice care?"

"A little." Her mother's voice cracked.

"I can have someone come and discuss hospice with you in the morning. At least that way she can be in the comfort of her own home."

Her father nodded. "Thank you."

Dr. Taylor forced a smile and placed a hand on her mother's shoulder just before he walked away to the nursing station. Her parents didn't return immediately, though. Under heavy eyelids, she could see them in a quiet embrace in the hallway.

She wanted so much to say something to them right now, but there was nothing she could say that would make this any better. But the thought of it continued to rattle through her drug-addled brain: *It's okay. I'm not afraid to die anymore.*

CHAPTER 2

WITH A NEW COMBINATION of pain killers, Nikka managed to sleep through most of the night, although she remained plagued with dark dreams that continued to assault her. And because of the heavy drugs, she was unable to awaken to clear her head. When she opened her eyes, the room was lit from the window again, but the tak-tak of rain spattering against the glass signaled another storm outside. The sky must have been thick with dark clouds because she could read the arms of the clock, and at two o'clock in the afternoon, it should have been much brighter outside.

At some point during the last fourteen hours, the nurse must have removed the oxygen mask and replaced the nasal cannula. She felt the small prongs shooting wisps of moistened air into her nostrils. *That's a good thing*, she thought. Her oxygen saturation must be much better today if they took off that godforsaken mask that smelled like plastic.

Nikka glanced to the chair across the room and saw her mother, her head resting back against the wall and her arms wrapped in the shawl she had made at Christmas. The woman had never looked older, and it was all Nikka's fault. This horrible disease not only ravaged her, but it took its toll on her parents as well. With no other children, she knew that they were going to lose their family soon.

This time of day usually meant that her father was working. It was no secret that leaving the hospital every day to go to a cold building downtown, not knowing if his daughter would be alive when he returned, was torture to him.

"Good afternoon, Nikka," the nurse, Caroline, said as she walked through the door and approached the bank of monitors and IV hooks at her bedside. Today, she wore her blue scrubs with cute little ducks printed across the top. Every day the print was something new and adorable so the other kids on the floor could see that she was on their side too.

Nikka forced a smile, but it felt like her dry lips were ready to crack.

"Looks like you slept better," the nurse said and she withdrew her syringe and injected a clear fluid into the IV port. *Probably another dose of the pain killer.* They always seemed to keep up on it, and she was grateful, even if it did give her bizarre dreams.

She could feel the dryness of her throat, but she forced words out anyway. "Did they meet with hospice today?"

The nurse lost her fake smile and for a moment she glanced away. Nikka understood this. She got this a lot when they had to talk about difficult subjects.

"Yes, this morning," the nurse said, her voice dropping in volume as if she didn't want anyone to know she was talking to a terminal patient about her final plans.

"Did they take it okay?" Nikka asked, shooting a glance to her sleeping mother.

"As well as expected."

That meant her mom cried and her dad hugged her as he tried not to cry but he did anyway. That's just how it went these days.

"Can I get you anything? Feel like eating?" Caroline said in a quick change of subject.

"Maybe bring the head up," Nikka said, pointing to the head of the bed. "And some water. I've got some fierce dragon breath here."

The nurse let out a little laugh, but Nikka could see the woman's eyes glistening. She raised the head of the bed up enough for Nikka to see the television above her bed. The nurse excused herself as Nikka searched her fingers along the bed to find the TV control attached to the side of the mattress.

She was not going to die watching chatty women's talk shows or soap operas in the middle of the day. Some good old science fiction channels or a zombie movie would do just fine. Her cold fingers found the channel dial and she flicked through until she found some series talking about ancient aliens and postulating that there was historical evidence of an early alien invasion. *Whatever. Good enough.*

The show droned on, more in the background than anything else. She didn't really care about historical evidence of alien technology in the Mayan culture, but it was something besides the ICU, the nurses, her tragic mother sleeping in the chair across the room. It would not be long before she would feel the need to sleep again, but she forced her eyes to stay open this time. No more nightmares. There were too many of them last night.

Nikka sipped at the water the nurse had brought her, but it just hurt her stomach to swallow too much of it at once. At least it wet her mouth and tongue, and that was all she really wanted anyway.

Midway through the third episode, this time about aliens among the ancient Egyptians, something changed in the air. She didn't know how she knew it, but the room felt charged, electric. It made bumps rise against the surface of her skin and sent a clatter of shivers down her spine. Rumbling thunder rolled through the hospital, rattling at the windows as the rain pounded against the glass. Even her mother must have felt it because she awoke with a start and sat up straight in the chair.

Nikka turned her gaze from the TV to the door and saw a figure standing at the threshold. She couldn't see him well, but from his silhouette, she could tell he was probably another doctor. White coat. Periwinkle blue scrubs. The usual. Only, she had never seen him before this moment.

Her mother rose to her feet to greet him. The doctor stepped into the room and Nikka could see his face. As her mother shook his hand, Nikka saw his mocha skin, the hair on his head cropped very close to his scalp like a Marine or something, and he was built like a Marine, too. Probably six foot four, she could imagine him in desert camo fatigues. He was cute, and she remarked to herself that thoughts like that came to her rarely around here. Even his thin wire-rimmed glasses added a touch of class to that handsome face.

"Hello, Mrs. Connor," he spoke, his voice smoother and softer than Nikka would have expected. "I'm Dr. Smith. I was sent to consult on your daughter."

Her mother shook his hand and tried to smile, but her face just looked tired and worn. "Well, I guess I wasn't expecting anybody else to see her. We spoke with hospice this morning and they're arranging a transfer to home. Dr. Taylor said there was nothing left to do."

The handsome doctor glanced at Nikka. She saw his hazel eyes and was startled at how remarkable they were against his mocha skin. He flashed her a genuine smile, which was rare these days. Everyone always faked it, but deep inside she knew that they only did that to make themselves feel better about thinking she was going to die soon.

"I came as a treatment consultant. I spoke with Dr. Taylor last night and provided him with some new information that has recently been released. This is a breakthrough therapy with remarkable success."

She could see that her mother didn't know what to say. The doctor stepped up to Nikka's bedside, close enough that she could smell his delicious cologne. Usually, fragrances tended to make her nauseated and trigger the vomiting, but this was calming and settled her nerves, hints of sandalwood and lavender. He looked far too young to be a doctor, like he was barely a few years older than she was. Those eyes looked down on her, and she felt very exposed. For the first time since this all started, she felt that she looked like a hairless cat, with hideous bulging eyes and wrinkled pink skin. All but the horrible, whining meow.

But he didn't seem repulsed by her. He placed a warm hand on her shoulder and she felt the heat course into her chest. "I have no doubt that this medicine will cure your daughter."

The shawl fell from her mother's shoulders and crumpled in a heap to the ground, but she didn't seem to notice or care. "What are you saying? You can save her?"

"Absolutely."

The woman searched for the words to understand, but she only stammered.

"I understand that this may come as a bit of a shock," Dr. Smith said. "But it is nevertheless true." The way he spoke had a cadence she wasn't familiar with, like his native language wasn't English, but that it was so long gone only a hint of hit remained.

He knelt down by Nikka's bedside in order to look directly into her eyes. "This is a one-time treatment, not chemotherapy. It will stop the pain. It will give you unlimited strength and life without fatigue."

"Wait a second," her mother interrupted, rubbing her thin fingers against her temple. "Why haven't we heard about this before now?"

Those beautiful eyes turned up to her. "Because I just arrived. Now," he said as he stood again. "I can administer the treatment today; right now, in fact. We must act quickly."

Her mother clasped her hands and held them to her mouth as she looked down at her sick daughter, clinging at the edge of death. This would be a hard decision, and Nikka knew it. They had so many promises of effective treatments during the last year, and it only resulted in pain, nausea, and hair loss. Another setback would be devastating, but what did she have to lose? She only had a matter of days and Nikka was well aware of it. She felt herself slipping every day and the nightmares were getting worse. Somewhere in the back of her mind she knew those dreams were harbingers, death's little servants come to warn her that her final breath was near.

"I don't know what to do," her mother finally spoke, tears welling in her eyes. "My husband will be back at six—""

"There is not time to wait," he said and placed a hand on Nikka's head just like her father would sometimes do. He leaned down toward her, close enough she could feel his breath on her ear. "What are your wishes?"

As she looked into his kind eyes and felt the warmth of his skin against hers, she had all the faith in the world that he was telling the truth. Somehow, he had come to them and it would be a miracle. At least that's what she had to believe.

Nikka took in a breath. "Yes."

Her mother grasped her hand and squeezed. This always made her hands feel so bony, but she grasped her hand as well.

"We must go immediately," he said and worked at getting her IV's redistributed to the hooks on the bed. He disconnected the oxygen tubing and the remaining cardiac monitors.

"Can I be there with her?" her mother asked.

"I am afraid not, Mrs. Connor. This is very sensitive , but she will be back in no time at all."

He seemed to be rushing to get the bed unlocked and rolling out the door. Nikka released her mother's hand as the woman placed a quick kiss on her forehead. Then she was out of the room that had been a prison for weeks. Harsh fluorescent lights zoomed overhead as Dr. Smith pushed the bed. Nikka closed her eyes against the light, feeling the turns and bumps of the bed as he moved it through the halls of the intensive care unit. Two pounding bumps shook the bed, triggering her nausea, but she swallowed and opened her eyes again.

They were now in an elevator as the doors hissed to a close. The car moved down, and the motion threatened to make her sick again. The lack of the oxygen in her nose now became brutally apparent as she felt the weakness take over every wasting muscle in her body.

In that brief moment, he grasped her hand. She looked up to his face that was framed in the overhead lights of the elevator. "We are almost there."

The elevator finally slowed to a halt and the doors slid open. In an almost frantic pace, he pushed the bed into another hallway, the bumps at the threshold jolting the gurney again. The lights here were different than the rest of the hospital, darker and less sterile. The walls were coated in a plain gray, not the crisp white of the ICU. It smelled damp here, like the mouth of a cave.

And there was another smell mixed with the scent of mildew, an odor she remembered from anatomy lab in Biology class. Preservatives. Formaldehyde.

The cart careened around a corner and slid through a pair of double steel doors. The air grew much colder as the gurney came to a sudden halt. Dr. Smith stepped around the bed, locked it in place and hurried around to the far side of the room. For the brief seconds that he was gone, Nikka raised her head the best that she could and saw the series of steel cabinets set about the room as well as a steel table in the center – a steel table affixed with a drain in the lowest point of gravity.

He had taken her to the morgue.

A cold sweat beaded up on her forehead as she struggled to push herself up. The doctor turned back to her and rushed up to her bedside. Her weak hands grasped at the side rails, trying to lift her body over the edge. She wasn't sure what she was going to do if she succeeded in getting over the rail. Her legs would never hold her up and it would be useless to try to crawl away from him.

"You lied to me. Take me back," she said, her voice shaking and her brain starving for oxygen.

"I cannot do that," he said, his voice still gentle. His warm hands rested on her shoulder and the weight made her collapse back against the gurney.

"Nikkola, I am your last chance at life. I never told you or your mother a lie. I can truly save you."

The panic alarms in her brain would not stop, though. Her bony hands grasped at his wrists, but she had no strength to fight him off.

He withdrew a syringe from his lab coat and this made her stop struggling for a moment. The liquid swirled and seemed to change colors within the vial. It emanated a faint light like a glow stick.

"I can give this to you, but only if you swear a promise," he said, the timbre of his voice now taking a desperate edge. "With this, I promise you strength, power, and life. It does not come free, though. You will owe allegiance to humankind. You must vow to protect them, no matter what you may lose. Do you swear this?"

The fierce nature of his voice and his gaze stilled her. Her fingers still clasped tight to his wrist. The liquid in the syringe swirled and cast its light against her pale skin.

"And what if I choose not to?" she spoke.

"Without this, I promise that death will come to you by 10:37 tonight. That is when your heart will take its last beat, and you will be lost to the world forever."

This doctor didn't even know her, and yet she could see the sadness in his eyes as he said this. It was the first time she could feel the tremble in his grasp. He really did want to save her, but what was this talk about protecting humankind? Was this some sort of "pay-it-forward" thing? She could do that. She could do anything if she was no longer sick. Whatever it took, she could raise money for leukemia research, be there for kids like her when they got sick and could no longer tolerate the chemotherapy.

The grip on his wrist relaxed as she nodded her head. "Okay—I swear."

His face relaxed. The doctor backed away from her to find the IV port. He connected the unusual syringe and injected the liquid into the IV line. The swirling blue-purple fluid coursed through the line until it finally entered the vein.

Dr. Smith's eyes turned to hers, but the sadness continued to dwell in his gaze. A wave of extreme relaxation spread through her muscles like a warm blanket. He placed a hand against her cheek.

"God speed, warrior. I will see you on the other side," he said just as a wave of light enveloped her. Her eyes closed as her body rose from the surface of the gurney and into the warmth of the glow.

CHAPTER 3

THE WHITE LIGHT FELT WARM, even welcoming, at first, but that soon changed for the worse. The glow surrounded her, just like the fog in her dream. It lifted her from the bed and almost blinded her, but she could see enough to know that she was no longer in the morgue. There was somebody else there, and it wasn't Dr. Smith. Whoever stood beside her now did not have his kindness.

Many hands grabbed her from all directions, holding her arms and legs. They thrust her down against a hard surface, pinning her until she could barely move. There was no peace in this light; only what seemed to be cruelty.

Then the pain came like a white-hot brand. This was the first moment she realized that she lay naked against the hard surface as something seared into the skin of her legs, inching its way up her legs and across her abdomen. She had never experienced anything as terrible and twisted as the pain that now bled under her skin and worked up to her shoulders.

Then the hands held her with a vice grip and flipped her over into a supine position on the cold surface. The pain started again, threading like spiders across her flesh from her legs up to her buttocks and over both flanks. There was no holding back anymore. She felt the tears fall down her cheeks as she screamed in agony. That only made the pain worse, but she couldn't stop the screaming. It was the loudest sound that had come from her throat in months, and it was all she could do to stay awake through the torture.

Death could not come soon enough. The chemotherapy and radiation and nausea that had plagued the past year of her life were nothing compared to the torture she now experienced. Her hands clutched into fists as she tried to struggle against the hands that held her, tried to escape the fire against every inch of her skin. The muscles in her arms twitched, but she couldn't fight anymore; the only thing left was to cry and scream with every second of the pain.

Then a stabbing shot through her chest, taking her breath away in a fraction of a second. The scream choked silent in her throat. She squeezed her eyes closed as her lungs filled with smoke and fire, threatening now to scorch her from the inside out. The fire spread into her heart, gripping it with a fist of death. Her lungs fought for her last breath.

Her ribs rebelled against the pain, expanding in a quick gasp. The cold air filled her chest. In that instant, the pain subsided, her lungs cleared of the fire and smoke. Her body twitched and trembled, waiting for another round of the torture that seemed to go on for hours, but there was nothing.

Hot tears streamed from her eyes, trickling down her temples, as she cried. There was nothing she could do to control it. Her quaking hands moved to her mouth to cover the sobs that escaped her lips.

Before she could open her eyes, she knew the light had disappeared. The room had grown cold, and she could feel the sweat that covered her skin now chilling in the still room where she lay on a cement floor. She let her eyelids open with caution, her hands still at her mouth.

The room was definitely dim, lit only by a single bulb in a socket somewhere in the corner. It looked like some sort of utility room, with pipes and electrical conduits running along the ceiling. A coating of moisture had condensed along the walls, leaving a scale of calcium like starter bumps of stalactites. Even the mineral film had affected the light bulb, causing the light to look jaundiced.

Nikka pulled her hands away from her face and caught sight of them in the dim yellow light. Black marks streaked from her wrists and up her arms, like tribal tattoos etched into her skin. The marks stretched over both her arms and up her shoulders. But beyond the unusual marks, there was something else and unbelievably more striking. The bony appearance of her hands had morphed into full-fleshed fingers, without the ghastly protrusions of tendon and bone so typical of a starving and dying person.

Her muscles still twitched occasionally with the memory of the searing pain, but she forced herself upright. The action was something that she had not been able to do in months, but moving to her feet felt liberating. The chill of the room crept into her joints, and she clutched her hands to her chest—her bare chest. She realized that she was completely naked.

As she looked down her bare torso, she saw more of the black tattoos stretching across her lower abdomen and down her legs. They were nearly everywhere except her chest. Her hands moved to her thighs, to the markings that curved across her skin. Under her touch, she felt the full and healthy muscle below the flesh. She turned toward the light to better see herself.

Despite the dim light, she could see the soft but strong curves of muscles that shifted and moved with her, from her arms, down her torso, and her legs. Even before the cancer, she never remembered having a six-pack, but there it was. She gripped her hands into fists, feeling the strength in her arms.

Whatever was in that light did exactly what Dr. Smith had promised: it gave her strength, and power.

What else did it do?

Her fingers reached up her cheeks, and she felt the eyelashes across her lids as well as the brush of eyebrows. A small smile played across her lips. I have eyelashes again.

Excited, she moved her fingers up her temples and to her scalp, but found that it was still smooth and bare. Whatever this "treatment" was still had not given her hair back. Perhaps it would take more time. All this was more than she could have hoped for so far.

As she stood in the light, a glint from a dark corner of the room caught her eye. Her bare feet stepped toward the shadows with caution, the cement making her feet grow colder with each step. She approached the object that rested on the ground.

Even in the dim light she could see a long blade catching the light of the bulb. The blade extended down to a hilt that still remained shrouded in shadows. Her brow furrowed as she examined the strange artifact, lying here for no apparent purpose. It appeared to resemble the blades of old Japan, a katana, if she could remember correctly. It looked like something she had seen in a Bruce Lee movie once. She could only assume that for some reason it was left here for her.

She crouched down and grasped the hilt of the sword. As though it had a life of its own, the object began to vibrate and hum ever so slightly once she held it. A flash of blue light, like a propane fire, erupted down the length of the blade. Her fingers quivered, and she dropped it to the ground with a loud clang. The light dissipated as did the faint hum, but her fingers still vibrated like aftershocks from an earthquake.

This was no ordinary katana; that was clear. But what had just happened? Looking at it now, lying half in shadow, it seemed simple and harmless. The vibration ebbed into her arm, and she longed to feel it again, the curve of the hilt in her palm and the hum singing in tune with her soul.

Nikka grasped the hilt again, feeling the subtle vibration move into her fingers. The blue flame enveloped the long blade, casting the room in a ghostly blue light. Everything about this sword screamed that it was hers; it was meant to be in her possession all along, but for what purpose she didn't know.

After a minute of examining the blade, she remembered that she was standing naked in a strange place, and that any moment somebody could happen upon her in this condition with a glowing sword in her hand. She turned away from the light and saw a single door at the opposite end of the room. With quiet and cautious steps, she padded to the door and opened it slightly, revealing a hallway lit with fluorescent lamps every few feet. The lamp light made her squint, bringing brief flashes of the light and the pain that she had just endured. Once her eyes adjusted, she glanced down the corridor, keeping herself concealed behind the door.

The hall looked to be part of a building engineering floor. The smell of laundry detergent and the humidity in the air suggested that somewhere nearby she may find some clothes. There were no people within sight of the hall, but she would wait a few minutes. She would just die if somebody saw her running naked down the hallway.

When she assumed the way was clear she tucked the sword close to her body and stepped into the corridor. Her feet stepped along the cold cement as she approached the edge of the laundry facility entryway. She could see several large machines lined in rows along the walls, the driers tumbling away with loud bangs. Five women and two men worked between the washers on pressing machines, filling them with white sheets that fed into the rollers and spit out perfectly flat linens.

She spied a cart of clothing, stacked in order of colors, resting at an angle between the doors and the pressing machines. Scrubs. She must still be in the hospital. With the noise of the washers and dryers, she knew that nobody would hear her open the doors. She crept into the room, sidled up to the cart and snagged a scrub top and bottom. They could have been extra large or extra small; she didn't know and didn't care.

Nikka held the scrubs against her torso, hiding the sword behind them and tiptoed down the hall to an area indicated as a locker room. She slipped inside and felt so much more comfortable to be out of the corridor.

The scrubs were just a little big, but they would suffice for now. It must be her lucky day, too, because she found an assortment of shoes lined up against the lockers. She slipped on a pair that fit, satisfied to have something between her feet and the cold cement. With the clothes covering her skin and something to warm her feet, she needed to warm her hands that still trembled with the memory of the last several minutes.

She stepped into the bathroom where she found a sink and turned on the hot water. As she allowed it to warm up, her eyes glanced up to the mirror before her. This stopped her for a moment. It had been so long since she looked into a mirror. When her hair started to fall out from the chemotherapy, she stopped using mirrors altogether. It was too painful and sad to see herself falling apart like that. Now, she froze as she met her own gaze. She saw the bare scalp, something that she had never wanted to see before. But in the harsh light of the bathroom, she could see more of the tattoos etched over the skin of her scalp and tracing down the back of her neck and onto her shoulders.

Steam rose from the sink, but she couldn't look away from her blue eyes, now against flesh that no longer sunk into her skull. Pink lips traced a faint line over her teeth, now devoid of the cracks and chapping that came with the dry oxygen pumped through a face mask. The steam eventually condensed against the mirror, and she couldn't see her reflection any longer. This jolted her back to her situation, and she clutched her hands into fists, resting them against the sink.

Get a grip, she chided herself.

She ran her hands under the water. Even as hot as it was, she felt no pain from it as it thawed the chill in her fingers. The trembling eased with the heat of the water. She splashed some onto her face, the warmth smoothing over her eyelids and nose.

It was time to take control of her situation, which could be so much easier now that she had clothes and shoes. If she was still in the hospital, then she would find her way back up to the ICU, locate her parents and tell them what happened. Yes, they would be shocked, and a little dismayed to see their only child covered in tattoos, but that could be overlooked given that she no longer seemed to be suffering from cancer. *Hey, we can all look on the bright side, right?* She could just march up there, get some real clothes, return the scrubs to the hospital, and return the shoes that she was about to steal with a "sorry" note attached.

Nikka stood straighter now that she had a solid plan and she marched out of the bathroom. Then she saw the sword resting on the bench where she left it. Now, how to explain that would be much harder. Well, she would approach that subject when it became necessary.

Along the wall she found a dark gray hoodie and slipped it on, covering her head with the hood. At least that would cover the tattoos on her scalp so her mother wouldn't freak out from the start. Then she found a long overcoat hung on a collection of coat hangers. She slipped it on and concealed the sword neatly against her body.

Hoping that she didn't look like a female Unabomber, she took in a deep breath and smiled to herself. That didn't hurt, for the first time in months. She let it out and stepped from the locker room with hopes that she could find her way out of the basement and into the ICU.

CHAPTER 4

THREE PEOPLE WERE getting into the elevator when she approached the lobby. It would have been nice to be in there alone, but that would have been difficult being in the city's largest hospital. And it would look suspicious if she lingered outside the elevator bank waiting for an empty car.

She tucked the hood over her forehead and stepped inside, shifting her way to the back of the car so as not to be too noticeable. Once she was tucked into the back corner, her hand pressed against the outside of her coat and felt the firm blade against her thigh. She let out a careful breath and waited for the ride up to the seventh floor.

Thankfully, nobody seemed to notice her or act like she was out of place. *Good.* It was embarrassing enough having to steal clothes and shoes to get around. Getting caught with a dangerous sword that glowed with blue fire would just be the last straw.

She was the last one on the elevator when it opened onto the seventh floor: the cancer ward and cancer ICU. The smell hit her as soon as she stepped out of the car. It was the same odor of antiseptics and alcohol that she had lived with for so long. She gave a single glance to the nursing station and saw her regular nurse, but her back was turned as she charted on a patient. Nikka slipped past the desk and made her way down the hall to room 752, the place where she had lived and where her mother now waited.

An orderly moved past her, but paid her no attention as he pushed his cart of unfinished meals. Moving down the hallway, she glanced out the windows of the individual rooms. The sky was black outside, and rain still pelted the windows. How much time had she lost from the time she entered the morgue until now? It had seemed like an hour tops, but it was pitch black outside. She must have been out longer than she thought.

The room loomed closer, and she reached for the doorknob. With nervous fingers, she opened the door, ready to reveal everything to her parents. They must be sick with worry, given the late hour. Hopefully someone sent word to them that she was okay.

The door opened and she crossed the threshold, but stopped as soon as she saw the bed in the center of the room. A little boy, no older than eight, lay still in the bed, his mouth attached to a ventilator that pumped and hissed with each breath that it delivered. The woman at his side glanced up at her from where she sat at his side, her eyes red and puffy with days of crying. She recognized that look: the appearance of lost hope.

"Can I help you?" the woman muttered.

Nikka stood there, confused and silent for a moment. "I'm sorry. I must have the wrong room."

The woman sniffed and wiped her nose with the tissue wadded into her palm. "That's okay, honey."

She backed out of the room and slid the door closed as quietly as she could. Something must be wrong. She checked the door number again. There was no way she would have forgotten which room she had been in for so long. Why would they have switched her out of her room when she went down with Dr. Smith?

Great, she thought. She was going to have to talk to somebody at the desk in order to find her parents. This promised to be embarrassing, but the circumstance left her with no choice. The nurse would know where they were moved.

She approached the nursing station and stepped around to where her nurse worked on her charts, but she was no longer wearing her blue scrubs with little yellow ducks. Now, it was pink with white cats.

"Hey, Caroline," Nikka whispered, hoping not to draw too much attention from the other nurses and floor secretaries at the desk.

The nurse looked up from her chart. "Can I help you with something?"

"I'm looking for my parents. Somebody moved my room since I went downstairs."

"Are they patients here? If so, they would be in the adults ward which is down the left hall" she said.

Confused, Nikka furrowed her brow and shook her head. "Caroline, it's me. I went down for treatment and I just came back to find someone else in my room."

The nurse slid her chair to the computer at her right and began typing. "What room did you say you were in?"

"Hey, it's me, Nikkola Connors. Room 752."

Caroline typed in the name. She seemed to be studying several pages as she clicked through the screens. "Hmmm. Nothing's coming up. Are you sure you were on this floor? Were you registered under a different name?"

"No," she said and shook her head. The trembling started again and she felt her stomach begin to flutter as though she was on a roller coaster. "Caroline, you took care of me for months. I know I look a little different, but come on . . ."

"I'm sorry," the nurse said with a fake smile. "I look after so many people. But I just don't see your name in the patient registry."

"I was just in my room a few hours ago," she said, trying to keep the volume of her voice to a minimum but it was getting harder with the passing seconds. "Dr. Smith took me down—"

"Honey, there is no Dr. Smith on staff. You must be mistaken."

Nikka's jaw almost dropped. This can't be happening. "No, I talked to him. He gave me a treatment down in the morgue, and then I woke up by the laundry room."

Caroline's jaw now set hard as she reached for the phone at her desk. "Ma'am, just excuse me one moment." She held up a finger in an attempt to silence her as she put the phone to her ear. Even though she turned away from Nikka, she could still hear some of the conversation. ". . . there is a woman up here claiming to be a patient, but she is just going on about some really crazy stuff. I think we need security right now."

The nurse continued her conversation in hushed tones, but Nikka backed away from the desk. Some of the other nurses now looked at her after hearing some of their discourse. Her heart pounded against her ribs as she slipped into the elevator, this time all alone.

This can't be happening; this can't be happening, she repeated as she pressed herself into the corner of the car. How did she wake up into this bizarro world? Was this another one of her fevered dreams fueled by morphine?

The elevator opened and she stepped out into the main lobby, the sword pressed against her thigh. To drop it here in front of so many people would be disastrous, especially since she was now fleeing from hospital security. She slipped through the rotating door and out into the cool night air, moist with falling rain.

Thankful for the layers of the coat and the hoodie, she tucked her head down and walked along the sidewalk to the busy street. Enough people walked along the sidewalks that she could easily get lost in this crowd and no security officers would know any better. The cold rain soaked her hands and she tucked them into the pockets of the overcoat. Cars, taxis and delivery trucks moved along the road, the traffic congestion much better this time of night. She crossed the street at the next intersection and sought the relief of an awning overlooking a bakery, its windows darkened and door locked. At least this place gave a brief respite from the cold rain.

Where would she go from here? She had no cell phone and no change for a pay phone. She had no money to pay a taxi to take her home, but perhaps she could hail the cab and take it anyway. Her father would pay the cab driver without question as soon as she arrived home. It was the only logical solution to this predicament, however strange it was. No matter what, she had to get away from the city and out of the rain. It wouldn't do her any good to be cured of leukemia and a few hours later die from the cold.

She worked at hailing a cab, and it didn't take too long for one to pull up next to her, the tires sending shoots of water rushing out onto the sidewalk. The driver rolled down the passenger window and leaned over to speak to her.

"Where to?" he asked.

She felt a tickle across her skin moving over her arms and legs. Those tattoos were really starting to itch and she scratched at her arms as she looked over the taxi.

Nikka crouched down, ready to relay the address in the northern suburbs, at least a good 30 minute drive. But something wasn't right. At first she saw a middle-aged man, his mustache peppered with gray and his hair cut a little too short for his round face. Perhaps it was a trick of the light and the rain, but his face changed right in front of her. His skin melted off his bones, leaving only a layer of black, decaying skin. The eyes morphed into black slits surrounded in yellow. A foul odor seeped from the car and into the night, an odor too familiar to her. It was the stench that she remembered from her dreams, when the beast in the fog opened its mouth and spoke to her.

She couldn't speak and staggered backward, falling into the puddles of the sidewalk.

"Lady, what the hell's wrong with you?" the cab driver called out to her.

The stench emanated from the vehicle even stronger, as though the car was filled with the bodies of slaughtered animals. She struggled to her feet and ran as fast as she could down the street, glancing back once to see the cab drive off into the street and through the stop light. Nikka darted into a side street, then she curved around a silent and closed restaurant. The air moved in and out of her lungs rapidly, and she leaned over, trying to slow her pounding pulse and catch her breath.

What the hell was that? The image of its black flaky skin sickened her and she retched, but her stomach was so empty that it was only saliva.

She's going crazy. That was the only explanation. Whatever Dr. Smith gave her turned her insane.

Her hands quaked as she squatted back against the wall to gather her wits. The sword protruded through the front of the coat and she tucked it back into the folds once again. She rested her head in her hands, trying to come up with a better plan. If indeed she was losing her mind, she needed to find help before she was too far gone and died right here in the street.

The rumbling of a car exhaust caught her attention. Before she looked up she could tell the car was slowing down. Oh, please, don't let it be the cab. She lifted her head from her hands to see an 80's era sedan slowing down at the curb, its windshield wipers going at full speed. She couldn't see the driver well ,but she could tell he was looking at her.

No more of this, she thought and stood up. Hoping to slip away into the dark of the street, she turned and walked away from the main street, her hands tucked into her pockets. The rumble of the engine revved again and the car drove away, leaving her in the dark street alone. She let out a sigh of relief and continued onward, to where she was not sure yet, but she decided she would just keep walking. At least that way she could try to stay warm.

She saw an open park at the end of the dark street. Her mother always warned her it was best to stay away from those places at night. You never knew what was hiding out there. Plenty of people get robbed and raped in secluded places like that. Another street intersected her street just before her. She could just follow that until she found someone who could help her.

As she approached the cross street, the sound of the rumbling engine erupted out of the dark. The same sedan turned the corner and pointed its headlights right at her. Her heart raced: what if it was another one of those things, like the monster driving the cab? She couldn't face it again and she did the only thing she could: she ran toward the park. The car could not follow her there, and she would hopefully lose it.

Nikka bolted for the park fence and climbed over it without effort. She could hear the roar of the engine behind her as it followed her, taking the road around the edge of the park.

The rain pounded into sloshing puddles in the grass, soaking through her tennis shoes as she ran and darted into a thicket of trees. The branches scraped at her coat, whipping against her face as she moved. But she didn't care. It was better than facing whatever was following her.

She emerged into a clearing that opened up to a small hill. The grass left her footing slippery as she scrambled up the hill and onto a gravel road. But as she clambered to her feet again, the headlights swung from around the hill and the car came barreling toward her. It stopped with a screech of tires on gravel, blocking her forward escape.

Whoever this was would not take her that easily. She turned back down the hill and let herself slide down the wet grass. She heard the car door open quickly behind her, but this only made her run harder when she came off the slope. Footsteps pounded behind her, barely audible over the rain. Another bank of shrubbery emerged in front of her. She moved to plunge into them when a heavy weight landed on her back, dragging her to the wet ground.

The assailant held her down as the rain drenched her face. She cried out as he turned her on her back, ready to fight him against anything he might try to do. The man grasped at her flailing hands, his head and torso covered with a black hoodie that shadowed his face. No matter how hard she tried, though, he grasped her wrists and pinned her to the soggy grass.

The only thing left to do was scream, even though she knew that nobody would hear her at this hour and in the shadows of the park.

She filled her lungs, when his voice came to her from under his hoodie.

"Nikka," he said. "It is okay, Nikka."

This stopped her for a second as she stared at him. He released her hands and moved his weight off of her. She crawled away from him, at least far enough so that he could not grab her again and watched as he pulled his hoodie from his head, revealing his mocha skin and short-cropped hair.

"Dr. Smith?" she gasped. "What the hell—"

"Actually, it is Gideon. I am no doctor. Just Gideon," he said as he rose. He offered his hand to help her off the ground.

CHAPTER 5

IKKA'S HAND FUMBLED in the coat and felt the hilt of the sword. The moment her hand touched the sword, the blue glow enveloped the blade and lit the small space between them. She pointed the tip of the katana at him, even though the sword trembled with the quaking in her hands.

He took a single step back, but kept his hand out to her. "It will be okay. I can help you."

She set her jaw tight and wiped the rain from her eyes while keeping the sword pointed at him. "Like hell it will—"

"I am not going to hurt you," he said with the same smile he gave her in the ICU.

"Too late," she said, flashing him a bit of the tattoo that snaked from her wrist and disappeared under the sleeve of her coat.

Gideon crouched down and removed the rain-speckled glasses, slipping them into the pocket of his hoodie. "I am sorry about that, but it was necessary for the transformation."

"What are talking about? What's going on?"

"Come with me. I need to get you to safety. Once we are there, I swear that I will explain everything. Out here we are too exposed."

The sword continued to tremble even though she tried to keep it steady. He reached his hand out to her again, his unusual eyes seeming to glow in the blue light.

"You are the one with the weapon," he said. "I am just here to help you."

Even in the hospital, he had a way of making her feel that everything was going to be all right, and that didn't change now. Something in his eyes or his smile convinced her. If he had the answers to this strange night, then she would have to take him up on his offer. She didn't know how to wield a sword, but it seemed sharp enough and would do enough damage if he tried anything that she didn't approve of.

She accepted his hand and stood with him. The thunder rumbled again, the loudest that she had heard since she had come out into the storm. He helped her into the passenger seat of the sedan, and they drove away from the shadows of the park.

The windshield wipers flicked back and forth madly in the falling rain. Gideon turned up the heater, which was a welcomed gesture despite the years of dust that had built up in the ventilation system of the car. Nikka warmed her hands over her small vent.

"Are you okay?" he said.

She flashed him a sideways glance as the rain dripped from her hoodie over her eyes. "I'm so far beyond okay, it's not even funny."

"I do not understand."

"Forget it," she said and pulled back the hoodie from her head. "Where are we going?"

"A sanctuary."

"What does that mean? Why do you talk like that?" she asked.

"Like what?"

"Like that. All formal and stuff, like you were born in an English boarding school or something."

"I do not understand," he said, keeping his eyes on the road ahead of them.

Nikka shook her head and rolled her eyes. "Oh my gosh, you're like a robot. Whatever. I just want to go home, okay? I'm sure my parents are worried sick."

"Not yet. It will not be safe for you or for them right now."

That concerned her, especially the way he said it.

"Hey, you've got to tell me something. I'm freaking out here. First, you take me to the morgue—the *MORGUE!*" she said. "The next thing I know, I'm being tortured beyond belief, and then I wake up in the basement, bare-ass naked. Nobody seems to remember me; I can't find my parents. And then, whatever you gave me is making me hallucinate because I saw some guy's face in a cab just melt right off his bones."

He glanced at her with a startled expression. "You saw one already?"

"Saw what?"

Gideon took in a controlled breath. "You saw a demon—or a drone—to be specific."

"No," she said with a sarcastic laugh. "What I saw was a side effect of lots of narcotics and whatever you gave me."

The car turned off the main street and veered into a darkened road, heading out of the city.

"There is much to explain, and I promise that it will all soon make sense to you. What you saw was very real."

"That's not possible," she said and shook her head.

There would be no more from him during the car ride, she knew that now. He was talking in riddles that didn't make any sense. She gripped the handle of the sword at her side, ready to use it if necessary. The car moved onto a dark gravel road, winding up into the foothills in the outskirts of the far west suburbs. This made her particularly nervous; dark road out in the middle of nowhere, no traffic for miles.

The road curved through the thick trees, climbing the hill until they arrived in a clearing. If the moon had not been concealed by such thick storm clouds, she could have seen the structure before them better.

The car pulled to a stop before a towering building surrounded by a security fence labeled with a sign, "Danger: Condemned."

Despite the rain on the window, she could see the old building, perhaps a decrepit church that stood quiet and rotting on the top of the hill.

"What is this place?" she asked.

"A monastery. It has been locked up for about 30 years now, and this is our sanctuary."

Her jaw hung slightly open as she looked at him. "That place looks like it's about to fall down."

Gideon smiled. "Looks can be very deceiving."

He exited the car and stepped toward the security gate. She watched him from the car, hearing the pattering of rain on the roof. The water streamed down the windshield and puddled around the vehicle. Gideon stepped over the puddles and through a flap of loose chain wire at the bottom of the gate. Then he disappeared into the darkness that surrounded the foreboding structure.

The nervous flutter started in her stomach again.

"This is crazy," she said to herself, because she knew she had no choice but to follow him now. She could have just taken the car back down the hill; he left the keys sitting right there in the ignition.

But he did that on purpose. She knew that. This was a test of trust, but could she trust him to this extent? To follow him into a condemned building in the dark of night in a thunderstorm. It was all the makings of a horror movie, and she was doomed to play the dumb victim. But he was the only one who had the answers she needed.

"Damn it," she cursed and stepped out of the car, jogging through the dark and under the flap in the gate.

The area surrounding the monastery grew even darker as she approached the marble steps that ascended into the entryway. Thick trees and vines overgrew the steps and threatened to trip her as she made her way to the door. Through the shadows she could make out the door and thought it gaped open, but she was not sure. She stopped at the threshold and placed a wet hand on the heavy door.

Damp, heavy air breathed out from the room beyond the door. There was nothing but thick darkness beyond the threshold. She couldn't make her feet move any further, and she glanced back to the car, sitting in the rain.

Another rumble of thunder rolled over the hillside and rattled the ancient glass in the windows.

"Doctor. . . . uh . . . Gideon?" she called out into the dark.

Then she realized that she had a light after all. She pulled the sword out of her coat, grasping the hilt, causing the blue light to envelop the blade. The glow didn't go far, but it lit enough of her space to make her a little more comfortable. She held it out before her and pushed the door open further. The wood creaked on the rusted hinges as she stepped across the threshold.

Dried leaves and twigs littered the marble floor before the threshold and skittered across the room when the breeze kicked at them. The blue light cast a circle around her enough to see pillars of carved wood curving up and over the atrium. Every step she took echoed down an unseen hallway.

"Gideon?" she said, her voice faltering.

"There you are," his voice came from her left, startling her.

She almost screamed as she felt her heart pound in her ribs. The light of the sword shone on his face.

"I am sorry," he said as he lifted a lantern and lit it with a click of a button. The propane hissed and the filaments glowed a bright white.

"I did not mean to scare you. I wanted to find a lantern so that we could see better. This place is very dark at night."

Trying to catch her breath, she said, "Yeah, you're not kidding."

"Come, follow me," he said, holding the lantern up. It provided much better light than the sword, and she could finally see the unique craftsmanship of the carved wood along the corridors.

"This place doesn't seem very safe to me," she said as she stepped around a gaping hole in the floor at the base of the stairway leading to the upper floors.

"It is a sanctuary because it is hallowed ground. That never changed just because the previous occupants left the premises."

Hallowed ground? Who was this guy?

He started up the stairs that creaked with each step. Nikka held to the railing for fear a step would collapse below her. They entered a landing where the railing curved around and entered the wall. With the light of the lantern, she could see a hallway lined with doors extending several feet into darkness. Some of the doors stood agape, some were falling off their hinges, but a pair of double doors before them seemed in remarkably good shape.

Gideon pushed open the doors and it reminded her of Alice entering the world of Wonderland for the first time.

A rush of warm, sweet air greeted her when the doors swished open. The lantern light cast onto a clean floor, polished wood and comforting furniture. Gideon stepped into the space and leaned over a table, lighting another lantern. This set off a series of reactions throughout the room, ticking out flints along a circuit from the tables to a chandelier above the room. Filaments instantly flashed to life, setting the room alight.

Nikka stepped into the room, taking in its splendor. In its peak, the room must have been a large dining hall or something. In the middle of the wall was a huge brick fireplace with a blazing fire already in full maturity.

"Gideon, this place is beautiful," she said.

"I have spent much time rehabilitating this space."

"No kidding."

"It has everything we need. Running water. Power through natural gas. Ah, I even planned for supper." He stepped to the hearth where he worked at removing a short round cast iron pot. Once he opened the lid, she could smell something wonderful inside which set her stomach growling. She had not realized how hungry she was until that moment.

"This is amazing," she said

He replaced the lid of the pot and turned toward her. "Now, we will have a good discussion about everything, but first I insist that you warm up with a hot shower and fresh clothes. Then we will have dinner and talk."

That sounded like a great plan. "Okay, I can deal with that, just as long as you don't murder me in the shower."

He stopped, his eyebrow cocked in confusion as he looked at her. "Why would I do such a thing?"

A little laugh escaped her throat. "Never mind."

He guided her up a back staircase to a third floor that had been refurbished just as the main hall had been. This must have been the sleeping quarters of the former monks, and Gideon had made good use of them. Her room was nicely equipped with a soft bed and fresh linens. A room down the hall had once been a shower room, now retiled and with new fixtures.

At first she was skeptical, but the water was indeed hot and felt great against her chilled skin. She took much more time in the shower than she had expected, but she realized how cold she had been.

The bath towels felt brand new and never used as she wrapped herself up in them. When she returned to her room, she found a set of loose-fitting knit pants and a long-sleeve T-shirt waiting for her on her bed. Gideon was a strange guy, but he wasn't a bad butler. She had to give him that.

She dressed and found her way back down to the main hall. Gideon was absent at the moment, and she stopped at the door, thinking back to the sword that she left on the bed upstairs. She just hoped after all this that she didn't need it now.

The fire crackled in the hearth. She padded across the rugs and sat before the fire, feeling its pulsating heat across her skin. The fragrance of the meal inside the pot tickled at her nose, and she had a fleeting thought of stealing a bite.

The door opened, and Gideon stepped into the room carrying two mugs of steaming liquid. "I thought you might do for some hot tea."

"Oh, yes," she said and accepted the warm cup in her chilled hands.

He casually sat down across the rug from her and worked on scooping the stew into two bowls. At this point, she didn't care what was in the stew.

She started at it hungrily, and it was the best thing she had ever tasted. *There is no room for manners here*, she thought. She felt like she had not eaten in months, and it occurred to her that was probably true. The only food she had really taken was through an IV with the exception of horrible white stuff that had been blended and went down her throat like slime.

"Would you like more?" he said, and glanced at her empty bowl.

She smiled. "Uh, absolutely."

He filled her bowl again and watched her down the second serving just as fast. The firelight flashed across his skin and his piercing eyes. His face lost the smile that he had since he came into the room.

"I promised you answers," he said. "Now I will give them, but you must keep an open mind, for what I am about to tell you will not be easy to accept."

That didn't sound good. She licked the last bit of salty broth from her lip and set the bowl on the floor.

"I will listen, but you have to tell me the truth—all of it."

"Very well, the truth it shall be."

CHAPTER 6

GIDEON'S PENETRATING STARE bore into her with those unusual eyes. "What do you know of the war in Heaven before the time of humans?"

"Uh, what?" she said, her left eyebrow raised.

"Hmm," he said, a look of disappointment sweeping over his face. "Have you studied the Bible in any capacity?"

"Well, sort of, I guess when I was a little kid," she said. "But not for a while. I wasn't raised in a very religious environment."

"Then I shall try to simplify as much as possible. Before Man was sent to earth, all souls lived in Heaven. There was a debate as to what should be done for Man to return to Heaven after he has lived his life on earth. Satan wanted all souls to be saved and that they would all obey Heaven's command. God did not agree with this, feeling the best course would be to give Man the gift of choice.

"Satan rebelled and started a war against God, taking a third of the souls in Heaven with him. Fallen Angels. This battalion became his legion. Those souls are the ones that Man would refer to as 'demons.' They never came to earth in human form, but they still wage their war for humankind.

"What you saw back there in the cab was a demon."

She felt an emptiness grow in her stomach as she watched him. "You expect me to believe that?" she said with a grimace.

"It does not matter what you believe. It is still out there, whether you believe in it or not. These demons walk the earth every day. The one you saw was a drone, a soldier sent to gather information. They are all over the place.

drones are the ones that the churches are always trying to exorcise. They are the easiest ones to spot."

"What, like Linda Blair?" she said, smiling.

His brow furrowed in confusion. "Who is this Ms. Blair?"

"Oh my gosh," she said and rolled her eyes. "Continue."

"But there are others: lieutenants, generals. They can infiltrate governments, corporations. They start conflicts and wars, inciting hatred and corruption wherever they tread. They perform the Devil's work, paving the way for the absolute destruction of humankind."

"What does this have to do with me?"

"Well, have you ever heard of the seraphim?"

Nikka shook her head.

"A seraph is a chosen being with the power of discernment and the ability to fight against the oncoming war. You, Nikkola Connors, are a seraph."

"Wait, what?" she said and rose to her feet. "Do you realize how crazy this sounds?"

Gideon stood to face her, his face serious in the fire light. "I understand that, but I swore to tell you only truth. Know that I am not lying to you."

"Okay," she turned away from him and headed for the exit. "I'm done here. I'm going home."

"You were chosen for this task, and I was sent to give you the gift of the seraph. The markings on your body are sigils designed to provide protection and to amplify your power of discernment. The sword is also a conduit for your power. That is why it glows when you touch it; only a seraph could do that."

She stopped but could not face him. As insane as this was, she had to admit she could not explain that sword, or how she got tattooed.

"If what you are saying is true, why me?"

"I do not have an answer for that," he said and stepped toward her. "I was only given the information that I needed to find you and complete the transformation."

"So what was in that syringe you gave me?" she said as she turned to face him.

"A serum, something that could heal your body completely and to provide the protection you needed to be among the archangels. Only they can create the sigils and empower them."

"What? Archangels?" Her head began to hurt. "And who are you in all of this?" she said as she folded her arms defensively.

A faint smile appeared on his lips. "I am a teacher. I am here to help you learn about your power and how to control it. But I am also a protector. I have many years of experience in teaching new seraphs."

"Wait. There are more of these . . . seraphs around?" she said with a wave of her hand.

He looked away for a moment. "No. When one dies, another one is called to take his place."

"So . . ." she started, but she could see the pain in his face. "Did someone recently die for me to be called?"

Gideon nodded. "Not very recently. It has been about a year. I have been searching for you for quite some time. My timing could not have been better. I almost lost you."

"You said that another is called to take *his* place. How many women have done this?"

For a moment he didn't speak but then flashed a glance up to her. "You are the first."

"The first of how many?" she asked.

"Thousands."

"So, is there a possibility that you could be wrong about me?" she said.

"No. The archangels would never have permitted you entrance if you were not the right one. And I have never been wrong."

"Never. How many years have you been doing this?"

"Thousands."

Her head was spinning now. She placed her hands to her temples as she felt a headache coming on. The fire crackled again and that seemed like a nice place to be right now. She sat down on the rug again and closed her eyes.

"This can't be happening," she whispered.

"I understand that this is a lot to accept. You are not the first of my pupils to want to reject it. In fact, King Arthur disappeared for almost a month after I told him."

Nikka laughed and opened her eyes. "Ugh. Just—stop." She took a sip of the tea, almost forgetting that it waited for her by the fire. "Okay, assuming that this is all true, I still think that you have the wrong girl. I'm thankful and all for curing me, but there is no way that I can go out there and fight demons. I mean, really? Demons?"

Gideon knelt down on the carpet before her. "And that is exactly why I believe you were chosen. This war has waged for millennia, and the seraph is always a soldier, a king, a great influencer of many. The other side will never see you coming. They will underestimate you."

He took her hand where it rested on her knee. "With this gift, you can see them before they see you. You have the power of a seraph now, and with this comes limitless strength and capabilities. I can teach you how to hone this power, to use the sword to your advantage. You will be able to exorcise demons and rid them from this earth."

She took in a nervous breath. "Sounds like a tall order."

"I am not sure what that means, but if that means a large burden, then yes, it is. We shall start tomorrow, but in the meantime, rest well, and I will see you at dawn."

With that, he left her at the fireside to contemplate the things he told her. She wanted to be sick, but that would bring more memories of post-chemotherapy nausea and she wanted nothing of it. She slipped into bed, which was amazingly comfortable, and it was not long before the fatigue of the night set in. For the first time in months she slept without nightmares of creatures in the shadows and the fog.

The next morning, Gideon awoke her with the harsh light of his lantern and his constant shouts to get moving. He was ridiculously annoying in the morning, something she would definitely not forget. After she found the appropriate clothes that he indicated she would need for today and the sword in her hand, she followed him to another large hall on the third level.

Morning light shone through the stained glass windows here, illuminating balance beams, exercise mats, punching bags and other gym equipment. Clearly, Gideon had prepared this room just for her as well.

"This is where we will train from 6 a.m. to 4 p.m. every day. In the afternoon, you will study the things I shall prepare for you," he said while he walked across the large blue mat that covered most of the room.

"But first things first; put away the sword," he said and faced her.

"Where?"

"Away," he smiled. "You can easily keep it hidden until you need it. Are you right-handed?"

"Yes."

"Then take the sword in your right hand and slide it behind your right shoulder."

She was skeptical at best with this, but he seemed convinced that this would work. With the sword in her right hand, she drew the blade over her shoulder and pointed it down her back.

"Now let go," he said.

Nikka released the hilt, but she didn't hear the crashing of the sword falling to the floor. She looked about her feet and there was no sign of it on the ground. "Where did it go?"

"It is still with you. Whenever you are in need of it, just reach back there and take it."

Her fingers reached behind her shoulder, feeling the hilt again. The sword pulled free and she looked at the blue flame surrounding the blade. She replaced it, much more smoothly and with more confidence this time.

"Whoa, that's so cool," she said and laughed.

"Now, come with me," he said and walked her over to the punching bag. "We will start with personal defense. Hit the bag." He positioned himself behind the hanging bag and looked at her.

Boxing had never really been her thing, and she knew nothing about it. She stood before the bag, trying to imitate some of the boxers she had seen on television with one hand in a fist against her chest. She hit the bag with her right hand.

"All right," he said and showed her how to fix her stance and hold her arms. "When you strike, make sure it comes from the torso. The arms are not the strongest part of your body. Your torso holds much more power. Try it again."

She positioned herself like he told her and struck the bag again. This time the bag moved much better.

"Yes," he nodded. "Now hit it harder. Much harder."

"Okay."

She balled her fists and held them before her, feeling the strength now coming from the stance that he taught her. The power swelled in her torso, just like he said. It felt like everything moved so much slower than it probably had. She twisted her torso, allowing the power to rise through her shoulder and down her arm. Her fist struck the bag with such force that she had no idea where it came from. The chain holding the bag broke, sending the bag across the room with Gideon behind it.

She almost couldn't breathe for a moment. *Did I do that*, she wondered as she gazed down at her fist. Gideon rescued himself from under the bag and stepped toward her with a smile.

"That is what I was waiting for," he said. "That is the power of the seraph. Now let me show you what else you can do."

Now that she knew what that power felt like, she could call it up whenever she needed it. The first few times were not her best, but once she got the hang of it, it was like she had always been able to do it.

Within hours, she felt like she could balance on the beam and back flip off of it like an Olympic gymnast. She sparred with Gideon like she had been a black belt martial artist all her life. Before she knew it, their time was over for the day, and Gideon had to remind her that they must stop until tomorrow.

With this kind of ability, she felt like she could do anything. The thought of it now made her giddy and she couldn't wait to try it again tomorrow.

CHAPTER 7

ALTHOUGH THE SUNSET HAD CAST the ruins of the church in shadows, Gideon burned the natural gas lanterns in the room that he called the study. It was one of the larger bedrooms on the third floor that he had furnished with a long oak table and shelves along each of the four walls. A broad collection of dusty books, some that looked centuries old, filled the shelves, and Gideon pulled one down occasionally and placed it in front of where she sat at the table.

"First," he said and opened a book before her. "We will go over the origin of the demons."

The painting on the page looked like something from the Middle Ages, when knights and kings insisted upon frescos like these be painted on the walls of castles. It depicted a creature covered in fur and squatting beside a blazing fire. Its horns spiraled above its head, and a forked tongue splayed from a mouth full of teeth.

"Part one will go into the origins of the drones," he continued. "From your own experience, you can see that the picture does not do it justice."

"Yeah," she said. "You're telling me."

"These are the lowest of the demons. They are basically sent out for reconnaissance, to gather information and to get a feel of the environment before the other legions arrive."

"Legions?" she asked and looked up at him.

"We will get into that later," he said with an air of annoyance. "Now, the drone is your typical demon, in the sense that humans view them. They can be exorcised even by humans, but it can sometimes be very messy and may result in the death of its host."

He opened another book in front of her, this one more modern, with photographs of priests in the act of allegedly exorcising a demon from some unnamed woman.

"While possessing the human, the presence of the drone will cause the flesh to begin to rot. There is often a decaying odor about them. The longer the human is possessed, the flesh may start to peel and crack. It can be very devastating to the host and the sooner it is removed, the better."

Nikka couldn't turn her eyes away from the pictures of the exorcism. The woman sat in a chair with two men holding her down by her shoulders. Her eyes had rolled back in her head, and her mouth was open wide in a scream. The priest hovered over her with his rosary and a vial in his other hand, filled with what Nikka assumed was holy water. The photo was depicted in black and white and the people in it appeared to be dressed circa 1965. Despite the old feel of the photograph, the woman's face sent chills down her spine.

"You will be able to remove these entities with your own hands," Gideon's voice sounded close behind her ear. This startled her and she glanced back to him.

"The power that you now possess is no match for the drones," he continued. "You can drive them out and save these people before the demon does its damage."

"How is that possible?" she asked.

"The tattoos can act as a type of sensory perception of the demon's unnatural power. You may even notice that they burn or glow when you are in the vicinity of such a creature. You can use this ability to detect when one is nearby.

"The marks on your body are also there to channel your power. It comes directly from Heaven and the demon will recognize it. Once you have cleared it from the host, you can destroy it forever. A simple human exorcism just sends the demon back to Hell, just for it to return again. But only you can kill it."

Gideon reached around her and closed the book with the disturbing photographs. "Since we are discussing this point, there is a very important thing I must tell you."

He walked around the table and sat across from her so that he could look at her as he spoke. "Once a demon knows your identity, it will summon the legions and reveal you to the hosts of Hell. It is important that once you have made yourself known to one that you destroy it before it can alert the legion. Do you understand?"

Nikka nodded but felt her pulse begin to quicken.

"For this reason, you must conceal your marks. They will recognize them the moment they see them. Let no one else see them but me."

She found herself moving her exposed arms and tattoos under the table. "I understand."

"Good," he said and stood. "Now, the next in the demon rank is the lieutenant. This is a far more cunning creature than the drone. It will possess a host, but its presence does not incite decay. It can occupy a human for days, weeks, even months or years. These demons attempt to infiltrate society and create chaos. But they do this for the purpose of serving the general.

"A general is a rare demon to come across, but they are the most dangerous. They possess a host in much the same way as the lieutenant. Both of these creatures are difficult to detect because they are hidden so well in their hosts that your senses cannot penetrate their defense unless they wish to reveal themselves.

"Once the pathway has been created by the lieutenant, the general will come and take command, often bringing the legion. In regions of the world plagued by great turmoil and wars, the general has already taken control. Once that happens, it is very difficult to reverse."

"So," she said, "can I exorcise them too?"

"Excellent question, but no. Both of these demons are very powerful. They cling to their human hosts so strongly that any attempt at exorcising the creature will result in the human's death, and a tortured one at that. That is the purpose of the sword. You must sacrifice the human to kill the demon."

He found another book on the shelf and opened it to another painting for her. It was a depiction of a grove of trees and an opening to a great garden. The entryway was guarded by a being surrounded in white light as it held a sword enveloped in blue flames.

"Does this picture remind you of anything?" he asked.

She shook her head. "Should it?"

"When Adam and Eve were banished from the Garden of Eden, God placed a cherubim and a flaming sword to guard the entrance. This way, they had to go out and experience the world and could not reenter the garden."

"Wait a sec," she said and pulled the book closer to her. "You're saying that this sword is the same one that I have now."

"Yes."

Nikka stood and reached behind her back where the sword rested in its unseen scabbard. She withdrew it, and the blade appeared in her hand, with the soft lick of blue flames swirling down the length of the sword.

"Only God's chosen can wield it, and with it you can destroy the upper level demons. Cutting off the creature's head will eliminate it from both this world and Hell below."

Her brow furrowed. "But that will kill the host too."

"Unfortunately, yes. But it is a much kinder death than the demon would grant."

She examined the blade, feeling the weight of the hilt in her right hand. The glow of the flame illuminated her skin as she felt along the edge of the metal. The flame teased at her fingers but carried no heat.

"That is a sword given to you by God, which means that the demons would give anything to take it from you. Just like your marks, you must keep it safe. If you keep it concealed with you, no other can take it by force. They will try to destroy it, because without it you cannot kill the upper level demons."

"So, I'm assuming that the Devil is real and involved with this whole thing?" she asked.

Gideon stiffened and looked away from her. She could see that he tried to find the right words. "Very real."

"And do I fight the Devil?" She felt sick at that moment and hoped that he would say no.

"He rarely shows himself in this world."

Something about that nagged at her. That wasn't exactly the no that she was hoping for.

"Are you afraid of him, too?" she said.

"The Devil is not involved much with the struggle here. He has no need to be. His armies do his dirty work while he watches from a well-hidden location. What man believes is the work of Satan is actually the work of his minions."

She didn't want to press the issue anymore, but she was now sure that Gideon was terrified of the Devil and really didn't want to talk about it.

"That's good," she said with a fake sigh and glanced back down to the book. "I'd hate to run into that guy."

He withdrew another book from the shelf, this time one that was much smaller and could be carried in her pocket. "I would like for you to study this. It is a composition of the names of all the lieutenants and generals that are known to us. To know a name and understand its capabilities can give you the upper hand in a battle."

"Just knowing a name can do that?" she said, skeptical.

"Names have power," Gideon responded, his face shadowed against the light over the table. "To know a demon's name will create a temporary restraint. If you call out the demon by its name, it will give you a brief window in which you will have power over it. The same goes with your name. Once they know your name, they can find you."

"So when do I learn how to do an exorcism?" she said with a smile.

"In time," he said. "But you must learn the names before you can do such a thing."

She wrinkled her nose and accepted the small book. "Fine. I'll work on it." She flipped through the pages, seeing no pictures. This promised to be very boring.

"What is your place in this whole thing? I mean, I know you're a teacher and stuff, but why you? You live forever or something?" she asked and glanced up at him.

Gideon looked away and turned to busy himself with the remaining books on the shelf. "Well, uh—"

"Sorry," she said. "I don't mean to pry."

"No, it is fine. I was called to this duty to provide a service. It was something that I owed and I gave my word to fulfill it. With this calling I was given the ability to live a very long time."

"So you can't die?"

He shrugged his shoulders. "I am not terribly sure. I am not created the same way as the seraphs."

"What do you mean?"

A sigh escaped his lips. He turned around and faced her. "A seraph is very . . . durable. You, too, can be immortal."

She was taken aback by this. "Serious?"

"Immortal. You can live forever."

46

"That can't be right, because you said that when one of us dies that another one is called—"

"I did not say that you cannot be killed."

"I'm confused," she said, frustrated.

"You have the ability now to live forever, but a mortal wound is a mortal wound. Yes, you have the ability to heal quickly, but if you sustain a death blow there is no life after that."

"So, you mean that the others were . . . killed?"

He nodded. This made her sick to her stomach at that moment. The implication of what Gideon told her was clear: a true battle was a very real possibility and it could end in her death at the hands of a demon. Immortal did not mean invincible.

Gideon cleared his throat. "That is enough for your first day. You should go upstairs, get cleaned up and I will have our meal ready in about two hours." Then, he departed the uncomfortable silence that their discussion had created.

Nikka walked up to her room with a numb feeling that crept into her muscles. Instead of undressing and climbing into the shower, she crawled into bed and wrapped herself in the comforter. She didn't bother turning on the light; she simply wanted to gaze out the window that overlooked the valley.

The lights in the city sparkled through the glass, looking like stars in the dark. Many of the stars moved among the others: cars winding through the streets. So many people down there knew nothing of the things that she learned today. They had no clue what was going on around them, and now she wished she was one of them too. But those blissfully ignorant people milled around in their busy and uneventful lives, not knowing about the danger that walked beside them, a wolf in sheep's clothing. These demons had been all around her—her family—and they never knew about it.

Her family. This made her bolt upright in bed. They had to be warned about it. Somehow, she would have to get word to her parents. She knew Gideon would not like it, but she had to persuade him to let her talk to them soon. Perhaps at dinner she could talk him into it. He would just have to understand how important this was to her.

CHAPTER 8

A FTER CHANGING INTO JEANS, a T-shirt and some comfortable shoes, she ran down to the main hall, where she could smell the night's dinner cooking. When he saw her, Gideon smiled and brought her a plate of pasta and tomato sauce. She sat at the table and watched him as he settled into his chair.

He began eating, but Nikka couldn't force herself to pick up the fork. She rubbed her forefinger and thumb together until they felt raw.

"I need a favor," she said.

Gideon glanced up to her. "Of course."

Her throat seemed to suddenly dry up like she had not drunk water all day. "Everything you told me today got me thinking. I need to alert my parents. Just one phone call—"

"I am sorry," he said. "But that would not be a good idea."

"Why?" she said as she stood. "Why won't you let me just talk to them?"

"It is complicated—"

"No, it's very simple," she said and paced to the door. The sound of his footfalls were right behind her, and she quickened her pace down the darkened stairway to stay well ahead of him. She neared the atrium when he rushed around in front of her, blocking the exit.

"Get out of my way," she demanded.

"Please, just listen—"

"Why? So you can continue to keep me hostage here?" she said and grabbed at his arm that held the door fast. "My family needs to know what's happening out there. They need to know that I'm okay."

"It will not do you any good, or them for that matter."

"LET ME GO."

"They will not know who you are," he said.

This quieted her for a moment as she took a step away from him. The moonlight shining through the atrium windows cast a silver glow across her face. "Just like the people in the hospital."

"What are you saying?"

He stepped closer to her. "You have no family. You were never a patient in that hospital, at least as far as anybody can remember. Your history has been erased."

"That's ridiculous—"

"Is it?" he said and took another step, but she backed away from him. "The staff in the ICU had never heard of you, had they? You were never in their hospital."

"Yes, I was." Tears began to collect in her eyes.

"Your parents never had a daughter, and they never suffered through the agony of watching her waste away to cancer. They are blissfully unaware that any of that happened."

"No," she cried and backed against the wall. Her knees wobbled beneath her and she slid to the ground.

Gideon crouched down in front of her. "This was all in order to protect them. If the seraph has no connections, then she will not be compromised. Your family can stay protected because they do not know you."

She let her forehead fall to her knees and she felt the hot tears flow down her cheeks. Everything was gone now. She had nowhere else to go and nobody to turn to.

"I am truly sorry," he whispered.

"No, you're not," she muttered. She rose to her feet and rushed back up the stairs to her dark room.

Nikka crawled into her bed again and gazed out the window. The city below continued to move like it always had. Far in the west suburbs, her parents were home and safe. And no matter what, she could not tell them that she was okay.

This was the price she paid for her cure, she decided. She gained her health and strength, but lost everything else that ever mattered.

CHAPTER 9

THE MORNING STARTED just like the previous day, with Gideon waking Nikka so early that she could barely walk straight. She must have slept fitfully because her neck hurt and her head still swam with anger. But, Gideon didn't ask how everything was going, and she wasn't going to talk about it anymore. They just needed to get to work and do what she was here to do.

The hours went by as she sparred with him, this time getting the feel of the strike from her torso and through her arm. It must have been effective, because he asked for a 'time out' and walked away looking a bit sore.

Today would be the day she would finally learn how to use the sword. She wished he would move a little faster with his lessons. It was so dull just learning parry and thrust and where to keep her feet. And he wouldn't even let her use the actual weapon; he made her use a wooden pole for now.

When she failed to hold her stance again, he turned to her, frustrated. "You need to keep your knees bent."

"I'm trying."

"Not hard enough." "

She looked away and held her stance again, not saying anything else to him.

Gideon stopped for a moment and clasped his hands in front of him. "I know it is hard with everything that you have learned in the last 24 hours."

He paused for her, but she continued to stare straight ahead, too angry to look at him right now.

"This is important," he said. "If you step wrong, even by an inch, it could mean your life."

Her gaze never flinched.

"Your family is still your family, even if they do not know it," he said, and this time her eyes flashed to him, and her knees faltered. "You will be protecting them by learning the most that you can. They cannot afford to lose you, and neither can I."

This created a hollow pit in her gut that she wished she could fill. She hung her head, unable to look at him. It was too hard to hear him say it.

Then she raised her head and grasped the rod even tighter. "I won't fail."

He smiled. "I know you won't."

She stood in her stance once again and held the rod before her as she went through the motions that he taught. Images of her parents continued to bubble into her consciousness as she took each careful step, wielding the rod that would eventually be her sword. She had to do this for them, even if they never knew it. She moved faster, feeling the power rise in her torso just like it did when she sparred. The force filled her limbs, energizing her strikes and keeping her stance strong. This made all the difference in her movements. Utilizing this power would keep her defense and attack powerful, no matter what form she used.

She could see the change in Gideon's face as soon as she began to feel the power coursing through her body. He knew that she could feel it now; that calling it up could change everything for her. It was then that he moved her into more than just basic stance and hold, but he entered with his own rod and encouraged her into sparring with him. He stepped behind her, his hands moving over her arms to position her just right. Nobody had bothered to touch her like that in so long that it gave her goosebumps at first. Since the first time she met him, he never treated her like something fragile that needed to be handled with care. He treated her like someone who had strength.

As soon as she remembered her feet and the rod's position, it was almost as though she could predict what he would do and that sensation grew more precise when she energized her arms with her power.

She couldn't help but smile with each strike, backing him into a corner. Just as she was ready to make her last strike, a cell phone chimed and echoed across the gym.

Gideon held up a hand to stop her and fished the phone out of his pocket as he walked away. The cell phone in his hand was an old flip model, and she was surprised that she didn't see him pull out a little antennae from it before he started talking.

Twirling the rod in her hand, she glanced back to him from where he stood on the mat. She tried to hear the conversation, but only caught a word here or there.

Finally, he nodded and ended the call.

He turned to her, his face almost grave. This startled her. "What is it?"

"It is time," he said and turned away from her, pacing to the exit.

Nikka jogged to catch up to him as they moved to the main hall. "What do you mean? Time for what?"

"Get dressed and cover your marks," he said as he worked at collecting a duffle bag and rummaging through a set of drawers in the corner.

"Will you talk to me, please," she pleaded.

"We are going out," he said, and his penetrating eyes turned to her. "It is time for your first exorcism."

The air in the room grew colder as the last word fell from his lips. She took a step back from him. "W-what?"

"I was hoping for more time, but it came sooner than expected, and now we must go," he said and continued working in the drawer. "Now go, and be back down in five minutes."

"Gideon, I'm not ready for—"

"Go," he said firmly, but without anger. There was a hint of concern lacing his voice and rippling off his shoulders.

"Okay," she stammered and ran from the room.

She removed her workout clothing and slipped on a pair of jeans, sneakers and her T-shirt. The hoodie, which hung over the back of the chair, would work to cover her arms and head. Hopefully, it was everything that she needed.

A wave of nausea passed through her, and she hunched over, her hands on her knees. Trembling started in her fingertips and moved into her chest.

An exorcism.

She was definitely not ready for this. Gideon had not yet taught her what to do. She had barely started to memorize the demon names. She had no idea how to exorcise one of them. All she knew about it was what she had seen in the movies.

"Nikka, now," Gideon called from down the stairs.

She took in a shaking breath. "Coming."

There was nothing left to do. She stood up straight, feeling a whorl of dizziness swim in her head. "Get it together," she whispered to herself. "You can do this." She forced her legs to move as she walked from the room and down the stairs to meet Gideon.

It felt like she had been trapped in the old church for a month when Nikka emerged into the afternoon light and climbed into the car with Gideon. He situated a leather satchel between the seats and started the car.

The sedan wound down the hillside road and then curved out into the south suburbs. The edge of the city turned into well-manicured lawns and colonial style houses that must have had at least six or seven bedrooms each. The drive remained quiet between them, and Nikka could feel the tension emanating from his shoulders. She tried not to let it affect her as she gazed out the window, to soccer moms on their jogs with a baby stroller or mailmen dropping off today's mail.

Everything seemed so mundane and simple. The beautiful American dream right here in this neighborhood. It was hardly the denizen of the Devil.

Gideon continued on the street and turned down a long driveway through rows of trees on either side. The branches overhung the road, dropping orange leaves to the ground. In this tunnel of trees, the light seemed to darken. A gust of wind blasted against the side of the car, picking up leaves and swirling them across the gravel. The car emerged from the tunnel and curved into a rounded pull through before a two-story colonial home and an attached garage.

Then Nikka realized the sky had darkened significantly since they entered the driveway of trees; it was not her imagination. Dark thunderclouds collected, drawing the afternoon light away. The wind continued to blast at the car as the clouds thickened.

"They can affect the weather," Gideon muttered as he undid his seatbelt. "Whenever one is about, they can cause storms. The larger the storm, the more powerful the demon. Hurricane Sandy was one such storm. That was a big demon: a general."

Nikka gazed up to the gathering clouds. The dark gray thickened into a deep blue-green that carried the wind against the car. Leaves scattered over the lawn and collected at the foundation of the house. She caught sight of the windows and saw a curtain pull back very slightly as someone gazed out to the driveway.

"The church will sometimes call me when they have a difficult case," Gideon continued. "Just follow my lead and do not reveal your marks until I tell you to do so."

"But you said—"

"I know what I said," he spoke. "Just follow my instructions. Call up your powers when I tell you, and you will know what to do. Just remember, once you make yourself known, the demon must be destroyed before it has a chance to leave."

She nodded and glanced back to the house, where the door opened and a man filled the threshold. There were so many more questions she wanted to ask, but her mouth was too dry.

Gideon collected the satchel, opened his door and exited the car. The butterflies swarmed in her stomach as she watched him move around the sedan and toward the door. Even from here she could feel that there was something awful inside that house and she really didn't want to see it, but Gideon left her with no choice but to follow him. Pulling the hood over her head, she climbed out of the car and followed him to the front door.

The cool autumn air brushed hard against her legs, swirling the papery leaves around her feet. With each step toward the house, she could feel the prickles of dread crawl up her spine. The trees that lined the driveway swayed in the wind, branches crashing into each other and leaves spraying into the air. She approached Gideon where he stood at the door, talking to the man that held it open.

Whatever discourse they had, she had missed it in her hesitance to approach the house. The man, with an unruly bunch of white gray hair on his head and tired eyes, let them into the house and shut the door behind them. It sounded like the closing of a tomb.

She stood beside Gideon as the two men whispered in the darkened atrium.

"This is my apprentice," Gideon said to the man.

"She is the one you said could help?" he asked.

Gideon nodded. "Yes." Turning to Nikka, he said, "This is Father Beyers." Then he signaled them further into a darkened corner of the entryway. "What have you learned so far?"

The priest swallowed first and glanced behind them to the sitting room. "The husband says it started two weeks ago after his wife came home from work. He thought it was depression or anxiety. He took her to see the doctor, but medication didn't help."

Nikka glanced back to the sitting room, following the priest's gaze. A single grandfather clock ticked away, standing against a wall perpendicular to a dark fireplace.

"Then he says it got worse," the priest continued. "Scratching on the walls at night, cold spots, voices coming from rooms when nobody else was around. Then, three days ago, he woke up and couldn't find her in bed. He came downstairs to see her sitting in the TV room, but the television was just static, no broadcast. He tried to get her to come back to bed, and he says she began speaking in a language he didn't understand."

"Have you determined which language?" Gideon asked.

"I heard it myself. Sounds like Sumerian."

It seemed as though Gideon winced a bit.

"Why does it matter?" Nikka whispered.

"The language can sometimes tell you how long it has been around. Sumerian is a supremely old language, and the demon is, therefore, very old." Gideon said and turned to the priest.

"Have you received a name yet?" Gideon whispered.

"Not yet. I've tried everything I could come up with, but nothing. I can no longer reach the woman. It has her completely possessed."

Gideon nodded. "Very well. We will proceed. The husband?"

"In the kitchen, waiting for you."

"And the woman?"

Father Beyers cleared his throat and pointed upstairs. "Bedroom."

Nikka's glance moved to the stairs and up to the ceiling. Above them, a demon waited, tormenting a woman that had no idea what was happening to her.

And, somehow, Nikka was expected to exorcise that monster.

CHAPTER 10

THE PRIEST LED THEM through the sitting room. Although large colonial windows opened on two sides of the room, the space felt dark and empty. Nikka was happy to be free of that place as they walked into the kitchen, although it was not much brighter.

As they entered, a man stood from his chair at the dining room table. He appeared no older than forty, with a slick of well-manicured blonde hair on his head. The anxiety on his face was evident as he extended his hand to the group that had just entered his home.

Nikka met his eyes as she shook his hand and she could sense his concern upon looking at her. It was justified, she thought. She just looked like some street kid that was here for the ride. He glanced one more time at her, disapprovingly, before turning to the men.

"Sean," the priest spoke to him. "These are the people I told you about. This is Gideon and his apprentice."

The man nodded but appeared to be at a loss for words. Father Beyers placed his arm around the man's shoulders. "They are here to help, and I have no doubt that they will cure your wife."

Nikka wished she could give him the same sentiment, but she didn't have the confidence in herself that the priest or Gideon seemed to have.

"Has she said anything to you in the last few days?" Gideon asked.

He shook his head. "Nothing. She just stays in the bedroom. Frankly, I keep the door to the room locked now. I can't risk her leaving the house like this, although it's not like she will, but I'm just afraid of . . ."

"What do you mean?" Gideon said.

"Well, she just sits there, staring at the wall. She doesn't eat. She doesn't speak. The room is cold as hell no matter what I do to the heater. I just keep the door locked and sleep on the couch downstairs."

Gideon nodded. "Any children?"

"Two, but they have been at my mother's house now for about a week. They have no idea what is going on and I would like to keep it that way."

"Understood."

Sean shifted his weight and cleared his throat. "I am sorry to pry, but what makes you more qualified to do this than Father Beyers?"

Gideon smiled and glanced at Nikka. "Well, we have a secret weapon. And I promise, that your wife will be healed by the end of the day."

Sean smiled, but it was forced and showed the lack of faith he had in Gideon as well as Nikka.

"What is her name?" Gideon asked.

"Beth," Sean said with a hint of reverence.

Gideon nodded. "Very well. We shall begin," he said. "I only ask that you please remain down here with Father Beyers, no matter what you hear."

The color drained from the man's face as he nodded and took his seat at the table again.

Gideon turned away and moved back into the sitting room as Nikka followed close behind him. The oppression of the room crept back into her bones, chilling her as she stayed with him. They moved to the base of the stairs, and she gazed up each carpeted step that opened onto a darkened landing.

Nikka felt a chill move down the staircase, as though someone had opened a deep-freezer and left the door ajar. Gideon started up the stairs, but it took Nikka much more effort to move her legs. The cold penetrated deep into her joints and made it difficult to move.

"Do not reveal yourself until I say," he whispered.

She couldn't speak; her throat was too dry.

"Use your power, and it will guide you in what you are supposed to do," he continued. "I cannot tell you how to do it."

They entered the landing, where the shadows penetrated every corner. At the end of the corridor, the bedroom door stood with a ring of light around the edges.

Gideon continued down the hall, and they approached the door. The air was so much colder here, and Nikka could see her breath move in small white puffs from her lips.

He touched the lock and turned it with careful precision so as not to make a sound. His hand moved to the doorknob and opened it.

The bedroom was lighter than expected; someone had removed all the drapes from the three large windows. A king-size bed stood in the center of the room, the linens in severe disarray over the mattress. And at the far edge of the bed sat Sean's wife, silent and staring at the wall across the room.

The woman did not flinch or move in any way when Gideon opened the door and placed the satchel against the wall of the bedroom. Her strawberry blonde hair fell in waves, concealing some of the dirty nightgown that covered her thin shoulders. Her shoulders slumped over, only moving with her slow breathing.

Frigid air filled the bedroom, but beyond that, Nikka gagged a little at the smell. It was that same rancid odor she had experienced when she faced the cab driver downtown. The smell seemed to emanate from this woman with every breath.

As they moved around the bed, Nikka could see Beth's face and arms. The skin that covered her appeared to be stretched thin over a web of fine blue veins. Her lips had chapped, and a trickle of dry blood painted her chin. Her eyes stared unblinking across the room, seemingly unaware that Nikka and Gideon were even in the room with her.

Gideon crouched down to look into her eyes, but kept his distance.

"Beth," he said. "I am Gideon. We are here to help you."

The woman made no effort to move or speak. She merely continued to stare beyond him. Wind beat harder at the windows, shaking the glass in the frames of the sill. Although Beth never moved, Nikka was sure that the woman was making the glass tremble.

Gideon stood, gazing down at the woman. "I now address the creature that infects this host. I command you to name yourself, before God and the power of Heaven."

Beth never twitched, but her eyes grew unusually pale and turned up to gaze directly at him. Her dry lips moved into a smile, cracking the skin open again. "You have no power here, and you have no God."

Its voice was pinched and inhuman with a subtle growl, not the sweet voice of the small woman that sat on the bed.

"I know you," it said with a slight laugh as it gazed upon Gideon.

"Name yourself, demon," he said.

The woman suddenly stood, her joints creaking as though she hadn't moved in years. Her thin frame never wavered, but her fingers moved in rapid succession as though she was trying to write invisible letters. Nikka stepped back against the wall, feeling the surge of panic begin to rise in her gut. Before her was an inhuman creature that appeared like it could kill her with one glance.

This beast, an inhuman monster inside a human shell, exuded hatred and vice. Its eyes pierced a viscous glare through the space that existed between it and Gideon, its mouth resting open and revealing the deep cracks in its lips. The woman's pupils appeared to have swallowed the iris as she looked at Gideon with such malice that it would have made any other man shrink away in terror.

The temperature of the air plummeted as the woman's body leaned forward, but she continued to stand on her tiptoes. Her eyes rolled into the back of her head. As she tilted forward in a very unnatural slant, a black and oily fluid poured from her mouth. The creature inside her growled and laughed at them as it stared out from her blank white eyes.

God, help me, Nikka thought as she watched everything happen before her like a scene from *The Exorcist*. The cold penetrated into the joints of her fingers and she wrapped her arms around her in protection from the monster that infected Beth's body.

"I demand your name!" Gideon spoke, his voice rising with authority.

The creature continued to lean forward, the fluid still pouring from her mouth and now pooling on the floor. The smile left her cracked lips, as her blank eyes stared toward Gideon.

A grumble rose from her throat as her lips began to quiver. The sound coalesced into words, but nothing that Nikka had ever heard before. The creature blabbered in the strange language as though neither of them were present in the room.

Gideon watched her for a moment and then shot a glance to Nikka.

"Sumerian," he muttered, but flashed his gaze back to Beth.

Yes, the ancient language the priest said that Beth began to speak when she started to change. And Gideon had said that it made the demon very old. Well, she didn't care how old it was; this monster was easily the most terrifying thing she had ever seen.

The woman still hovered at a 45-degree angle to the floor, only the tips of her toes touching the ground, her cracked lips moving in trembles with whispered incantations. Another voice spoke in unison with her own, something that came from deep inside her chest and spoke the words at the same time. The sound was subtle enough that Nikka barely heard it, but it still came out as a low growl with each word she breathed. Fingers twitched in strange and painful angles at the joints as the demon babbled. As Nikka pressed back against the wall and away from the demon, the woman's eyes turned entirely black, like a spill of motor oil had swallowed her orbs. The muttering from the demon's lips grew louder, as did the growl that hovered just behind each word. The stench of decay drifted over her as the woman spoke louder.

"What's it saying?" she whispered.

"It is reciting old Sumerian scrolls, sacrificial rites," he responded.

The words stopped and the room fell silent. Even the sound of the wind and the rattling of the windows ceased.

Beth took in a wet breath as she turned her blank eyes toward Nikka, the host's neck crackling with the sounds of tendons and dry skin rubbing against bone. The black liquid dripped over her cracked lips as she stared at Nikka.

"What have you brought me?" the creature growled and smiled at her.

Gideon stepped into her line of sight. "I demand your name, demon."

The monster laughed mockingly. The silence was then broken as the floor posts on the bed rattled against the hardwood floor. Then the nightstands on both sides of the bed shook with an unseen force. The sky above darkened with a swirl of late autumn thunderclouds that beat a fierce wind, shaking the house once again.

Before they could see it happen, the nightstand lamp rose from its place and moved suddenly across the room. Gideon dodged it in time, but Nikka failed to move as fast. It brushed her shoulder as she tried to jump out of the way. The lamp crashed with such velocity against the back wall that it shattered into a thousand pieces and left a dent in the drywall.

Gideon glanced back to Nikka where she crouched on the floor, her eyes wide with terror. Puffs of white escaped her lips in little breaths. The white of her knuckles now shone clearly through the skin of her clenched fists.

"It is time, Nikka," Gideon said.

CHAPTER 11

I T WAS INEVITABLE. Gideon had told her that she would have to do this; but he also said that the power she held would tell her what to do. Well, the "power" was staying silent on the subject right now.

Her mouth felt full of cotton balls. Time for what, exactly? She still didn't know what she was supposed to do. But Gideon stood there and expected her to perform, as though the knowledge of this whole thing would just wash over her.

Oh, well, she thought. It would be now or never.

She stood, and her eyes drifted to the demon that now stared at her with its blank white orbs. Beth remained in a sharp slant forward, her arms at her side with her hands still twitching.

For a moment, Nikka closed her eyes, keeping the sight of the possessed woman away from her for that brief second of time. She pulled her mind away from the sound of the pounding winds and the furniture rattling and scraping on the floor. The cold drew away from her fingertips as a warm sensation tingled across her skin and worked its way up her arms.

Without asking, she willed the first embers of her power to life within the core of her stomach. She felt heat spread across her arms and legs as it began to surge along her nervous system. As the power grew, her fears began to ebb away with each swell of heat sizzling under her tattoos.

The demon continued to watch her as its host tilted back into an upright position and stood near the edge of the bed. The air crackled against Beth's throat as it took in a breath.

"You are not as you seem," it growled and pointed a shaking finger at her.

Nikka let her eyes open and faced the creature. Her fingers no longer trembled as she unzipped the hoodie. She pulled the garment from her shoulders and allowed the hood to slip from her head. Before the hoodie even hit the ground, the demon gasped in a guttural howl.

The tattoos on Nikka's arms glowed with a faint blue-white light, sparkling like miniscule twinkle lights under her skin. The light moved up her arms, coursing over her shoulders and up her neck along each tattoo that marked her flesh.

A horrific growl shook the floor and the furniture rattled more violently than it had before. The bed overturned and flung itself against the wall as one of the nightstands rose into the air and raced toward her. Nikka could see the object move toward her, but everything was much slower than it should have been. She dodged the nightstand by a few inches and moved toward Beth. The furniture crashed into the back wall and splintered in a clatter to the ground.

The demon screamed with an unearthly voice that rumbled from deep within the human's throat. It clawed at Beth's chest, its face twisting into an angry grimace.

"Seraph," it hissed, black oil spitting from its lips as it spoke.

It screeched and lunged toward Nikka, its hands outstretched into claws. Windows rattled and burst inward in a shower of tiny glass shards. The sound startled Nikka for a moment, and the demon took that second to leap onto her, its hands at her throat.

The two fell into a tangled mess of limbs against the hard floor. The demon moved to scratch at Nikka's face, but that gave her a moment to move her foot against the demon's abdomen. With a strong kick, she forced the creature off her, and it crashed against the upturned bed.

The creature screamed again and scrambled to its feet. Nikka moved into a crouch, eyeing the monster from where it leaped at her again. This time she was ready. Nikka didn't know how, but she knew where the demon would step and when it would be on her. As it bounded into the air, coming straight for her throat, she swiped her arm across the creature's torso. It fell to the floor beside her, just as she knew it would.

She twisted around, pulling the demon close to her and straddled it with its arms pinned under her knees.

Finding itself suddenly bound, a violent howl erupted from the creature's throat, shaking the rafters of the house.

It fought against her, kicking and trying to bite at Nikka's hands, but she stared down at the creature as the power surged up her spine. As it entered her head, her vision became clearer than she had ever experienced. The light that sparkled under her skin escaped in an ethereal glow through her eyes.

As she gazed down on the demon, it screamed and fought harder as though it knew it had foreseen its own fate. Nikka knew what she had to do; Gideon was right. The power would guide her through this.

She moved her steady hand to Beth's forehead and gazed down upon her. As soon as she touched her skin, the demon screamed and closed its eyes. In that moment Nikka could see the face of the real woman that was fighting against the demon that infected her body. Beth appeared almost as a spirit under Nikka's steady hand. The woman opened her eyes and looked at Nikka. Tears sparkled in her eyes.

"Help me," she wept and looked pleadingly into Nikka's eyes.

Nikka had not expected to see her in the face of the demon, and this made her hand falter. The ghostly image of the woman faded, and the demon opened its blank white eyes again.

But Nikka grasped the power again before it faded, and felt it pour into her fingers, telling her what to do.

"What is your name?" she spoke steadily.

The demon grimaced, its lips twisted into a pained growl. "M—M—Moloch," it stammered as though it struggled to keep its secret..

Nikka placed her hand against its chest as it continued to scream. A light erupted in her fingertips. The creature howled as though the light burned its flesh.

"Ab—abad—it comes—" Moloch screeched.

Gideon scrambled over to them and grasped Nikka's hand. "Wait!" he spoke to Nikka, and then turned to face the creature. "What did you say?"

"Abaddon!" it screamed. "He comes for you now, and he will avenge me!"

Gideon released Nikka's hand, and she allowed the light to flow into her fingers again. From under the skin of Beth's chest, she could feel the demon squirming within the woman. Nikka's fingers melded into her chest like there was no substance until she found the body of the demon Moloch. She wrapped her fingers about its spine and ripped it from the woman's body.

Beth gasped painfully as the monster was torn free from her soul. She arched her back in agony as every last bit of Moloch peeled away from her.

Nikka stood with the writhing monster in her grip. Gideon wrapped his arms around Beth and pulled her away from the horrible scene about to unfold. The demon, at first a form of hazy smoke, solidified into a serpentine black monster, its tail whipping violently as it struggled in Nikka's grasp. Three rows of sharp, glass-clear teeth lunged at her throat with a brisk snap. The smell of rotting flesh now filled the room and poured into her nostrils.

She could not kill Moloch this way; somehow she knew that. In a quick decision, she hurled the demon into the corner, knowing exactly what it would try to do.

Moloch hit the floor with a heavy thud and then swiveled around to come back at her again. Nikka reached for the hilt of her sword and produced it with a quick sling of the blade. The blue flame licked the edge of the weapon as Moloch bore down upon her. She swung the katana down just as the creature came at her with claws and teeth that dripped of anger and hatred.

The blade pierced Moloch's head and sliced cleanly down the center to his neck. The monster stopped its advance, its outreached arms falling to its side. Before it could topple to the ground, Nikka swiftly turned with the blade and cut through the neck, beheading the creature.

She held her stance for a moment as the head fell to the ground in a splatter of black oil, blood and gore. The body toppled into a heap. As it hit the floor, the body and the head dissolved into a pile of ashes and embers, leaving no sign of the demon that had terrorized the woman in Gideon's arms.

Nikka didn't move until the demon disappeared. The glow left her eyes and tattoos as she let the sword down to her side. The blade dripped with black blood that landed in tiny splatters on the wood floor.

Once the power left her body, she felt the shaking in her human form. Adrenaline surged through her veins, something that she had not noticed when she was filled with the power of the seraph.

Thank heavens, she thought. She never could have done that without the power.

She lifted her eyes to face Gideon, who held Beth as she cried on his shoulder and grasped at his arms. He gazed at Nikka with a faint smile on his lips, a smile of confidence, that said *I told you so.*

Well, at least one of us knew I could do it, she thought as she re-sheathed the sword.

CHAPTER 12

NIKKA WAITED AT THE THRESHOLD of the door, tugging at the hoodie that covered her head, while Gideon talked with the priest and the couple.

She couldn't help but overhear Beth with her occasional sobs as she retold her experience when she first became possessed by the demon Moloch. The clink of a glass half full of water would echo into the atrium every time Beth drank and set it back on the coffee table. Every sound from that room seemed to be amplified to her, or Nikka's hearing had become remarkably sharp since the demonstration of her power in the bedroom upstairs. Whatever it was, she hoped that it would go away because she was beginning to get a headache.

Gideon soon returned to the atrium, followed by Father Beyers. "I will get in touch with you soon," he said to the priest and signaled for Nikka to follow him.

She stepped toward the car and turned back to see Gideon reach into the satchel that he had brought with him. He withdrew a small glass vial, dabbed some liquid onto his finger and rubbed it along the bottom of the threshold of the door. Then he re-corked the bottle and slipped it back into his bag before he turned and hurried back to the car.

As Gideon climbed into the car, Nikka's gaze lingered on the door, wondering what he had just done. But then, she saw a face looking at her from the windows at the side of the door. The priest stood there, watching her with a stern gaze, sending prickles down her spine.

She opened the car door and climbed inside, hoping that the priest would soon lose interest in her.

When she rested her head against the seat, her muscles finally relaxed, as though she had been running for hours without a break. The fatigue of the previous hour caught up to her at last, making her head throb even more.

Even Gideon's strange behavior of rubbing the liquid from that jar on the door vanished into the swirl of other thoughts that pounded in her head.

The car started down the path to the road, and she felt every pothole and uneven surface of the pavement.

Despite the deep-set tiredness overwhelming her, there was something that continued to nag at her. She had kept quiet about it until now, fearing that bringing it up in the house would cause them problems.

"What did the demon mean? Who is Abaddon?" she asked and opened her eyes to glance at Gideon.

For a moment, he said nothing, but kept his gaze fixed on the road ahead. However, she could tell that he grew tenser the farther he drove. She could see the muscle in his jaw ripple and his lips tighten.

Finally, he sighed in defeat.

"He is a demon; a high general to be more precise," he said.

"He said something back there," she said and lifted her head from the seat. "He said that *he* is coming."

Gideon only nodded.

"I take it that's bad."

Gideon nodded again. "He is a leader of legions. And if he has already gotten word that a seraph has returned . . ."

"Wait," she interrupted. "You said that as long as I keep myself hidden, that they won't know who I am."

"What I told you is truth. They will not know who you are, but the moment you came into existence, the spawns of Hell felt it like a tidal wave. They absolutely knew you were here from the moment you first awoke."

Her throat went dry. "So, I'm gonna be seeing a lot more like that?" she said, pointing back in the direction of the house.

"Oh, no," he said and shook his head.

This gave her some relief, until . . .

"They will be much worse. That was an easy one."

Nikka closed her eyes and rested back against the seat again. She couldn't bear to hear anymore right now. The images of the black demon wriggling in her hand like a giant scorpion were still too fresh in her mind. Even the smell of the thing threatened to make her gag.

She remained this way for the duration of the ride back to the dilapidated abbey, feeling every sway of the car in the turns and the bumps in the road.

They finally arrived at their destination and she opened her eyes to see the old church towering over the small grove of trees. Its once great bell tower now barely stood on a stack of rotting bricks, yet the entire structure seemed much more majestic. Perhaps it was that she knew it stood on holy ground and that things like Moloch could never penetrate the walls.

At least, she hoped it couldn't.

Nikka stepped out of the car, but as soon as she stood she felt her knees buckle below her. She caught herself by the frame of the car door before she fell to the ground like a stupid fool. But Gideon had seen her, and that made things so much worse.

He rushed around the side of the car and wrapped an arm around her. "Are you feeling ill?"

She shook her head. "No. Just really tired."

"That happens the first few times," he said and helped her to her feet.

Her legs felt like jelly, and she was not sure how she was going to make it up all those steps.

"I'll be all right," she said and tried to wave him off, but he was not so easily appeased.

He scooped her up into his arms and began the trek to the entryway of the church. "Please, indulge me for a moment. I have never been able to pamper one of my charges."

A small smile crept over his lips, creating the tiniest of dimples to form on both of his cheeks. It wasn't so bad, she guessed, being carried to the door like some bride. She tried not to blush, but she remembered back to the first time she saw him in the hospital. Even then, his unusual hazel eyes contrasted his darker skin, and she'd been intrigued by him from that very moment. And this was the first time that he seemed a little less stiff and formal around her.

No matter if he saw her blush, she knew there was no way she could have come this entire way into the church without his help. She couldn't remember ever being so tired in her life.

He carried her up to her room and placed her on the bed.

"You did well today," he said as he stood and made for the door, but turned back once more. "You will find that your strength will return in about a day, and you will rejuvenate faster each time. Tomorrow we will continue our training, but for today, you must rest."

"You got no argument here," she said and rested her head back against the pillow.

She barely remembered him shutting the door after he left the room. As soon as she closed her eyes, she fell asleep.

When she awoke, the sun peeked above the mountains, sending sharp golden beams through the slats in her window shutters. She felt a little dizzy when she first opened her eyes and moved her head, trying to remember where she was and the events of the day.

If the sun was peeking through her window, it meant that it was morning, probably about seven o'clock. That also meant that she had slept for almost an entire day and night. She sat up, feeling every stiff joint begin to loosen. She rubbed the knots out of her neck.

As she blinked her eyes into focus, she noticed a tray on the nightstand. She smiled when she saw a peanut butter and jelly sandwich wrapped in cellophane as well as a bottle of water and a bag of potato chips.

"Gideon, you're the best, no matter what anybody says about you," she whispered to herself and started on the lunch that Gideon must have slipped into her room while she slept. It was the best sandwich she had ever tasted.

After eating, she cleaned up in a warm shower and slid her leggings and sports bra on, ready to take on another one of Gideon's training sessions. She pulled on a T-shirt and started out the door to the gym. She smiled as she opened the door to the gym, ready to start with a renewed sense of purpose.

But the place was quiet, without Gideon's usual remarks about how late she was. She called his name, in case he was busying himself on something where she could not see him, but only the echo of her voice responded.

That's strange.

She turned away from the gym and moved down the stairs to the main room. As she neared the door, she heard voices coming from the dining hall. This slowed her step, and she pressed back against the wall as she approached the door that stood slightly ajar.

"We only wish to know who you have brought into this situation," one man said.

Gideon spoke. "It is not necessary for you to know. Just know that she is my apprentice."

"This is highly unorthodox," another man said, his voice pinched and angry. "The Church never authorized the exorcism."

Calmly, Gideon responded, and she could hear the smile in his voice. "And yet, the woman is now free of the demon regardless of your authority."

The second man grumbled. "I want to know what authority you and this . . . this girl have to do this."

"Enough to cure the possessed of what ails them," Gideon said.

"Gentlemen," the first voice spoke again. "Father Beyers spoke with us the evening prior and said that his attempts had failed. He then brought you and your apprentice into it. We are simply concerned about a girl being involved with something so awful."

"I assure you that she was in no danger."

"Who is she?" the second man said.

Nikka felt her shoulders tighten as the man grew more hostile. She inched along the wall and peered into the room through the small opening of the door. Gideon stood among the two men, whose backs were toward her. The men were dressed in black, and she had to assume that they were priests. Both had tufts of white hair, but the second man stood nearly a foot shorter than the first priest.

As though he knew she was there, Gideon's hazel eyes flashed up to her for only a second. In that one glance, she knew he wanted her to remain hidden. He had the situation under control.

"Do not concern yourself with such trivial things," Gideon spoke and turned his eyes away from her.

She pulled away from the door and inched back into the shadowy darkness of the staircase. The stairs creaked slightly as she made her way back to the gym to wait until Gideon finished with the men.

It took longer than she had expected, but Gideon finally arrived at the gym with a smile on his face.

She stood as he entered, wiping her clammy hands on her leggings. The wait had made her more nervous than she first realized.

"What was that?" she asked.

"Just the Church," he said. "They always get themselves frustrated over what we do."

"Is it something to worry about?"

"It never is," he said and signaled to the gym equipment. "What are you waiting for? Let us begin."

Frustrated with such a short explanation, she turned to the mat and started her warm up. The routine went as usual from there, with no further discussion about the priests that had seemed to be upset with her. But as she sparred with him, the situation became clear to her. The Church did not know about the seraphs, and Gideon would never give up her name. He apparently did not trust the Church.

With that thought, she felt her spine loosen a bit and she struck stronger against the sparring pad with each hit. The feel of her sword in her hand spurred the surge of energy in her limbs again. She concentrated with her forms as she held the sword and positioned her legs the way Gideon had taught her.

In the evening, after her studying and dinner Nikka retired to her room. She was eager to be rid of Gideon's company for a while because she had been thinking of trying something new, something that might help her move her training on a little faster.

If using her power made her tired, and it would soon get better, then she would practice with it every night. Using it a little each day and increasing her time with it should get her more used to feeling the power, and hopefully she wouldn't be so hung over after a while.

She crawled onto her bed and crossed her legs as she gazed into the dark of her bedroom. The door remained closed and hopefully stayed locked for now. She wasn't sure how Gideon would respond to her doing this, so she had to keep it to herself for now.

A slant of moonlight shone through the window, giving her enough light to see.

She closed her eyes and concentrated on the power that dwelled some-where within her. Now that she knew what it felt like, it was easier to find on demand. The tingle of it started in her fingertips and began to flow like warm water up her arms. The room lit up in a faint blue light that sparkled from her tattoos. Soon, every mark twinkled like tiny points of fiber optic cables under her skin. The room glowed with a ghostly blue light, shimmering and waving in undulating ripples over the ceiling.

The light intensified at her fingertips as she willed it to. With enough concentration, she was able to pull the light into a small, sparkling ball just above her palm. It was only the size of a golf ball, but it stayed strong for a few seconds before she grew too tired to control it any longer. The light faded, and the sparkling along her tattoos ebbed away until there was no light left.

Tingling continued at her fingertips for a moment after the light faded. Feeling the energy fade away, she smiled because she had controlled it for even a moment when she wanted it. The power was now a part of her, and she welcomed it.

CHAPTER 13

A FTER HER TRAINING the next morning, Gideon said something most unexpected.

"I am taking you to the university library now for your studies. You have read everything I have here, and the library has an excellent selection in their Medieval section."

That was a surprise. So far she had felt captive to the monastery, and now he was willing to let her leave the confines of the church. The thought of getting some fresh air was exhilarating. He surprised her even more when he produced some things that he wanted her to take.

He drew a few shopping bags to the table in the main hall. The first thing he pulled from the bags appeared to be a wig. "This will help you blend in a little better." He slipped the wig over her head and slid it into position. The strands were a honey blonde that fell in straight locks just below her shoulders. The bangs fell down and slid a little to the right above her eyes.

"I hope it works okay for you," he said. "I just thought of you as blonde."

Nikka slid her fingertips through the hair, something that she had not done in over a year. Her own hair had originally been long and pretty close to the same color. "I love it," she said with a smile. She had not realized how much she missed having the feel of hair falling in her eyes and tickling her face.

Then, he withdrew a box from another bag and opened it, revealing a cell phone. "A cellular telephone, so that we may keep in contact when you are away from here. The man at the store suggested that I should have one just like it, so I purchased one as well."

She laughed a little as he placed the phone in the palm of her hand. "It's a smart phone, dude."

"I am sorry. Did I make a mistake?"

"No," she laughed again. "The phone—they are called smart phones because they can do so much more than just make calls. Nobody calls them cellular telephones."

Gideon glanced down to the black rectangle in his hand as if he had seen it for the first time. "I really had no idea. This is very different from the one I have had."

She slid it in her pocket. "I'll show you how to use it sometime."

"I also have this," he said as he pulled out a simple backpack from the last bag. "I observed many of the students at the university wearing these. You will appear to be one of them if you wear it."

"Thanks," she said and accepted it from him. She wanted to say something, but she felt a little nervous. He may not understand what all this would mean to her. "Really, thanks for all this."

"Of course," he said as he met her eyes. For a moment he didn't move or speak, but only looked at her as though he had truly seen her for the first time. Then, he cleared his throat and set to busying himself with cleaning up the grocery bags. "I will take you to the library in the afternoon. The section on Christian mythology is going to be the most beneficial. In the bag I have included writing material with which to take notes."

Nikka slung the backpack over her shoulder. "This'll be exciting. I was planning to go to college before . . . well, before all this."

"Please understand," he started with a hint of concern in his voice. "You are not attending university. This is research. You must learn all you can about your foe. Being out there could put you in very serious danger. Do you understand?"

He was not speaking harshly to her; at least she understood that. The look in his eyes was one of deep worry, and she realized that taking her from the safety of the monastery must be very difficult for him.

Nikka nodded. "I do."

"As you have learned, it is a far more dangerous world out there than anyone else realizes. You must keep to yourself. Do not reveal yourself to anyone. Trust no one. Remember, the drones you can see, but others hide themselves very well. They only need one look at your markings to know who you are."

This made her tug a little on the ends of the sleeves of her hoodie, pulling them well below the level of her wrists. "Okay," she said.

It was enough to appease him for now. Even with his doomsday outlook on everything, though, she was still excited to get out there and see the light of day.

When he had finished his preparations, they left the church and climbed into the car. It was a significantly nicer day than the one she had witnessed the last time she was outside. The sun shone in bright beams through an azure sky without a single cloud. The air remained calm; a stark contrast to the storms that had swirled overhead when she had gone to perform the exorcism.

The car travelled down the hill, and she couldn't help but stare out the window and watch the trees rush by. The outskirts of the city soon came into view, with the afternoon traffic moving by in a slow procession through the main streets. Soon, the university campus came into view, with its main student building rising above the surroundings like a cathedral spire. Oak trees and shrubs lined the streets around the outer edges, breaking occasionally to allow a small peek into the vast inner campus.

Gideon drove to the far north corner of the campus and pulled to the side of the street. "I will pick you up here at six o'clock this evening, but please use the phone at any time if you need me. The gentleman at the phone shop included my number in a list he called 'Favorites' when he set it up."

"I'm sure I can find it then," she said with a smirk and opened the car door.

He leaned over the chair and looked up at her from where she stood. "Please call if you need help, and do not speak to anyone."

"Okay, Dad. I won't talk to strangers," she grumbled and shut the door. Before he could say anything else, she jogged across the street and entered the campus between the arching boughs of two massive oak trees. She refused to look back at him because she knew that he was still there, sitting in his car worrying about her safety.

It made her feel a little bad that he was so concerned for her. She promised herself that she would do everything he said and more. Gideon had taught her so much, and disappointing him would be the worst at this point.

The cool autumn air filled her lungs as she looked out over the expansive green lawn littered with orange and yellow leaves. Sidewalks cut through the green carpet, snaking to the various red-brick buildings that surrounded the campus. To her right, she could see the science building and the department of engineering. More spires of a large building loomed over the center of the lawn, and she had to assume that it might be the library since there were several students milling about the building and absorbing one of the last warm days of the fall.

Her fingers held her backpack in place as she walked past a group of students chatting and laughing on their way to class. She instinctively lowered her head as she passed them, but they barely noticed her. A deep breath released from her lungs, a breath she had not even realized she was holding. *Damn you, Gideon.* He had made her so nervous that she knew she must be drawing attention to herself by just being anxious.

Just smile, she told herself. She raised her head, smiled and straightened her spine. A guy with tousled brown hair and thick-rimmed black glasses passed by her with a smile. She gave a little wave and continued on her path to the library.

See, she thought. *I'm just one of you.*

The entrance of the library came into view. There were two glass-paneled doors that opened into an expansive atrium. Rows of wooden desks lined either side of the atrium where the librarians worked, checking the books in and out of the computer system. She continued deeper into the library and entered the main room.

It opened into a large space, with books stacked on dark wood shelves set in rows along the far wall. Tables with lamps filled the main floor under the gaze of high rising colonial-style windows that shone down into the room. A staircase rose onto a second floor with railings that bordered a view to the first floor. More shelving of the same dark wood filled the upper floors as well. There were students studying at the tables, and some were sprawled on the floors along the walls with their books and papers strewn around them. A bank of computers along the far left wall interrupted the ancient gothic appearance of the library with a flare of the modern era.

She had never seen such a beautiful building in her life.

And it was so big. How was she supposed to find the section she needed? She wandered through the rows of tables to the back and noticed the number labels on the ends of the shelves: the Dewey decimal system. Ugh. She remembered this from school, but never really bothered to use it in her school library. The computers would help, but she was sure she had to be a student to log into them. Asking a librarian would be talking to a stranger. That was on Gideon's "no" list.

Oh well, she thought. She had the time. She would simply have to walk all the rows until she found a section that might look like something that she could use. Her fingers re-situated the backpack on her shoulder as she began her scan. After walking through every row on the main floor for the last hour, she sighed and trudged up the stairs. When she got to the upper level, she groaned in frustration. There were so many more shelves up there, and it would take hours more of her time just to scan them.

You've gotta be kidding me, she thought.

She stepped along the railing and faced the first row. Well, she would never find it just standing there. She started gazing at the books again, shelf after shelf. Biology, physics, anatomy. All the major subjects covered in the first ten rows that she scanned. The math section covered three rows all on its own.

She rounded another corner and nearly ran into a cart stacked with various books.

"Whoa there," the man standing behind it said and grasped the cart before it rolled into him.

She gasped in surprise as her leg banged into the cart. "I'm so sorry. I didn't know anyone was over here."

The man smiled, and this was the first time she had actually looked at him. He appeared to be one of those guys that really didn't give a damn what people thought of him. Straw blonde hair fell in long waves below his ears and matched the color of his goatee. Stark blue eyes glanced up at her under long lashes.

"You okay?" he said, his voice a little graveled, as though he had smoked at some time in his life.

Would this qualify as a stranger to Gideon? She didn't know and frankly didn't care at this point.

"Yeah, you just scared me for a sec," she said and rubbed her thigh where she hit the cart.

He grasped a book from the cart and placed it back onto a shelf just above his eye-level. "Anything I can help you with?"

As he placed the book on the shelf, his long sleeve fell away from his forearm, revealing a mélange of tattoos spreading up his arm and under his shirt.

"Help me?" she said, confused. "You work here?"

He gave a little laugh. "Yeah. I know, right? Like I look like a librarian."

Nikka smiled and realized she was staring at him. It was hard not to stare: those blue eyes were stunning and he was pretty cute with the whole "bad-boy" thing going on.

"So, you need help?" he said again and glanced at her.

"Um, yeah," she said and looked away. "I can't find the Christian Mythology section."

"Oh, easy. I thought you had a hard question for me," he said with a smile that made his face light up. She suspected he had dimples under that goatee somewhere.

He turned around and pointed across the library to the rows under the windows. "The 200's, over there."

He turned back to face her.

"Thanks," she said.

"Anytime," he said and went back to work, re-stacking his cart of books.

She slipped around him, trying not to look at his butt in those dark jeans with the silver chain dangling off to the side of his leg. Nikka continued on to the other side of the library but could not help but smile. *Just don't look back,* she thought and gripped tight to her pack as she made her way to the rows that he had mentioned.

While the thought of him slowly faded away, she scanned the rows and could tell he had led her in the right direction. This section was filled with books on religion, cults and philosophy of worship. She moved over the sections to find a large book with a worn leather spine. The gold words printed on the side were barely visible, but she could see that it was titled *Encyclopedia Daemoniorum.* She pulled it from the shelf, and it was even heavier than it looked. There were several other books next to the large book that she collected in her arms until she couldn't carry any more.

She moved her stack of books to a nearby table and sat down to continue her work. With the pen and notebook that Gideon had supplied her with, she started in with the large book. She opened the book and heard the spine crackle with each page she turned. The pages smelled musty, as though the book had been stored in a damp basement for fifty years. The edges of each page had yellowed over time and seemed ready to crumble to dust.

Thick, black ink curled in dizzying lines where the book displayed old wood etchings from various demon cults through the ages. Every page was written in longhand, a feat that must have taken years since the book was clearly over one thousand pages.

The next problem she encountered was that every word was written in Latin.

The book suddenly became a useless artifact, nothing more than a collectible relic. She sighed, frustrated, as her eyes scanned page after page of illustrations accompanied by the description in a language she couldn't read.

But a thought flickered in her brain. It was something so impossible, but what if there was a way that she could read it?

Nikka closed her eyes and concentrated on the smallest twinkle of power in her fingertips. It always seemed to grow from her fingertips up to her shoulders. She didn't want enough to make her tattoos light up like a Christmas tree, but just enough to make her hands tingle. The longer she focused, the stronger the sensation got. When it was the tingle she wanted, she concentrated to keep it steady. The power flowed up and down her fingers in predictable waves, steady and rhythmic.

She opened her eyes and willed the power to fill her sight. It shifted, fluctuating in a thin arc up her arm. It threatened to spread into her marks and spark into a fresh light, but she controlled it as it inched up into her neck. The sensation disappeared for a moment, but then her vision flashed into a chaotic meld of colors, almost like looking at a negative of a picture. Blacks were white and vice versa. The light flashed once more, and her vision was restored.

She held her breath for a moment, expecting to feel a powerful headache, but there was nothing but the ticking of the clock above the stairs and the bright afternoon sunlight pouring through the windows. The tingling had subsided and her shoulders slumped. It didn't work.

Her fingers moved to close the book when her eyes met the page. She stopped in an instant, reading the illustration description which now appeared in routine English.

" . . . the Daemon Aerborus being cast out of a farmer by the Bishop Edwards . . ."

The entire page now appeared to be written in English. She flipped through several pages and she no longer found any Latin. Whatever she had done had worked. She wondered if Gideon even knew that she could do that.

With the excitement of her newfound talent, she began reading the tome from the beginning, hoping to find some reference to Abaddon. The book seemed to be written by someone who had travelled throughout old Europe, witnessing many forms of demon possession as well as various exorcism rituals. Every ritual was different as was every possession. The Catholics varied in their requirements for possession from the Protestants and Jews. But one thing was constant: they all agreed on the existence of the demon.

She found lists of demons that she had never seen in Gideon's books, some from all religions and some going back thousands of years. The book never seemed to stay on a single religion or practice of exorcism, either.

Then, she saw the name she had been seeking.

Abaddon is known in Greece as well as among the Hebrews. He is king of locusts, master of the Abyss. He is the Destroyer.

Nikka swallowed as she felt her heart race. She sat back against the chair and glanced up at the window. The time had passed so quickly that the golden rays of sunlight had given way to the dark pink and gray hues of twilight. The absence of the light made her hands grow cold as she thought on the words she had just read. *He is the Destroyer.*

On the adjoining page there was a full color illustration, painted in the Middle Ages, of a creature with piercing almond-shaped eyes and two spiraled horns emanating from the top of its head. A forked tongue protruded through a row of sharp teeth. The creature sat atop a mound of naked bodies, bleeding and torn to pieces. His muscled legs with blackened claws rested on a ledge of bleached white skulls.

The monster's yellow eyes stared back at her as though it could look directly into her soul, almost like it could see her right now.

She shuddered and slammed the book closed. A poof of dust escaped the edges of the book as she did it. She had not expected the loud echo that slamming it would create, though. She glanced around the upper level and even back to the stacks where that guy had stood, but she was alone. He was long gone and there were no other students up there with her.

Then her eyes caught sight of the clock and saw that it was 6:15.

"Oh, crap," she muttered and gathered her things into her backpack. She had lost track of time, most of it wasted in trying to find the right books. But now that she had discovered what she needed to read, she didn't really want to stop. Gideon would be worried; he probably was already pacing around his car waiting for her.

She slung the bag over her shoulder, gathered the books and replaced them on the shelf. The last thing she needed was some librarian, especially the cute guy, looking at what kind of books that she was studying. That would be too embarrassing if she ran into him again and he knew that she had been reading about demons. He would probably think she was some cult psycho.

When all the books were re-shelved, she dashed down the stairs and out the front door of the library. Most of the students that had been surrounding the library during the day had left, and there were only a few walking from building to building across the deserted campus. She jogged faster along the sidewalks and then cut across the lawn to find the spot between the trees where she had entered the campus.

Just as she had expected, Gideon leaned against his car where he had parked it under the trees. He had the phone in his hand, attempting to operate it, but was so far unsuccessful.

"Hey," she called to him as she ran across the road.

He looked up to her and his expression melted from one of worry to relief. "Where have you been? I said six o'clock."

"I know," she said, panting for air. "I just lost track of time."

"I cannot seem to get this contraption to work," he grumbled and tossed his hands into the air. "The old one was so much simpler."

"I'm sorry," she said and grasped the phone out of his hand. She pushed the center "on" button and the screen lit up. "Just push that. Then touch the symbol with the phone in it. You can find Favorites in there."

He accepted the phone from her and gazed at the screen. His fingers moved over the screen just as she had said and pushed the button. Within seconds, the phone in her pocket began to ring.

"See," she said. "Easy."

Gideon did not look up at her but continued to stare at his phone. The silence was uncomfortable, and she could tell that he was too upset to speak.

"I am sorry," she said and touched his shoulder. "But I'm okay. Really."

His hazel eyes flashed up to her for a moment as he nodded his head. She was unsure why, but she reached her arms around him and hugged him. It seemed like the right thing to do at the moment. She felt his hands slowly move around her, and he placed his chin on her shoulder.

"Please don't worry so much," she whispered.

"I cannot help it," he said. "You would too if you had seen what I have seen."

CHAPTER 14

GIDEON WAS MOSTLY SILENT during the physical training the next morning. Nikka was worried enough about it that she was afraid to hit him too hard during sparring. But she realized he could see the lack in her effort and was able to drop her to the mat, knocking the air from her lungs.

"You are not trying your hardest," he said as he walked around her like a predator surveying its kill.

"Sorry," she said and moved to her feet. "I'm sorry that I was late last night."

His brow furrowed in confusion. "What?"

"I can tell it's still bothering you," she said and started unwrapping her wrist braces.

Gideon turned his back to her and walked away from her.

"Hey," she called after him. "I can take care of myself. I'm not just some woman in distress."

"I know that you think you can take care of yourself. You are not ready to face the worst of these things yet."

"How will I know if I never see anything?" she said. "And I was just fifteen minutes late last night. It's not like I broke a curfew or anything."

"I know that you want to see more, but you are not ready yet."

"Whatever," she grumbled and turned away from him.

She had thought about telling him of the trick she learned yesterday, where she could suddenly read Latin, but now she was just mad at him. He didn't deserve to know her new talent, not when he was acting like such a jerk.

The remainder of the training session continued in silence, and Gideon was absent for most of it. It didn't matter; she could do this without him at this point.

It still surprised her that he mentioned going to the library again as she walked out of the gym. She was sure he would never take her there after last night. As soon as she showered, changed and collected her things, including the wig, Gideon walked with her to the car.

The sky appeared cloudier than the day before, but the warmth of the previous day still held onto the ground. The leaves fell heavier today as they drove down from the hills. Gideon parked the car in the same place as he had previously. Nikka stepped out of the car, ready to shut the door again, when he spoke from the driver's seat.

"Six o'clock," he said.

She rolled her eyes and slammed the door shut. Without looking back at him, she jogged across the street and plunged into the campus as fast as she could.

Why did he have to baby her so much? It's not like he was even family. He had no right telling her what to do and when to do it. She was an adult and could make her own decisions. Yes, she could agree that he was well experienced with the . . . things . . . that they had been dealing with, but she was learning so much. When was he finally going to trust her?

He wasn't her dad.

This made her stop midway through the lawn on her way to the library. As the thought skittered through her brain, she felt her hands shake and her mouth go dry. She knew she shouldn't do it, only because it was something Gideon didn't want her to do. Nikka reached into the pocket of her jeans and withdrew the phone. The screen lit up when she pressed the main button. The small icon at the top corner illuminated, indicating that the signal was good.

She could call her parents. Just one call. Just to hear their voices.

The phone trembled in her shaking hand, and the screen became blurry as her eyes flooded with tears. No matter how long she looked at the phone, though, she could not force herself to touch the Call icon. Her thumb hovered over the green symbol for too long.

Maybe Gideon was right about this one thing. What could she possibly say to them? Hey, I'm the daughter you forgot about. How ya' doin'? She blinked away the tears and shoved the phone back into her pocket. It just wouldn't be a good idea right now, whether or not Gideon told her to stay away from them.

She wiped her cheeks with the back of her hand, took in a deep breath and continued on to the library. *Just clear those things from your mind*, she thought. *You have to concentrate now. It's time to show Gideon that he was wrong about you.*

Several students stepped out of the library doors just as she slipped in behind them. Without stopping, she went upstairs and walked along the railing toward the section where her books were located. At first she tried not to keep her hopes up, but she found herself glancing through the rows for any sign of that guy, but was soon disappointed when she saw that she was alone in the upper level of the library.

Stop worrying about him, she chided herself.

She shook her head, collected her books, and returned to her desk where she set up her camp, as she liked to think of it. Now that she was comfortable with it, she called her power with more control and will this time. The Latin changed to English as soon as she called the power. With a smile, she started where she had left off the night before, only this time, she tried to avoid looking at the painting of Abaddon on the opposing page.

As she continued, she glanced at the clock periodically. Being late again would be the worst right now, since Gideon was being such a pain in the ass about the time. So far, so good, though. There was still plenty of time.

She turned through the pages as the hours ticked by. She approached another collection of pictures and found several biblical references. Luckily, the library had various versions of the bible and she pulled one out to search out the reference. The first she found in Revelations, Chapter 9. Again, this brought up the demon's name.

> *And they had a king over them, which is the angel of the bottomless pit, whose name in the Hebrew tongue is Abaddon, but in the Greek tongue hath his name Apollyon.*

This passage called him a king, and this confused her. She jotted down the reference in her notepad and glanced over the illustrations—more of the same horned creature in various formations of battle, sometimes against angels and other times against men. They all had something in common, though. Every picture showed him as the superior warrior, destroying all those around him.

A squeaking sound caught her attention and drew her from the book. She glanced up and saw the guy and his cart again, a single wheel squeaking as he pushed it between the rows of shelves. He was placing books on the shelves.

For a moment, she realized that she might be blushing as she looked at him. He must have sensed her looking because he glanced up and met her gaze. He smiled, and she swore she could have seen dimples this time. The cart wheel squeaked one more time as he jutted his chin up in a simple "how you doin" gesture.

She smiled in response and looked down at her book again. *Don't stare at him,* she thought. *He's going to think you're stupid or something.*

But she really wanted to see if he was still there. She glanced back to the rows again and saw him busy with his work, not concerned about her at all.

Just concentrate, she scolded herself. *He barely even notices you.*

She continued reading, but it was so much harder to follow the words now. Her mind drifted back to him, those gorgeous blue eyes and that killer smile. What was a guy like that doing working in a library? He clearly didn't put out that "librarian" vibe, but instead, looked like he could be in a motorcycle gang. Hell, he just might be in a gang. Those tattoos on his arm looked like they could have been gang related.

What did she know about gangs? Nothing. That's what.

Stop it and just read.

Nikka glanced back to the clock. Five o'clock. One more hour.

She couldn't help but flash her gaze over to the rows again, but the cart was gone and so was the guy. Too bad.

No. It was a good thing. She only had an hour left and she had to get in as much studying as possible in that short time, with plenty to spare to make it across the lawn to meet Gideon.

She returned to the book, taking notes as she continued and erasing any further thoughts of the cute librarian. She could save those thoughts for later when she wasn't trying to learn about the worst demon in biblical history.

The light of day began to fade, and the library grew even quieter than it was before, just as it had the previous night. Twilight had come, which also meant that her time there was drawing to a close. She gathered her things, slung the backpack across her shoulder and hastened out of the library. A quick glance at the clock before she walked out told her that she had five minutes to spare. Perfect.

She stepped across the lawn where the sodium night lamps lit up the grass and sidewalks, leaving shadows around the trees where the light could not reach. The night was darker than she remembered, but it could be that she was running to see Gideon last time and she hadn't noticed. The lawn was empty now, most of the classrooms and buildings shut down. Many of the night classes didn't begin for another hour, so the quad was quiet and dark. Very dark.

The shadows at the edges of the lamps unnerved her. She wasn't normally so easy to spook, but there was something about the air tonight. Perhaps it was Gideon's talk about such horrible things that got to her tonight.

It couldn't be that. There was something wrong. It wasn't just her imagination.

When she felt the first tingle in her fingertips, she knew what the problem was. Her power began to surge into her arms like a ready-set alarm system, and it was doing it all by itself without her will or control. She could see the break in the trees ahead where Gideon would be waiting on just the other side of the street. The tingle moved up her arms as she quickened her pace toward the tree line. The power coursed up her arms and into her torso. She knew that under her clothes, the tattoos were lighting up like fireworks.

A dark figure emerged from the shadow of the Engineering building. He stepped in her path with his long black coat drifting around his legs as he walked. His head had been shaved, but the hair growth on his face said he hadn't attended to it in over a week.

"Hey there," he said, his thin face spread in a smile. The yellow of his teeth gave away his extensive drug use, and she could smell the cigarette smoke from across the sidewalk. "You need someone to walk you home tonight?"

Her fingers clutched at the pack as she stopped. The man walked toward her and intercepted her path.

"No, I'm fine," she said as she stepped onto the grass in an attempt to bypass him.

"It's no problem," he said and moved into her way again. "I got all the time in the world for a bitch like you. What d'ya say?"

"No, thank you," she said and moved to step on the other side of him when he grabbed the other strap of her pack and pulled her closer to him. The power seemed to burn along her skin as his other hand grasped her arm.

"Thank you? So polite," he said, his teeth stained yellow in the light. "What else have you got for me?" The hand on her arm moved down to her torso and caught the waist of her jeans.

She felt the power erupt into her vision, just as it had when she read the book from Latin into English. Her sight cleared, and she no longer saw her attacker's face. Instead, his meth-addled appearance had given way to a creature with twisted features and razor-sharp teeth. Nikka reacted fast, pulling away from him as quickly as she could.

"I don't think so," he said. She could still hear the man's voice within the creature's throat. The smell of rotting meat emanated from his mouth when he spoke.

He lunged at her and the vision of the creature faded back to the man's face, but she now knew what it was. And she knew what she had to do.

Nikka dropped the pack, stepped quickly into position, and landed a powerful kick to his face. The man staggered back in surprise, almost losing his balance. He caught himself and scowled at her.

"You're gonna pay for that one," he said and came at her again.

She dodged to the side and he almost fell, but he caught her around the waist and she went down with him. He dragged her to the cold, wet grass, hitting hard on her side. Nikka gathered her strength again, feeling the surge pour into her limbs. She dropped her elbow hard into his throat and scrambled to her feet again before he could take another breath.

The power continued to fuel her, but she felt something else now. Anger rushed through her veins. It made her hands shake and her heart race. This demon had no idea who it was dealing with.

She clutched at his shirt and pulled him up to face her as she landed a strong hit in his face and then slammed him into the trunk of the tree. The man grimaced in pain for a second and then growled at her, clawing at her arms.

The power swam just under her skin now. She willed it up like a geyser and it exploded through her tattoos and into her eyes again. The light glowed through her eyes and her fingertips began to sizzle with the heat of it.

The man now realized what she was when he saw the glow of her eyes. He opened his mouth to scream, but it sounded like the roar of an animal.

His eyes rolled into the back of his head as black liquid seeped from the corners of his mouth and down his chin. Hands raked at her skin where she held him to the tree trunk.

She could see the demon just under his skin now, writhing against its inevitable end. She didn't care what the demon was called: it was going to come out just because of her power. Her fingers plunged into the ether of his chest, through the layers of clothes and skin and bones that only felt like a cool chill until she felt the twisting carapace of the demons at her fingertips. It pulled and snapped at her, but she clutched her fingers around its thrashing spine. The light intensified, and the man screamed as the demon tore through his soul. The beast appeared under her hands, wriggling and screeching at her grasp. Nikka pulled it free as the man collapsed to the grass. Screams, grunts and wails echoed back through the quad, rebounding off the empty buildings as she held the demon in her grasp.

With a quick reach, she drew the sword and thrust it into the demon's abdomen. It screamed and fought at her, but its effort began to wane. She dropped it to the ground and swung the sword across its neck. As soon as the head was separated, the residual of the demon faded away into ashes.

The trembling in her hands continued, but she controlled it as she placed her sword back in its invisible scabbard. The embers of the demon's body sparked for a moment and then went black. She took in a deep breath of cool air and calmed the power back into dormancy.

"Nikka," Gideon's voice called to her from the edge of the trees. She glanced up to see him running toward her as fast as he could.

"I'm okay," she said, trying not to sound so out of breath.

"But I heard it scream," he said. He neared her and touched her arm, examining the grass stains on the sleeve of her shirt.

"I said I was okay," she said. "I got it."

"You did?"

"Don't sound so surprised," she said with a laugh and dusted off the grass from her jeans. "I could feel him coming before I saw him. Then I just reacted. Pulled it right out."

Gideon smiled. "What was its name?"

"Didn't get one. Just pulled it out instead." She continued to pick the dead blades of grass out of her hair and started to turn away from him.

"What did you say?" he said and stopped her.

"I just pulled it out. What?" she asked.

"Well," he stammered. "I have never seen a seraph just take one out before getting control of it by its name."

She winked at him. "Well, I guess you haven't been working with the best."

A groan drew their attention, and Nikka glanced back to the man on the ground. He looked confused and tired. Blood dripped from his nose where she had hit him in the face.

"Wh—what happened?" he asked as he tried to stand up, but collapsed against the tree again.

"Are you okay?" she said, kneeling down beside him.

"How did I get here?" he said as he looked around the lawn. "Who are you?"

"Never mind that," Gideon said. "Do you know your way home?"

"Sure," he slurred like he had just woken up from a deep sleep. "I just feel like hell."

"I bet," Nikka whispered. She helped him to his feet until he was steady enough to walk. "Go home, get some rest." He simply nodded and walked away into the shadows of the trees.

She grasped her pack and turned to face Gideon, who was staring at her in awe. "Stop being weird. You're freaking me out."

"I am sorry," he said and shook his head. "You were right."

"I like the sound of that, but right about what?"

"You are not just some woman in distress. There is much to talk about tonight," he said and walked with her to the car.

CHAPTER 15

"SO, YOU JUST PULLED IT OUT OF HIM?" Gideon said, stuffing his mouth with another dinner roll. The meal he had made for them was more extravagant than usual. It felt like a reward.

She couldn't believe that he kept asking her that same question, as if her answer was going to change sometime. Nikka laughed and drank another sip of water. "I told you a thousand times: yes."

"Then you have learned faster than I would have expected," he said and shook his head in disbelief.

It was time to tell him, she decided. There was no way she would be able to keep her secret much longer anyway. She cleared her throat. "And there's something else, too. Apparently, I can read Latin, and probably other languages. I didn't check them all yet."

He looked at her. "What do you mean?"

"Well, I just concentrated my power and the words changed from Latin to English. I found a great book up there that was all written in Latin."

"I have never heard of that happening before," he whispered almost to himself. "How did you know to do that?"

She shrugged. "I don't know. I just thought of it and it worked."

"Amazing," he said and stared at her like she was a new treasure.

"I guess I'm like a superhero or something."

"I do not know what that is," he said.

"Are you kidding me with this? You don't know what a superhero is. You don't know how to use a smartphone. What century are you from?"

"Well," he said after he finished another sip of water. "I live in the current century, but I have been witness to many more."

Nikka shook her head with her hands over her ears. "This is going to make my head explode."

A look of concern crossed his face. She stopped and smiled. "Not literally. Come on. In all that time, haven't you seen a movie or watched television or read a book?"

His face brightened. "I have read the Bible."

She mumbled under her breath. "I'm dealing with a Puritan."

With a deep sigh, she looked at him across the table. "A superhero is someone who is an ordinary person who is going about their everyday life and, through no fault of their own, becomes a person with extraordinary powers."

His brow furrowed. "What happens to them to create this consequence?"

"Anything," she said with a shrug. "A spider bite, or maybe he saw his parents murdered by the Joker, or he got blasted with gamma radiation. It doesn't matter. What matters is that now they have special powers that enable them to save the lives of the innocent and to battle evil."

"So," Gideon said, his face etched in concentration, "that would make you a superhero."

"Looks like."

"You were an ordinary person, as you put it, who was a chosen individual to be given the powers of Heaven, and now you use your power for good."

Nikka raised her glass in a toast. "Exactly."

"Where are these other superheroes?"

She laughed. "They're not real. They're stories. Comics."

"I do not understand. You said they help eliminate evil."

"They do," she said and placed her glass back down. "In stories, they do. And then others have turned those stories into movies, so that those people who aren't into reading the comics can still enjoy the story."

"I am still very confused," he said. "How can they fight evil if they are not real?"

Nikka shook her head in frustration. "Oh my gosh. Don't you have a computer or something?"

His smile returned. "Indeed, I do. A laptop. I believe that is what you call it." He rose to his feet and walked to the cabinet across the room. He produced a black case and withdrew a black-backed laptop. The screen illuminated after he opened the computer.

Nikka walked to his side as he sat upon the sofa and rested the computer on his knees. She sidled beside him on the couch and stared at him in disbelief. "You can't use a smartphone, but you have one of the most high-tech laptops I've ever seen. How is that possible?"

"Oh," he said. "I utilize this device to track weather patterns and follow possible sightings of the demons. That is how I found you."

"Seriously, Gideon?" she said with a smirk.

He clicked on the keys with his index fingers until he pulled up the screens for weather patterns across the world. "Remarkable technology. This has improved my tracking. It is so much easier than using weather balloons or windsocks."

"Well, haven't you ever done anything else with this thing?" she asked.

"Like what?"

"I don't know. Search the internet or something. Check email. Look at porn. Anything."

"I have not had the need for anything else."

"All right," she said and grasped the computer from his hands. "Let's expand your mind." She clicked through onto the server and navigated through to a popular movie website.. "This is one of the best movie and TV download sites. Let's set you up on your own account."

After joining and logging in, she moved through the page, pulling movies into his favorites group.

"There. I am going to make you watch a few things. This will be your study time."

A smile formed on her lips as she finished the download. She placed the computer on his lap again and demonstrated the functions to him. "Just click here and it will show you all the movies I put in your cache. I love comic book movies, and these will be the most basic ones for you."

"These are the tales of the superheroes?" he asked as his eyes scanned the pages with awe.

"Yeah," she said and clicked on the first page. "My dad used to read me the comics when I was a kid. He was sort of a comic book nut. He had stacks of them in his study. My favorite was Spiderman."

The movie poster for Spiderman pulled up onto the page as she clicked it. Gideon watched the page open and stared at the picture as though he could not absorb the information fast enough.

"This Spiderman, he wears the colors of your nation. His iconography instills a sense of pride in your country," he said.

Nikka smiled. "I guess I've never thought of it that way, but yeah. He's a really good guy."

"Why do you enjoy the stories of this man?" he said and looked at her.

"Well, he was kind of a dorky, ordinary teenager doing ordinary things. He was bitten by a spider and his whole world changed. The spider bite gave him all these powers that he didn't know what to do with at first, but then he became this awesome superhero that could save everybody in the city from the Green Goblin or Sandman or Doctor Octopus. But he always remained that dorky, ordinary kid to everyone else."

He continued to look into her eyes. "Just like you."

"Are you calling me 'dorky'?" she said with a laugh.

"I have no idea what that even means."

"Well, you're probably right anyway." She clicked on the Play icon and the movie started. Together they rested back against the sofa and watched the story unfold from the beginning.

When the effects of all that food began to make her sleepy, she patted him on the shoulder and stood up from the couch. "I'm going to get some sleep. Enjoy."

As she walked to the door, she glanced back to him. He seemed to not even notice that she had left the room as he continued to watch the movie, enthralled by the story of Peter Parker.

When the sunlight flowed into her window, she woke up with a stiff neck. The room remained quiet and still, unusual for the morning. Gideon was always the first to wake her and it was usually before the sun rose. She would have already gotten in two hours of training before the sun even came up. But here she was, rising on her own, and it had to be well after eight in the morning.

Nikka climbed out of bed, wiping the sleep from her eyes, and padded out the door. After the last time he didn't wake her up, she was worried that there were more men having a concerning conversation in the main room regarding her. It was none of their business what she was doing or even how she was exorcising demons. The fact is that it worked. They must have been jealous that they couldn't do what she could do.

She stepped closer to the main hall but heard no chatter of angry men. There was a different noise coming from inside the room. She opened the door to see Gideon sitting on the sofa as though he had not moved all night. The computer remained on his knees, the screen flashing through images as he watched a movie. From her vantage point, she could see that he was watching The Incredible Hulk.

"Oh my gosh," she said.

Gideon jumped a little and pressed the space bar of the computer to pause the film.

"Have you been sitting here watching movies all night?" she said with a smile.

He glanced around as though he had been in a stupor for hours. "I must have lost track of time. I am sorry."

"Don't be sorry. I got to sleep in."

He closed the computer and stood. "You are correct. These stories are remarkable. They are modern fables with much deeper meanings than one could determine from the exterior."

"Got it. They are awesome-sauce."

Confusion crossed his face again.

"Never mind," she said.

"And I would agree with your determination that Spiderman would be my favorite. His story is poignant, and his uncle has tremendous clarity and wisdom. His advice rings true to all of us."

"And what advice is that?"

"With great power comes great responsibility."

She nodded and shrugged. "Good advice, even though the movie screwed up the line a little bit."

"So," he said with a forceful voice. "We must be responsible with your power and complete your training for today."

Ugh. Her shoulders slumped and she leaned back against the door. She had hoped they might have a reprieve from the grueling training, but that didn't seem to be the case. Gideon was full of energy despite his all-nighter and he would probably make up for the time they had lost this morning.

She changed into her training clothes and completed her hours. Just as she had expected, he made up for their three hours lost. When they were done, he rushed her through lunch and to the car to make it to the library.

As she moved to exit the car, he leaned over the seat. "Six o'clock."

"But that doesn't leave me much time," she complained.

"It is dark by six, and I am not comfortable leaving you to walk back here all alone after what happened last time," he said.

"I thought we had this figured out. I can handle myself."

"This is true," he said. "But you are still my responsibility and I shall not leave you out to be hunted."

She slammed the door and shook her head. He was probably still talking, but she didn't care. Standing here listening to him would waste precious time, and she was already losing daylight.

She stormed across the quad, grumbling about him under her breath. After all that she did last night, how could he not trust her? He had even said that he had seen nothing like it before. So that must mean she was more powerful than her predecessors, right? So why did he still insist on treating her like his kid sister that he had to babysit?

With all the thoughts rampaging through her head, she almost didn't see the guy from the library, sitting on top of the picnic table in the quad. A golden beam of autumn sunlight fell through the trees onto the table, making his hair look angelic. He rested his elbows on his knees as he ate a simple peanut butter and jelly sandwich.

"Hey," he called out to her. "Back for more, I see."

Nikka stopped and bit her lip: was he talking to me? On the off chance that he was speaking to her, she stepped off the sidewalk and onto the grass toward him.

"I won't bite," he said with a smile.

She returned the smile and stepped toward the picnic table. "A little late for lunch, isn't it?"

"I usually eat late," he said and patted the space on the table next to him. "Have a seat."

The pack slipped from her shoulder and she placed it on the grass as she moved onto the table beside him. The cool air drifted past him, blowing through his hair and bringing the scent of a faint cologne from under his shirt. He smelled wonderful and not at all what she had expected.

"I'm Jason, by the way," he said and extended his hand.

"Nikka," she said and shook his hand.

He raised a package of cookies to her and she accepted one. "They're not my grandma's but they'll have to do."

She bit into the cookie. "It's good anyway."

"So," he started, "I've never seen you in the library before this week. You new here?"

"Uh, yeah," she said, trying to think of a lie as fast as she could. "I just started. Transferred from out of state."

"I figured. I'm sure I would have noticed you," he said and flashed a smile. Those blue eyes were even clearer up close.

"How about you?" she said, feeling her heart race as she looked at him. "What year are you?"

"Oh, I'm not a student. I just work at the library. It was arranged by my PO last spring."

She furrowed her brow. "PO?"

An uncomfortable laugh escaped his throat and he averted his gaze as he raised an eyebrow. "Parole officer."

Maybe Gideon was right. She never should have talked to anybody. She felt her spine go rigid.

"And there it is," he said. "The uncomfortable silence that follows my astounding revelation."

"I'm sorry," she said and took another bite of the cookie. "I guess that just took me off guard for a second."

"No, it's okay. I get it," he said and glanced back to her. "Did 18 months in County. Jacked some car stereos and sold 'em. I got paroled early, and they arranged for me to work here. It gets me familiar with the campus and I can get a letter of recommendation so that I can apply here next year."

"So, you don't just love libraries, then," she said and returned the smile. "Bummer. I thought we had something."

He laughed. "Actually, I love this one. It's been a good job. I've read more than ever; some stuff that I would never have looked twice at before."

"It'd be hard to come back from something like that," she said and brushed her hair from her eyes. "It sounds like you're trying to change your life for the better."

"Well, you're still sitting here, talking to me, so that's something," he said. "It usually scares people, and they come up with some excuse why they have to leave. So if you haven't run away screaming by now, then I've done something right."

"I promise that this isn't just an excuse, but I really do need to study. I'm sure I'll see you around," she said and slid from the table.

"Sounds good," he said. "Then I'll make sure to always have cookies in hand." He lifted the little plastic bag of snacks up to eye level.

She smiled and turned toward the library. As she made her way there, she felt the flutters begin in her gut. The blue of his eyes and feel of his hand in hers, rough skin and all, continued to linger in her senses like a good dream. Even the faint cologne that drifted from his neck played at her nose.

As she stepped back to the library with a smile, she felt the prickles of something that seemed to crawl up her neck. It wasn't her angel power; it felt nothing like that. It was more like the feeling of being watched, and not in the way that she hoped Jason watched her now. This was more like prying, studying eyes that she would never invite.

She glanced up from her path and her gaze darted over the lawn as her pace quickened. Students studied in groups over the green quad in the patches of sunlight that shone through the trees. Nobody seemed to give her a second thought, let alone stare at her. She looked back at Jason, who now devoured his meal from where he sat on the picnic bench. He wasn't even looking at her now. Then, she saw a man standing under a locust tree whose leaves rained down occasionally in the breeze. She recognized his face the moment she saw him.

Father Beyers.

He wore a broad-brimmed hat that shaded his eyes, but she was sure that it was him. There was nobody else with him. Not the angry priests that she had overheard talking to Gideon. Nobody. He stood there watching her with his hands buried in his long black coat. Even when she looked right at him, his gaze never wavered. It was the same look he gave her as she left the house of the exorcism. Why was he there? The prickles began up her neck again and she turned to run into the library. At least there were more people there, and if Beyers wanted to come after her, there would be too many witnesses for him to do anything to her.

She rushed up the stairs and stepped along the railing that overlooked the first floor and gazed down to the entryway, waiting for the priest to come in looking for her. Several minutes ticked by, each to the rhythm of her pounding heart. But she saw no sign of him. Maybe he figured there were too many people in the library as well. Maybe, he planned on just waiting for her when she came outside again. She let her shoulders relax as she settled into her usual table, occasionally giving a glance back down to the doors. When she felt that he was definitely not coming into the library, she was able to open her books and continue where she had left off the previous day.

She found the Latin book again and worked at interpreting the pages dealing with exorcisms in Europe during the Middle Ages. But the words kept slipping between Latin and English like ripples on the top of a pond. At first she thought it may be because of the priest she saw on the quad, but she soon realized that wasn't it at all. No. She kept thinking about Jason.

During the entire time she had been studying at this library, she had never had this much trouble concentrating. She felt like she was back in high school, hoping for the cute guy to talk to her before lunch hall or to send her a flirty text. Jason was the kind of guy that could just make you want to do whatever he asked just by the way he smiled. They had actually had a real conversation today, as short as it was. And she learned something about him, something besides just library stuff.

Okay, so he had been in jail once. But he was out now and trying to be a better person. That had to be okay, right?

She closed the book, feeling a headache coming on from the attempt at keeping the Latin away from the pages. The sky had already begun to darken and her time with the books was nearly spent.

At ten minutes to six, she packed her things away and re-stacked her books. As she stepped out of the rows, she saw Jason come up the stairs and caught his eye.

"Hey there," he said, out of breath from his run up the stairs.

"Hey," she said, confused as to why he was here, and hoped that it wasn't just to re-stack books.

"I know you're getting ready to leave, but I had to come up here," he said. "I was wondering if you'd be interested in just getting a burger or something tonight. There's a great place just off campus." He held his hands out as though he was presenting a wonderful gift. "My treat."

She cringed inwardly for a moment. She wanted to go with him so badly, but there was just no way she could get away with that tonight. Gideon would kill her if she didn't show up to meet him. "I would love to, but—"

"Ah, there it is," he said and averted his gaze. "The but."

"No, I really want to. You have no idea how bad I want to," she said and grasped his hand. "But it's my . . . my brother. I'm staying with him right now and he's really a Nazi about me coming home on time. I'll be in so much trouble if I don't meet him in like ten minutes."

"Okay," he said and forced a smile.

She slipped the pack over her shoulder and hesitated for a moment. Every second that she stood here was another minute later to meet Gideon. "Rain check?"

"Really?" he said.

"Yeah. I would love to try that burger place. It's been so long since I had one."

"All right, I'll catch you later then."

"And you know where to find me," she said, nodding her head to her usual table, and turned toward the stairs. But a thought raced through her head, something that Gideon would kill her for if he found out. She turned back and jogged toward him as she withdrew a pen from her pocket. He smiled at her as she approached and grasped his hand. With the pen she scrawled on the palm of his hand. "My cell number, just in case you maybe don't know where to find me."

She smiled up at him, meeting his eyes. That was the craziest thing I think I've ever done, she thought, but then shook her head when she thought of the demon she destroyed last night. Maybe not the craziest thing. She dashed back down the stairs, feeling his eyes on her the whole way. It wouldn't be cool to look back. Just leave them wanting more; that's the best way to go. Right?

CHAPTER 16

THERE WAS NO WAY she was going to tell Gideon about Jason or Father Beyers right now. Being so over-protective lately, he would probably flip out and wreck the car or something. They just needed to get back to the monastery and have their dinner. Perhaps if she could distract him with more movies, he would be willing to let her go on a date with Jason. But that was a big maybe. Perhaps she could get him distracted with other things when she told him. Especially about the priest.

Something about that guy still bugged her, and as much as she hated bringing it up, she knew that Gideon needed to be told about it.

When they sat down for dinner, she arranged his computer to start the volley of movies that could keep him preoccupied through the night and hopefully distract him enough to be light on her for talking to someone at the university. But there was the issue of the priest first.

Gideon placed a plate of chicken and pasta before her. She had to give him props: he was a weird guy, but he did know how to cook.

When he sat down, she looked at him with the fork in her hand and ready to eat. "Do you know why Father Beyers was following me today?"

He looked up to her with grave concern on his face. "What did you say?"

"Father Beyers," she said. "I don't think he likes me."

Gideon didn't speak for a few seconds. He appeared to be thinking hard enough to hurt, something that carved deep furrows between his eyebrows.

"He just stood there and watched me from across the lawn."

"This is very concerning," he muttered.

Then she felt the flutters begin in her stomach. The thoughts that floated through her mind disturbed her; things that she had never considered earlier today. "Is it possible that he could be one of them? One of these generals?"

He glanced up at her, and she didn't like the look on his face. "Well, I would previously have said no. He is a priest, and I have known him for some time now. But I cannot explain his presence at the university today. Did you speak to him?"

"No," she said more forcefully than she wanted. "The dude creeped me out. I just ran into the library."

"That is best for now. I would advise you to call me if you see him again."

Well, that settled her mind a little for now. For a brief moment, she had the thought that Gideon may have sent Father Beyers there to spy on her, but now she was sure that he hadn't. But there was the disturbing question of why he was there in the first place. Whatever those priests wanted, maybe Beyers was spying for them. Or maybe there was the far more concerning question of him possibly being a demon.

It was obvious now that Gideon was troubled by the information she had shared, and now was not the time to bring up Jason. *Baby steps,* she thought. *Give him only what he can handle.*

She finished her meal and excused herself after she set Gideon up with some movies to watch on his computer. This time it would be some *X-Men.* There were enough of those to keep him plenty busy for most of the night. If he watched them all night again, then she could confirm that he was addicted, and then Gideon could finally be considered cool despite being such a bizarre guy.

Nikka rested on her bed and opened the small book that Gideon had first given her to review. It had been some time since she opened it and read through the first few pages again. The content began to make more sense than it had before, especially since she had been studying the book at the library. There were a few names that were more recognizable for her since she had been studying demonology: names like Ashtaroth, Pazuzu, and Beelzebub

The digital ringing of her phone startled her and she silenced it before Gideon could hear anything. She glanced down to the screen and saw an unfamiliar number. She slid her finger across the screen.

"Hello?" she whispered, eyeing the door and listening for Gideon's footsteps outside her room.

"So you gave me your number," the voice said, "and I just wanted to see if it actually worked."

Nikka smiled when she heard Jason's voice. "Well, it does."

"Good. I was worried for a moment that maybe you just gave me a fake."

"Hmm. I wouldn't be able to think that fast," she said and leaned back against the wall. "So you're just calling to see if I lied to you."

"Nah," he said and she could hear his smile. "I just wanted to hear your voice again."

"Well, it's nice to hear your voice too." Was that too cheesy? Oh, gosh. She just didn't feel like she was good at this.

"And," he said with a little hesitation, "I was wondering if you would like to go on a ride tomorrow. I have the afternoon off and if you're not too excited to study, I would love to show you this place on the coast that I love. It won't be this warm for too much longer, and it's not so nice on a motorcycle when it's cold."

She really wanted to say yes so much, but then there was Gideon. There was no way he would allow it.

Jason must have sensed her internal struggle because he interrupted her thought. "I promise I'll have you back in time to meet your brother. He won't even know you were gone."

The butterflies swam in her gut. He was inviting her on a date. She would love to spend time with him alone and get to know him, but she always heard Gideon's voice in the back of her mind as well.

"I'll think about it, okay," she said.

"Hey, it's not a no. That's good enough for me," he said. "Either way, I'll see you tomorrow, and I'll bring cookies."

She laughed. "That would be nice. They were so delicious. Goodnight."

"Goodnight," he whispered, and she thought that there was no way he could have sounded sexier than he did just then.

She ended the call and just held the phone in her hands as though he was still there. Those blue eyes and blonde hair the color of straw continued to play in her memory. His smile, oh gosh, he was so gorgeous. The kind of gorgeous that makes it hard to breathe. She would tell Gideon some other time about him, and maybe invite him to meet Jason at lunch or something. But for now Jason would have to be her own little secret.

CHAPTER 17

WHEN GIDEON DROPPED NIKKA OFF at the edge of the campus, she barely heard him recite his usual time to meet him. The butterflies in her gut seemed to have doubled and made her nervous as she ran across the road and away from him. It had taken all her willpower not to say anything to him during training in the morning. She did her best to focus on the tasks during training, even if she was a little clumsier than normal, but Gideon didn't seem to take notice.

She had been careful to pick out her clothes today. The right jeans, the right T-shirt, even if she had to mostly cover it with her long sleeve hoodie. She had gotten so used to the wig that she hardly noticed it anymore. It was so natural to have hair brushing her cheek and playing around her ears. Just as long as it looked good and didn't look like a wig, then she was okay with that.

The pack hung from her shoulder as usual, a casual look that most of the students around campus portrayed. It gave her the appearance that she was okay with being a student and everything was cool. At least that was what she hoped it looked like. She just didn't want to look like a total dork when she met with Jason, who just oozed sexy.

When she saw him sitting on the picnic table with his elbows on his knees, she felt the swarm of butterflies go crazy, like crazy mutant insects flittering madly inside her stomach. He was scanning the lawn, evidently looking for her. His trademark smile accented with dimples appeared when he saw her.

"Hey," she said. It was all she could think of.

"So what's the plan?" he said and hopped off the table.

Up until this point she really had no idea what she was going to do, but the words just came out all on their own. "Let's do it."

"That's what I'm talkin' about," he said and she walked with him across the other side of campus to the side street.

It wasn't exactly a surprise, but not what she had expected, which would have been just some random generic motorcycle. Jason sidled up to a Harley with slick black paint and chrome highlights. He strapped on a simple black helmet and held a second one out for her.

"Safety first," he said.

She pulled the backpack over both her shoulders and then strapped the helmet on. "I've never ridden on a motorcycle before."

He straddled the machine and slipped on a pair of sunglasses. The look seemed to complete him: he was the hottest thing she had ever seen. "Easy. Just climb on back, wrap your arms around me and place your feet here." He showed her the pegs on the back side of the bike.

Unsure of herself, and not wanting to fall and look like a complete fool in front of him, she straddled the bike behind him. This was the closest she had ever been to him and it made her blush as she wrapped her arms around his torso. She could feel his lean muscles glide below his shirt. This is what he told her to do, but it still felt a little awkward with her breasts pressed to his back and her hands clasped just above the waist of his jeans.

"You got it?" he asked her over his shoulder.

"Yeah," she said. Damn right, I've got it.

He kicked the starter and the bike rumbled to life. "Don't let go," he said and then rolled the machine into the street.

Her hands clutched around his torso as they moved, and she realized she was probably squeezing him too tight, but the thrill of riding through the streets with the wind whipping through her fake hair was exhilarating. And she liked the feel of him so close to her. He maneuvered the motorcycle through the city streets and onto the freeway. Here, they moved with such speed that it felt dangerous. The afternoon sunlight felt warm on her cheeks despite the wind blowing past them.

The motorcycle turned onto an exit, one that she remembered from a couple of years ago. This would take them to the road that snaked along the coastline. The road also turned up the hill and to the cliffs that overlooked the coast, and that was exactly where Jason drove now. The road was mostly isolated, frequented usually in the summer by tourists, but the fall allowed the locals a near-private access to the cliff side stops.

Over the sound of the motorcycle's engine she could hear the crashing of the waves against the rocky shore below the cliff line. The salty spray drifted up the cliff face and filled her nostrils with a familiar scent that brought memories of playing Frisbee on the sand with her father when she was ten years old. The thought made her smile and she clasped her fingers tighter around his torso.

He turned the bike onto a small outcropping lined with a simple wooden railing. The bike slowed to a stop and he rested it against the kickstand. The engine died when he turned the key. She stepped off the bike, still feeling the buzz of it between her legs. He unstrapped his helmet and gazed out over the railing.

"This is it," he said. "I love this place."

She unstrapped her helmet and placed it back on the seat of the motorcycle next to his. The warmth of his body still burned in her hands and she clenched her fingers to keep that heat as long as she could. She stepped up beside him and looked out to the ocean.

"It's beautiful," she said.

"My mom used to take me here when I was a kid. I like to come here to just get away from everything. It helps me think," he said and then turned to her. "Sorry. That sounds so stupid."

"No," she interjected. "It's not stupid. I can see why you come here."

"I started coming every day after I got out of . . ." he started, but he trailed off. She knew what he wanted to say, but understood that it was embarrassing to say it. Jail. "It keeps my head clear, focused."

"Is your family still around here?" she said.

"Yeah, but I can't go home. Dad said not to come home until I do what I came here to do," he said and turned away from her, stuffing his hands in his pockets as he looked away from her. "So here I am, getting my life in order."

Then he turned away and leaned over the bike, producing a box of cookies from the bag at the rear of the motorcycle. "As promised."

She laughed and accepted a cookie. "I like a man who can keep his promises."

"I'll keep that in mind," he said and bit into a cookie.

"What about you?" he said.

"What about me?"

"You know. Family. You got anybody else here besides your brother?"

Gideon. It was easier to think of him as a brother than a guardian. "No. Just him."

"Well, I can see why he is so overprotective then," he said. "You're all he's got too. I take it he's your older brother."

"Yeah," she muttered. It was getting hard to lie to Jason. "He just doesn't let me do anything. I keep telling him I can take care of myself, but I just don't think it gets through, you know."

"Someday he will see you for the strong woman you are," he said and looked out over the ocean again. "He can't keep you forever."

Nikka looked at him, feeling a flush at the words he used. A strong woman. Is that how he saw her?

"Thank you for all of this," she said. "I haven't been out for so long. I forgot how beautiful the coast was."

"Anytime," he smiled. "I mean it. Anytime."

His hand moved to hers on the railing— hesitant at first, but she opened her fingers as he grasped her hand. She allowed him to entwine his fingers with hers. The warmth of his hand drove the autumn chill away from her fingers. She had never held hands with a guy who looked at her like this. It was nice.

"We can always get a burger some other time," he said.

"I bet you tell all the girls that," she said as she tilted her head toward him.

"No, just you."

CHAPTER 18

THE HOURS WENT BY LIKE MINUTES with Jason, and the time spent on the back of his motorcycle was too short. But he kept his promise and returned her to the campus with plenty of time to spare for her to meet Gideon. He even got her back in enough time to linger with her for a little while by the motorcycle.

She didn't want the afternoon to end. This was the happiest she had been since being diagnosed with cancer, which was a subject she wasn't sure she wanted to share with him just yet. It would have to come out eventually, since it was such a big part of her life, and she would have to reveal that her hair was all fake. She just didn't have to share exactly how she was cured.

When she looked at the clock on her phone, she knew she would have to leave him soon.

"I had a really great time today," she said.

His fingers intertwined with hers. She could feel his cold silver skull ring against her hand.

"Me too. Can we do it again sometime?"

"I would love to."

"Tomorrow?"

She smiled. "I'll have to think about it."

"So noncommittal," he said with a laugh.

She let her fingers slip from his and stepped away from the motorcycle. He straddled the machine and kicked it to start. The engine rumbled as he strapped on his helmet and flashed her his Hollywood smile.

"See you tomorrow then," he said and turned the motorcycle into the street.

As he disappeared down the street in the fading light, she felt the warmth of her T-shirt where she had been pressed up against him for the last hour as they rode. It was a feeling that she never wanted to give up. Nikka stepped back onto the lawn, watching him leave until she could no longer see him. The smile on her face made her cheeks hurt, but she didn't care. Those butterflies flitted around again, but it didn't make her anxious anymore. With the smell of him on her shirt, she slipped into the library until it was time to meet Gideon.

When the sky had darkened and the hour approached, she made her way across the lawn and found Gideon in his usual place. She slipped into the car, knowing that he could say nothing now to take away this feeling.

"You seem to be doing well," he said and put the car into gear.

"It was a good day," she said. "I got a lot done."

"Excellent," he said and turned the car in the opposite direction than they usually went. "We have a change of plans tonight."

This was strange. Did he know something about what she did today? "What's going on?"

"I thought a night out might be in order," he said, his voice without a hint of what he was doing.

She felt her grip on the backpack tighten. The car moved deeper into the city, among the skyscrapers and the busy shopping district. She felt her anxiety return: she wasn't ready to talk to him about Jason quite yet, but this was out of the ordinary and he wasn't being very talkative. Not that he ever was anyway. He pulled the car into a full parking lot and stepped out. She swallowed, feeling her mouth dry up, and stepped out of the car.

He encouraged her to walk with him across the street to a simple diner. The restaurant appeared to be nothing unique, smelling like plenty of fried food. The hostess seated them next to the window, as Gideon requested, and filled their glasses with water.

Nikka eyed him before she took a sip of her water. "What's going on? You're freaking me out."

"Just dinner," he said and scanned the menu.

Yeah, right, she thought. She glanced at the menu but hardly studied her choices. It was the usual sandwich, soup and salad place. When the waitress returned, he only ordered a cup of soup, and she did the same. She wanted to stay alert to everything Gideon was doing, no surprises.

When the waitress left with their orders, he leaned across the table and began to whisper. "Dinner and a stakeout, as the modern vernacular goes."

"What are you talking about?" she asked.

"Not just dinner," he said. "Look outside. What do you see?"

She glanced out the window. The city was dark except for the glow of streetlights and car headlamps that moved by the restaurant. People walked the sidewalks between shops and restaurants. Directly across the street stood a high-rise building, likely a high-end real estate company or law firm. Something huge and vague. It was obvious that whatever business they were in was a big money industry. The spacious lobby remained mostly vacant except for a security guard at the main desk.

An elevator door opened in the lobby, and a woman, dressed in a stylish dark gray pantsuit, her hair tethered into a French twist, stepped out. Two men, also in tailored suits and ties, followed behind her. The three of them stopped at the desk to speak with the security officer.

"I see cars and people. I see a building with business-type people ready to leave for the day," she said. What was the big deal?

"That building houses a private security firm that handles accounts from the Department of Defense," he whispered.

She glanced back to the building and the people talking at the desk. Gideon made it sound like they were about to get into some high level spy stuff. Where was he going with this?

"Okay, so?" she said.

"What else do you see?" he asked.

"Nothing, why?"

"Look with your other eyes."

Oh, right. She peered back across the dark street and willed her power to rise. The tingle moved from her fingertips as she directed it to her eyes. The vision of the street flashed for a second and she opened her eyes to gaze into the office building.

The two men stood on either side of the woman until she turned, then they followed her to the exit, where the security guard let them out. The trio stepped out onto the sidewalk and for the first time she could see their faces. The men's faces were twisted and blackened with eyes, pale and grotesque.

Drones. Two of them.

She focused on the woman, who appeared to be just as she looked: a business woman. There had to be something more, though. Gideon would not have brought her here just because of two drones. She willed more power into her vision. The colors of the light around her throbbed into hues of blue and purple until her eyes adjusted. At first she didn't see it, but she turned her head as if looking at an optical illusion. The effect was subtle, but she could see a flash of orange light in the woman's eyes as though they reflected an intense fire. Her face never twisted into the serpentine mask of the drone, but she was definitely not human.

"Whoa," she said. "What am I seeing?"

"A lieutenant," he said.

The waitress appeared just then and placed both cups of soup on the table. "Anything else?"

"No, thank you," Gideon said as the waitress flashed him a flirty smile, but he didn't seem to even notice.

"Dude," Nikka said with a grin as she watched the waitress walk away. "She was totally hitting on you."

"Focus," he said without a hint of frivolity in his stare.

"Sorry," she said and glanced back across the street to see the trio step into a cab. "So what are we going to do?"

"I have been doing some research, which has become particularly more productive since you showed me how to search the internet," he said with a thank you nod. "A demon like her working within a company that has access to the Department of Defense could be catastrophic."

Nikka took a sip of the soup, but it was a little too hot. "I guess I don't get it. There're demons everywhere. You taught me that."

"It is a gateway into the entire defense structure for the United States. If you can affect the nation's defense, you can control the nation. It is only a matter of time. This is exactly the kind of thing the demons would want to do. This is why you are here."

Her mind sorted through what he had said, and the grave possibilities began to settle. He didn't mean that she was here in this diner right now. She knew he meant that it was her purpose in being the seraph. "This is bad."

"It is not surprising to find a high-ranking demon such as her at a place like this. Something tells me there are far more inside that building. They get just one like her and they can infect everyone, and a firm like that could eventually work its way up to the Pentagon, the White House. Even the U.N."

"Um, this is kind of a big deal," she said, suddenly not feeling hungry at all. "Shouldn't we get somebody else involved?"

"Whom do you suppose could handle something like this?"

"I don't know. The FBI? The CIA? Somebody besides us," she said and wanted to yell at him, but tried hard to control the volume of her voice.

"They are no match for what lies in that place," he said, pointing his finger at the window. "You are far more capable of handling it than they are."

"Like hell I am."

"I have seen you. You can do this."

"Are you kidding me right now?" She leaned across the table and yell-whispered at him. "I have exorcised two drones. TWO. Now you're talking about taking on the Department of Defense."

He grasped her hand and gave her his strong stare with those powerful hazel eyes. "I have been watching them for days now. That woman is an entry level individual who has access to the upper levels. She is always flanked by the two drones. You take the three of them out and get her access badge."

"I can't do this," she said, feeling like she was ready to vomit.

"Inside that building could be the hub of the demon networks in this country. They could have valuable information on the location of other demon nests. You find the information, we could take down the network and get far ahead in this war. They may even have Abaddon's location."

She shook her head. "How do you know if any of that is in there?"

"Look closer," he said and pointed to the building.

She turned and focused her power into her vision again. She had been so intent on watching the trio leave the building that she hadn't seen anything else. As she looked from the street up the side of the building, she could see markings glowing as though they were painted in blue neon. The marks were similar to those on her arms and legs, but they appeared more twisted, broken. The symbols extended up the entire building and around the sides.

"Demon sigils," he whispered. "They are protecting something in there, something important. In all my years, I have never seen anything like it. Whatever they are doing, they do not want anyone else to know. Those sigils will keep out the eyes of angels, but not you. Even I cannot get in there. Only you can."

CHAPTER 19

GIDEON FINISHED HIS SOUP, but Nikka couldn't eat any more. Her stomach rolled and grumbled with anxiety as she thought over the implication of what he had just placed upon her. She said nothing to him on the ride back to the monastery, nor he to her. The streetlights moved by them in silence as the darkness of the night pressed in on the car.

He had not provided her with any more information; not when he wanted to do this or anything. Somehow, he expected her to be successful. It was evident that this was very important to him, and she tried to feel the importance as well, but she just couldn't do it. The possibilities were too frightening to consider.

They entered the church, and she followed him into the main dining hall. He crossed to the fireplace and started a fire, stoking it into brightness. The heat warded off the chill that had settled into her bones.

"When do you want to do this?" she said.

"As soon as possible," he responded and stood to face her. "I know that with the gift of your power, you will find a way to get into that building."

As simple as that sounded, she felt the weight of it on her shoulders and throbbing in her head. "I don't know what to do, Gideon."

He stepped to her and placed his hands on her shoulders. "I know you can do it. We need to get in there soon, tomorrow night. I will research more for you while you work on your part. No training, no library until we know what to do."

"What?" she said. She was expecting to see Jason tomorrow, every part of her wanted that, especially after spending the day with him today. "I have to go to the library."

"We cannot afford to waste any time," he said.

"Please, Gideon," she begged.

"These are the spawns of Hell," he said and gently placed his hands on her shoulders. "There is a demon nest in this city and we know exactly where it starts. We have never had the upper hand like this before. You have the chance to decimate their ranks. Do you grasp how important this is?"

Her hand trembled and her knees wanted to collapse. Of course she understood, but she was one girl against the legions of Hell. There was no way she could do this on her own. Right now, she only wanted to feel Jason against her as they rode his motorcycle up the hill and gazed out over the ocean, to go to a place that was still and calm and quiet. And safe.

But there would never be a place like that for her. Not anymore.

Nikka shook her head, but felt tears flooding her eyes, despite her best effort to stop them.

Gideon looked into her eyes and his voice softened. "You can do this. Remember, you are a superhero. What did Peter Parker's uncle say to him?"

She swallowed the lump that formed in her throat and looked at him. "With great power, comes great responsibility."

This was truer for her than ever. She was responsible for keeping this place, this world, free from the corruption of the demons. That had been her responsibility from the moment she awoke in the cold basement of the hospital. Otherwise, she would already be dead and buried in some cemetery. She never asked for it, but it was bestowed upon her and she would never be able to shake off that mantel.

"Okay," she whispered.

Then, Gideon did something that he had never done before. He wrapped his arms around her like a protective shield and held her close. She buried her face in his neck and closed her eyes. For a moment she forgot that he was her teacher, but only wanted him to be her protector, even though he could never be that.

But after only a few seconds, she pulled away from him. She couldn't afford to feel that she needed his sheltering. "I'll go get to work. I'll try to figure something out." Before he could say anything, she turned and rushed up the stairs to her room.

She locked the door and crawled onto her bed and pulled her phone from her pocket. With shaking fingers, she pulled up Jason's number and began her text.

Looks like I can't meet you tomorrow.

The phone made a swoosh sound as she sent it and then waited, watching the screen and trying not to cry. Within seconds, his response came back.

Too bad. I had a great time today.

I'm sorry. I really wanted to see you again. She tried not to let her tears fall onto the screen.

Maybe the next day, or night. :)

Yeah, right. My brother would never let me out of the house at night.

Jason didn't respond right away. She waited and watched the glowing screen, hoping to see his text.

Is your brother keeping you away tomorrow too?

She wasn't sure how much to tell him. Obviously, she couldn't just tell him the truth.

Yeah.

You haven't told him about me yet, have you.

No.

There was another pause, this time lasting a few minutes, and she worried that he was upset with her. Then the phone buzzed in her hand.

I guess I'm your dirty little secret . ;)

She smiled with relief as she typed her text.

You bet.

See ya soon. Goodnight.

Goodnight.

She turned off the phone and leaned back against the wall. At least she could talk to Jason, even if she couldn't see him. Now, somehow, she was supposed to come up with a strategy to get into the security firm without setting off alarms and without alerting anybody else that she was there.

Nikka closed her eyes and took in a deep breath, hoping to come up with some brilliant plan, but all she could think about was Jason's smile, the way he smelled and his fingers laced with hers. The thought of him relaxed her shoulders and before she knew it, she drifted off to sleep.

The dreams came as fast as they did when she would fall asleep after chemotherapy. But these were not fevered, angry or terrifying nightmares. She simply lay on her bed and she knew it was a dream when she looked over her room. It was the same monastery room that she had been sleeping in for weeks now, but it was bright and smelled of honey and sunflowers. She looked beside her and saw Jason laying there, his torso bare and his lower half under the scarlet blankets of her bed. He slept with one hand draped over her torso, his arms marked with tattoos up to his shoulders. The heat from his body permeated her skin, and she glanced down to see that she was naked under the blankets as well.

A surge of panic flooded over her and reached from her fingers up to her head. Her head was bare, devoid of any sign of the wig. Her tattoos were evident in the bright morning light, just as his were. But he only lay beside her in total relaxation and trust that she would be beside him when he awoke. His fingers had curled around hers at some point while he slept.

She sat up, letting the blanket fall from her body, but she didn't care. She wanted him to see her when he awoke—tattoos and all with nothing else to hide.

Then something caught her eye in the far corner of the room. She climbed out of the bed and stared into the dark corner. It was far too dark on a bright morning such as this, but she paced toward it despite the shadows that seemed to crawl from it. The shadows enveloped her, and she found herself in a different room, one with a single window and an old-style full-length mirror in a dark wooden frame standing in the center of the room. The window was dirty, letting in only yellowed beams of light through a spider web of mud and cracks in the glass.

But there was enough light to illuminate the single mirror.

Nikka stepped closer to the mirror and stopped when she stood in front of it. The light never wavered and the shadows stayed in the corners, but no matter how she looked into it, she could not see her reflection. Everything else reflected—the window, the corners of the room. She turned the mirror and it reflected everything else back to her except herself.

"This mirror doesn't work," she said.

"It works," Jason's voice came from behind her. She turned to see him standing there, fully clothed in the same things he wore when he took her to the coast.

"But I'm not there," she said.

"Yes, you are. It just can't see you," he said.

She awoke with a gasp and opened her eyes to the dark of her bedroom. The bright light of her dream had faded, as had the image of Jason in her bed or standing in the room. But the image of the mirror still lingered in her mind.

"It just can't see you," she whispered to herself.

She understood now what she had to do. It was something that she had never tried, but she had to see if it would work. Perhaps it would be just like turning the Latin into English. The power could do so much, and she prayed that it could do this as well.

CHAPTER 20

S HE WASN'T SURE WHAT TIME it was, but it was dark outside. "It didn't matter, though. She ran down the stairs when she was sure she had the solution. It was too hard for her to know if it would work without Gideon's input. This kind of test just couldn't be done alone.

She rushed down the stairs and into the main hall, where the fire was still blazing in the hearth. Gideon sat at the table with his laptop open, his eyes red from reading in the poor light.

He glanced up at her as she entered.

"I think I have a solution," she said, breathless.

He stood to face her. "Okay."

" I was thinking how I could get in there undetected," she started and rubbed her hands together. This was the only way to get enough of her power started in her fingertips. It seemed to require a lot in a short amount of time. "I started practicing a few things. I came up with this."

She forced the power to surge into her hands and then flood through her body like molten lead. The heat of it zipped through her veins, pulsating into her lips and eyes as well. She willed it to strengthen and mold to her whim.

As Gideon watched her, his eyes grew wide with amazement as her form disappeared into nothing. Every part of her seemed to dissolve into the background of the room.

"How did you do that?" he asked and stepped toward her. He reached out his hand to where she once stood. His fingers touched her as though she was a solid form. He moved his hands, and his fingers brushed dangerously close to her chest.

"Hey," she said, "watch where you're touching."

He snatched his fingers back as her form reappeared before him.

"I just started thinking about the Latin book at the library. I willed the words to change, but they didn't actually change. I altered how I perceived them," she said.

Gideon touched her arm as though he still did not believe that she was solid.

"So I just used that same logic on a larger scale—me," she said. "I figure I could alter the way others perceived me. Watch what else I can do."

She focused the power again to the same intensity as it flowed through her body. The force shaped itself around her cheekbones and lips. As soon as she looked up at him, he gaped at her with the same shocked stare.

It was understandable. She did it for the maximum effect. Gideon now looked at a copy of himself. Though it was an illusion, he saw himself in her face; the same curve of his mouth, the color of his skin and even his hazel eyes.

The power flowed just under her skin, but soon the deep fatigue began to set in, just like the first time she had used it. The illusion faded and she blinked her vision clear. The last bit of energy she had now fizzled out with the power, and she felt her knees shake. She grasped the arm of the sofa and eased down into the seat.

"That is incredible," Gideon said and sat down beside her. "That would definitely help you get into that building."

"The problem is that I can't hold it for very long," she said. "It takes a lot of energy to do it."

"You would not need long. Just time enough to slip past security and into the building. You get the information you need and slip back out again. How on earth did you ever think of this?"

She smiled. "Let's just say I had a dream."

Gideon nodded. "God works in mysterious ways."

"Keep working on it," he said. "We will be prepared for tomorrow night. It is just reconnaissance, an information gathering mission. If you can keep up the illusion, then there will be no need to fight. But I want you to be prepared if it comes to that."

"What exactly am I going to be looking for?" she asked.

"I am not sure. I am hoping you will know it when you see it."

That was reassuring, she thought. As she turned away to go to bed and try to get some sleep, she still felt the impossibility of what he wanted her to do. She didn't doubt that there was something out of sorts about that building, but she wasn't sure that she would be able to find what he wanted.

She collapsed onto her bed, but just stared at the ceiling, rolling the thoughts of her mission over in her head. Find something. Anything in that place. She allowed her eyes to close and tried to clear her head. The only way she could do it was to think of her dream again. Not the mirror part; just the Jason part.

When she opened her eyes, she decided that she must have gotten some sleep because the morning light was just starting to creep over the mountains. The brightest light had not yet peaked, but it wouldn't be long.

She remembered that Gideon had not planned training today, but she knew she had to do it. It would help her focus, and she could keep her muscles and joints limber for tonight. Despite what Gideon said, she knew that there would be no leaving that building without a fight. After all, she saw demons emerge from that place out into the city. Heaven only knows what they did after they got into that cab. She was not sure that she could just let them come and go so easily when she knew she could stop them, even if one of them was a lieutenant.

The workout felt more intense this morning, and she knew why. Each strike could be another one down, another minute of her life spared until she could get the information that Gideon needed. It would only be her alone in that place, and she had to be able to face anything that came at her.

It wasn't until she was done with the solitary punching bag that she turned to see Gideon watching her from the door of the gym.

She toweled off her face and took a drink of water from her bottle.

"Are you okay?" he said.

"What do you think?" she said and walked past him and out of the gym. She really couldn't handle him trying to big brother her right now. She needed to stay focused.

He turned to follow her. "I am simply assessing if . . . "

"I'm fine," she said and cut him off. "Let's just do this." She rushed into her room and shut the door on him.

She couldn't talk about it anymore; it only made her more nervous. Feeling nervous right now would just make her more vulnerable. She had to shake that off and keep going until it was done. After that, they could get back to their routine.

But she knew deep down there would never be routine again after this. It was bound to change everything. Gideon was going to be right about that place. There was something important in there.

After she showered and dressed, she stayed in her room and practiced on the illusion, altering it a little bit every time to see if she could sustain it any longer. Sometimes it helped, and other times, it just drained her even more. After a while of practicing, she couldn't take it anymore and leaned down against her pillow. The fatigue of it zapped her so quickly that it didn't take long for her to fall asleep. The dreams were fitful and violent this time, nothing like waking up next to Jason. Similar to her chemo dreams, she tried to fight the visions, but ended up coughing on the smoke and the blood that threatened to drown her. Instead, she woke up screaming and fighting off the darkness that pressed in all around her.

Enough sleep, she thought. Enough pretending that everything is going to be okay someday and it will all go back to the way it was. Nothing was going to be the same again.

She got up from her bed and pulled on a black tank top and her dark cargo pants. The black thick-soled boots that Gideon had gotten her seemed appropriate for such a mission. She stood in front of the bathroom mirror, gazing at the shadows around her eyes. The black marks were barely visible around her temples from this angle, but she could see the marks curve over her shoulders and trace under the straps of her top. The skin of her chest remained bare, framed by the tattoos that arced just around her breasts. Perhaps someday she would put a mark of her own there, one that she chose.

I will be strong, she thought as she looked at herself in the mirror. Nobody can stop me. I am invincible.

As much as she wanted to believe it, though, she couldn't convince herself, and looked away. It was now or never.

She stepped out of the room and met Gideon in the dining hall. He looked almost as worried as she did, but he continued to pack his computer and phone into his bag.

"Are you ready?" he asked.

"As ready as I'll ever be."

He nodded, and they collected everything into the sedan. He drove the car into the city, winding through the familiar streets to the downtown district. The swarms of bugs in her stomach seemed to transform into bees the closer they got to the building. He pulled the car over into a side street and killed the headlights.

Nikka felt like a stakeout cop in a movie as they both watched the building in silence. The lobby was lit just as it had been the night before, with the security guard at the main desk watching the monitors. The bank of elevators stood behind the desk, but remained still. When she focused her sight, she could still see the markings on the building just as they were last night. She turned her eyes toward the guard and focused deeper, but there was nothing.

"I think the guard is human," she whispered.

"That may be, but he is still employed by the firm to guard the entrance. He cannot be trusted."

Great, she thought. She watched the lobby with him for what seemed like an hour before anything changed. The elevator doors slid open, and the woman flanked by the two drones stepped out just as they had yesterday.

"There they are," Gideon said. "It's 10:13 now. They will return at approximately 11pm."

"Got it," she said and opened the door.

"Please be careful," he said just before she pressed the door closed.

She kept to the shadows as she watched the lobby of the building. The woman stood at the guard station, filling out the proper paperwork before leaving the premises. Nikka stepped across the street, keeping her eyes on the trio. Now, she planned on slipping into the shadows to the north side of the building behind the main doors. She knew Gideon would have a fit, but she could not tell him the rest of her plan. It was the only way it would work, and he would never understand it.

She heard the door click open with an electronic hiss. The trio stepped out into the cool night air, the woman's high heels clicking on the cement. Nikka had to act now.

Her muscles tightened just before she sprang forward. Like a limber cat, she jumped onto the back of one of the drones, pulling him backwards into the shadows. Before the others could react, she ripped the demon from him and let the human collapse to the ground as she drew her sword and split the demon into two pieces. The second drone came at her as the first fell into ashes. The woman stood back, smiling as her eyes erupted into circles of orange flames.

"A seraph," she said and stepped into the darkness. "Oh my. I never would have thought you would be stupid enough to show up here."

"You know nothing about me," Nikka said as her tattoos glowed. She formed the ball of blue light in the palm of her hand and threw it at the second drone. She had never done anything like that before, but something drove her to try, and luckily it worked.

The light tore through him, pulling the demon out with it as it struck the wall behind him. The man fell to the ground while the black demon screeched, pinned against the cement wall. Nikka lunged in and decapitated it. Then, she swung around into a protective stance as she faced the woman.

She laughed and clapped her hands as she watched Nikka. "Very impressive. I must say, I like seeing a female seraph. You know, Girl Power and what not."

Nikka watched her as the woman stepped around her like a hyena stalking its prey. Her eyes seemed to glow brighter the further into the shadows that she moved.

"Too bad I have to kill you now," the woman said.

As the last word disappeared from her dark red lips, she smiled and revealed a row of sharpened fangs. Saliva dripped like acid from the tips of her teeth. The creature lunged at her with outstretched claws. Unlike the drones, this creature moved with unusual speed and strength. Nikka dodged to the side, but the demon caught her and she fell hard to the pavement. The teeth snapped at her, coming awfully close to her jugular. Nikka planted her foot into the demon's abdomen and kicked her back into the shadows.

Nikka flipped up and landed on her feet just as the demon crawled out as fast as a spider toward her. She twisted and arched back into a flip, bounding off the cement wall and landing behind the demon. The creature must have anticipated something like this because it lashed out with a glowing red strand that emerged from the center of her palm like a whip that caught Nikka's ankle. The cord burned into her skin as the demon pulled and slipped her feet out from under her. She cried out as her flesh sizzled from the grasp of the cord.

The cold metal of the sword in her hand tingled in her palm. She swung the katana down and severed the cord. The glow immediately died as Nikka scrambled to her feet. The demon howled and came at her again, its muscles now rippling just under its skin. It crawled toward her using all four of its limbs like an insect, skittering easily over the pavement.

Nikka held her stance and swung at the creature as it came at her again, but the demon knocked the sword free at the last second. The weapon clattered to the ground when the beast grasped her wrist and forced her to the ground. It scampered over her, wrapping its claws around her neck. The flames in its humanoid eyes continued to burn as it gazed down at her.

"I thought you seraph types were stronger than this," the demon hissed as its face came down closer to Nikka's. "So disappointing."

The saliva dripped from its smiling mouth and landed on her cheek. The beast squeezed against her throat. Nikka gasped for air, but nothing would come. Her fingers grasped at the demon's hands, but she felt her strength slipping. The blood pounded in her head.

Her hand reached across the pavement to the sword. She felt the metal hilt just at her fingertips, but it slipped away with each attempt to grab it. The orange eyes came down closer to her as the demon hissed again.

At that moment, she forced her hands into the demon's face and pressed her thumbs into the creature's eyes. It screamed as she felt her fingers slip into the hot jelly of its face. The beast reacted and let its grip on her throat slip. She rolled to the side, grabbed the sword and the shadows lit up in a flash of blue flames. The demon howled, hearing her movements in the narrow alleyway. It lunged at her again as she spun around, katana in hand.

The blade flashed in the dark and struck the creature's neck. It sliced cleanly, sending the bleeding head careening against the far wall. The demon's hands clutched at its neck stump that now oozed black fluid. Then the body collapsed as the head rolled to the pavement with a sharp thud.

Everything was so still and quiet as she clutched the sword, afraid to move should the demon rise again. But it just lay there without smoldering into ash like the drones usually did. Instead, the twisted body now rippled and softened into the limbs of the woman she had seen at first. Even the head, with its sharp teeth and thick saliva, now morphed into the ghastly face of a dead woman, the mouth gaping half open and blood dripping from its empty eye sockets.

I just killed a person, she thought and dropped the sword. The blue glow faded when it lost contact with her. She felt her stomach heave, and she collapsed into the shadows as she threw up everything she had eaten in the last day. The smell of the blood permeated the alleyway, fueling her nausea even more.

She gasped and wiped her mouth. Her hands shook where she supported herself against the wall. With a hard swallow, she turned around to see the body lying in the alley.

Gideon's words still moved through her thoughts, and she knew that there was no other way. You can't just remove a lieutenant or a general from a human, not without torturing the soul, and the demon will kill it anyway. That was still a human lying in the alley, but she had been possessed, for how long, she didn't know. Killing her was probably a sweet release for her already tortured soul.

Nikka took in a deep breath of cool air and stooped to pick up her sword. Her muscles still twitched and trembled from the adrenaline of the fight. Her stomach still heaved a bit, and she couldn't force her eyes to look at the body. It was still just lying there, growing cold and oozing blood onto the pavement.

The sword shook in her hand. She was here for a reason. That woman had a security card that she needed. Now she had to find it, which meant she would have to look at the body. She would have to touch it.

She let her eyes move to the pavement, and they fell onto the shadows that angled sharply over the lifeless mass of torso and legs and arms. The sight made her queasy again and she looked away.

Get it together, she urged herself.

Nikka bit into her lip and held her breath as she wiped the small skim of blood that slicked the blade onto her pant leg and stepped up to the headless body. She placed her boot against the torso and pushed it over. The body rolled with a sickening thud, and she nearly gagged. She closed her eyes, feeling her throat tighten again. She took in a deep breath once more, held it and opened her eyes. Between the shadows, in the light of the distant street lamps, she saw a white glint from the edge of the jacket.

An entry badge.

She pulled it from the woman's jacket and glanced again at the photo on the front. Luckily it didn't have any blood or the black stuff that all the demons seemed to bleed when she cut them, because she wasn't sure if she could handle that right now. She backed away from the body and tried not to look at the severed head. With the back of her hand, she wiped away any tears that had collected at the corners of her eyes.

Focus. There's no time for this.

She held the badge into the light, quickly studying the woman's face. When she had the details memorized, she let the power take over from there.

CHAPTER 21

SHE WALKED INTO THE ENTRYWAY of the firm after she swiped her badge at the door.. The security guard stood as she neared the desk.

"Ms. Longmire," he said with a nod of his head. "Did you forget something?"

Nikka smiled through dark red lipstick. "Yes, I did. I need to go back up to my office. Forgot my laptop."

The guard hesitated for a moment and then handed her the clipboard. "Uh, okay. Can you please sign back in. It's protocol."

"Of course," she said and glanced down at the papers. She knew that nobody else came out of the building after the three demons. The last name on the paper was scrawled in a quick signature: Lisa Longmire, Suite 904. She scribbled in her best attempt at mimicking the signature and handed the clipboard back to him.

"Thank you," he said as she stepped away to the elevators. She slipped inside and held her breath until the doors closed.

She pushed the button to the ninth floor and glanced around the small space. Of course, she thought. A single camera gazed down to her from the upper left corner of the elevator. No doubt that the security guard was watching her as she waited in that elevator. She forced a smile and primped her hair that was pulled back tightly into a French twist.

The elevator dinged as it came to the ninth floor, and the doors opened. She exited into a hallway that was now partially lit since it was after hours. A scarlet carpet covered the floor as it opened into a pair of double glass doors. Gold etching painted onto the glass read, "Lisa Longmire, Chief Financial

Officer." She glanced down both sides of the hallway to see several cameras pointed at the elevator doors.

She stepped to the doors and pressed her badge against the reader to the right of the door frame. The doors clicked open and she escaped the hallway. The office was dark except for the lighting through the glass doors. She moved through the spacious waiting area, dotted with overstuffed leather chairs and glass tables topped with abstract art. The space opened past a secretary desk and to a hallway that moved further into the dark. A single wood door stood at the back of the hallway.

Her fingers found the brass door handle, and she held her breath, hoping the door wasn't locked. It turned without resistance, and she opened it. The room smelled of copier ink and wood polish. Her eyes adjusted to the faint light from the two windows at the far end of the room, but it was bright enough to tell that there were no security cameras in this office.

The illusion faded, and she could finally see through her own eyes without the effort to hold up the image of Lisa. She scanned the office and saw the usual shelves and books of a corporate executive: rows of binders and books on finance management. A picture of the real Lisa, with what Nikka assumed was her husband, stood on the end of the shelf—a harsh reminder that there was a human body now lying in the alleyway.

She slid around the edge of the desk and faced the computer monitor. It didn't take long for her to navigate the menus until she found what Gideon could be looking for. It was the only thing that looked like it might possibly have some significance to him, but she couldn't be sure. In the light of the monitor she searched the desk drawers and discovered a flash drive sitting in the pen holder. She plugged it into the computer and moved the files into the drive's memory. She copied the photo drive as well as the email files, just in case. Then, she slipped the flash drive into her pocket.

Her heart raced now as she stepped out of the office, willing the illusion to cover her body again. She slipped into the corridor and then into the elevator. The car moved down to the main floor and she steadied her breathing for fear the illusion would fail. The doors opened, but just as she moved to exit the elevator, the security guard stood before her.

"Can you come with me, ma'am," he said with his hands on his hips.

"I'm sorry," she said and tried to slip past him. "I am in a bit of a hurry."

"I have to insist," he said and grabbed her arm with enough force to bruise her flesh.

She jerked her arm free, but the loss of concentration made the illusion collapse. The guard stared at her in disbelief for a second as she pulled away from him. He reached for her and pressed the alert on his walkie-talkie at his hip. Nikka lunged back into the elevator, grasping the top of the elevator doors and kicked her legs out against him. He crashed back into the main desk while the elevator doors slid closed. She pressed a button down to the basement and the car began to move.

It slid down two floors and the doors opened to a parking garage with poor lighting. The place was mostly empty, with the exception of a few cars parked at the edges of the lot. A siren sounded from somewhere above the garage floors. She bounded out of the elevator and ran across the lot. Several running footsteps echoed from behind her as a group of security guards entered the lot from an emergency stairway.

She glanced behind her to see the group running toward her. She pushed harder, but felt her lungs burn and her muscles ache. The illusion had drained much of her strength, and she couldn't run much longer. She saw the driveway up to the second parking lot at street level. She turned up the drive and plunged into the shadows of the upper lot.

The guards followed her and split up as they emerged onto the lot. She dodged around a thick cement pillar as the guard in the lead spotted her. He ran as his talkie buzzed with chatter from around the building. He pulled his gun and rounded the pillar, but he could no longer see her.

Nikka held still against the pillar, holding the invisibility illusion. Her lungs ached for more air, but she had to control her breathing. The appearance would only be as effective as her silence. The guard stopped and aimed his gun into the shadows. He withdrew his flashlight and shined it into the furthest corners of the lot. Other guards came from the opposite direction in hopes of cornering her, but saw nothing.

"Where did she go?" one said as he gasped for air.

"She was just here a second ago," the lead guard spoke and shined his light around the lot. "She couldn't have gone far. Keep looking."

The guards turned away from her and continued scanning the parking lot. The exit was still across the length of the building, and many of the guards were still surrounding it. She couldn't hold the illusion much longer. She had to slip away as soon as she could.

From where she stood, she could see a steel door along the side of the wall closest to her. It would most likely be a utility closet. She just hoped that it wasn't locked.

She stepped as quietly as she could to the door and tried the knob. It turned with ease, and she slipped through and closed the door. For a moment she listened at the door for any activity that could have alerted the guards, but there was nothing. She stepped back and noticed she was at the top of a stairway landing.

The stairs led down into a darkness that smelled of sulfur and candle wax. The illusion was too difficult to hold any longer, and she let it fall as she stepped down the stairway. Her fingers felt along the cement wall as she descended into what she assumed was a sub basement. She hoped that there was another exit somewhere down here. Each step she took echoed into a large space in the dark. Then her fingers brushed against a light switch panel. She flipped the switch and squinted at the harsh light that sparked into life within the room.

The enormous room filled the entire space under the parking lot. A simple incandescent bulb hung from a cord in the center of the room and chased away the darkness within its radius of light. In that space of light, she could see a circle painted on the cement floor in red paint. An outer circle lined it, decorated with sigils similar to those that adorned the outside of the building. She could tell that many candles had been lit and burned around the outer circle, leaving puddles of hardened wax. The center of the circle was blackened, as though a fire had been set there.

Her marks began to burn and sparkle. The feeling raged just under her skin, and though she tried to control it, it burned like a fire poker piercing under her flesh. She staggered back as the power surged out of control. Whatever power lingered in this basement threatened to steal every bit of light from her body and devour it for its own pleasure. This place was something so awful, even if she had no idea what it meant. There would be no escape, and it was far worse down here than up in the garage. If her power felt that she needed to leave, she didn't intend to fight that feeling.

She fell back against the stairway and hurried up the steps, taking two at a time until she came back up to the door.

The power ebbed away, but not as quickly as she would have liked. It left her sweating and weak as she pressed her forehead against the door, listening for the sounds of the guards. When she had caught her breath and could no longer hear them, she gathered her strength and pulled on the invisibility illusion one last time.

She opened the door and peered out into the lot. There was no sign or sound of the guards anywhere, and she could see the lot exit from here. She stepped from the door and ran across the lot until she emerged onto the street that led away from the building. She continued to run, even though she could feel the illusion slip in waves from her body. Her legs carried her across the street where she could see Gideon's car waiting.

Sweat poured down her neck as she ran as hard as she could. Gideon stepped out of the car and ran to meet her in the middle of the street. She collapsed just as he reached her, collecting her in his arms. He scooped her up and rushed her to the car, then fired up the engine and drove away into the night.

CHAPTER 22

THE STREET LIGHTS ZOOMED by as Gideon maneuvered the car through the city, but Nikka barely noticed. She pulled her knees up to her chest and buried her face. The shaking continued in her hands, weakened by the use of such power for so long. The image of the woman's face and empty eyes continued to swim in the background of her thoughts. She could still smell the blood mixed with the sulfurous odor of the demon's breath.

"Are you okay?" Gideon spoke as he raced the car toward the hills.

The words echoed like a hollow roar in her ears. Her fingers clutched around her knees, hoping to bind herself together for fear of falling into a million pieces. If she moved, if she breathed, her world might shatter.

The glare of the city lights gave way to the dark of the woods and the winding hill road back to the monastery. Gideon stopped the car and ran to the passenger side. He opened the door and lifted her out of the car, carrying her into the church. The feel of his chest against her cheek felt like stone. He seemed to be rushing to get her inside the building. Once he moved up the stairs, he pushed open the main hall doors and rested her on the plush sofa, but he never left her side.

His hand touched her face, now wet with tears. The warmth of his touch didn't matter to her though. She grimaced and turned away from him as the tears flowed from her eyes. Here it was: the shattering of her soul.

She could still feel the steel in her hand as her blade cut the woman's head off, followed by the spray of blood and black ooze. Then she felt the sinister evil of the basement that crept into her bones. Her body trembled as she tried to pull her legs up to her chest again. But Gideon wouldn't let her. He lifted her up from the couch and held her in his strong embrace.

Her veins felt like ice water, rushing through every vessel and into her heart.

"I killed someone," she cried as he held her tight.

"I know," he said. "I saw everything."

His hand moved to the back of her head and the smooth skin that curved down to her neck. The embrace he gave her now helped to hold her world together just a little bit.

"There was no other way," he said. "You did what you were commissioned to do."

Her fingers clutched at his shirt, hoping he would not let her go. "There has to be some way. She had a husband. She was a person."

"She was possessed," he said and pulled her away just enough to hold her face in his hands and look at her. "You released her from Hell on earth, and by doing so, you may have saved countless lives in the process. Such is the torment of the seraph."

Nikka hung her head. "I can't do it."

"And this is why you were chosen—for your heart and your suffering," he whispered as he leaned in closer to her. She could feel his breath on her ear. "Now you must rest. Gather your strength."

As she looked up at him and wiped her face with the back of her hand, she withdrew the flash drive from her pocket and handed it to him. "Just plug this into the slot on the side of your laptop. It has a bunch of files that looked like something we could use."

He nodded. "I knew you could do it."

"And there was something else," she said, but felt her hands shake as she thought about it again. "I found something in the basement; a big circle painted on the ground with lots of candles around it."

"Was it scorched in the center?" he asked.

She nodded. "That place is pure evil."

The color drained from his face. "It sounds like a portal. I was right. That building is definitely important."

"What's a portal?"

He shook his head. "Let us not worry about that right now. I want you to rest. We shall talk about it tomorrow."

That was fine with her. Her mind still swam with guilt, and she wasn't sure that she could even focus on what he would be saying tonight. She turned and made her way up to her room, where she collapsed onto the bed.

In the dark and alone, she felt the tears flowing again as she clutched her pillow to her abdomen. Sleep would not come soon enough. As tired as she was, she couldn't stop the images of the demon and the woman from tormenting her thoughts. Every time she closed her eyes, she saw the framed picture of the real Lisa standing next to her husband, the wedding ring on her finger sparkling in the sunlight of the summer day when they had the picture taken.

Everything that had happened tonight felt like it now stained her soul. These things would forever be there, always recalled whenever she felt scared or helpless. It was like the time she watched a scary movie when she was young, and her father had warned her that it would be too scary for her, but then she couldn't get the images out of her head. They just kept replaying over and over again every time she closed her eyes.

Sleep came with horrifying dreams of black creatures and claws that scratched at her limbs. The blue sword could only light the space around her, but she was afraid to use it. There was always the possibility that she would hurt someone else.

And then she felt a warm hand on her wrist. She turned to see Jason's face, the only thing in the dark that she could see. The blue glow of the sword illuminated his face like an angel, but he looked at her with sad eyes and touched her face.

"What can I do?" she said to him.

The sounds of monsters in the dark silenced, leaving just the two of them.

"Don't let me die," he whispered to her just before everything disappeared in a flash of white light.

She awoke with a gasp, beads of sweat dripping from her brow and down her neck. The remnants of Jason's touch on her face still warmed her skin and she bolted upright in her bed to see the bright morning light through the shutter slats on her window. She wiped the back of her hand across her forehead to clear the slick of nervous sweat. Her breathing slowed as she oriented herself to her own bedroom, but the aftershocks of the dream continued to tremble down her spine.

She rose on shaking legs and knew that her strength had still not fully returned from last night. The heat and humidity of the shower helped, and she was able to examine all of her new bruises and the burn mark around her ankle when she was fully unclothed. She dressed in jeans and a white T-shirt before going downstairs to meet Gideon for the day. It didn't matter what he said, there was no way she could muster the energy for training today.

The fragrance of hot pancakes and scrambled eggs greeted her at the doors of the hall. When she sat down, he poured her some orange juice and sat down next to her with his own plate full of breakfast.

"How are you today?" he asked.

She shook her head. "I don't want to talk about it."

Gideon nodded. "Very well, but I would like to share some of the things I discovered. I was able to review the files you downloaded. Very intriguing. It appears that you found the right information."

He arranged a collection of printed photos and documents around the table. "There were lists of places all around the city and the state where I believe they have demon nests established."

"What about the portal? My power sort of freaked out when I got close," she said.

"That building is housing a gateway. That portal is meant to be the entry way into this world. I believe that they want to use it as a rapid entry point for an army. There are not many portals in this world, but it appears that you found one. I imagine that is why you were called to be a seraph, in this city at this time. This is the largest demon nest I have ever seen."

If he was trying to make her feel better about the events of the previous night, he wasn't doing a very good job.

"One very important thing I found," he said as he selected a page from his pile. "They do not refer to him by name, but I believe Abaddon has already come through the portal. There are several mentions of The Destroyer, but no specifics on location. If this is true, I believe that he may be in the city already."

"Great," she forced a very fake smile and drank her orange juice. She stood with her now empty plate and carried it to the kitchen.

"When are you taking me to the library?" she said as she walked back through the room.

"There is no time for that," he said and gathered his research. "We must establish our next move."

She set her jaw and glared at him. "I am going to the library today. Either you drive me or I am going to walk."

He looked at her in confusion. "Very well. Perhaps you can find information there to help us. Collect your things and I will take you."

They didn't speak much on the drive back into the city. She just looked out the window at the falling leaves for most of the way. The sky had become gloomy and gray, threatening a rain shower at some point in the day. Tree branches began to look like skeletal arms reaching into the air. She could feel Gideon's gaze on her occasionally, but she didn't care.

Somewhere in the back of her mind, she wanted to blame him for this guilt. If he had never come to her in the hospital, she would never have killed that woman in the alley. Yes, she would be dead from the cancer, but she would be free of this shame that she felt. She would be free of the burden that he had thrust upon her.

He pulled the car to the curb beside the campus. This time he said nothing to her as she got out and slammed the passenger door. It didn't matter what he said anymore. She never wanted to hear it again. She walked across the road, but slowed as she started onto the campus.

The prickles began on her neck, and she knew that there were eyes on her. Gideon had already driven away. She glanced back along the row of cars parked at the curb and saw the source of her uneasiness. Father Beyers watched her from a silver sedan down the street. He made no attempt to hide from her, nor did he avert his gaze. He watched her from under the brim of his hat with one hand on the steering wheel.

She stepped toward him. She was going to find out why he was following her. But just as she moved toward him, he pulled the car away from the curb and sped away with screeching tires.

What the hell was going on?

A cold wind gusted, blowing crisped leaves across the road. It penetrated through her hoodie and whipped strands of hair from her wig across her face. It didn't matter if he left her now. She was sure he would be back to continue spying on her, and when he did, she was going to confront him. She pulled her backpack close to her shoulder and walked toward the library.

She spotted the picnic table where she shared a cookie with Jason, but it remained empty today. Not a surprise. It was about twenty degrees colder now than it had been all of last week. Most of the students had sought shelter indoors and away from the wind and threat of rain.

She hurried to the entry doors of the library and stepped into its warm environment. At first she glanced around for any sign of Jason, but there were many more students on the main floor than usual, probably because of the weather.

Nikka moved up the stairs, scanning the rows of books as she entered the upper floor, but she still could not see him. Her nervous energy began to bubble in her stomach: what if something happened to him? The dream last night felt so horrible, and now she began to wonder if it was some kind of premonition about him.

Don't let me die.

She rushed to her usual table and gazed out the window to the quad.

Rain had begun to spatter against the windows, streaking down in thin streams. Tree branches rustled in the light breeze. She scanned the lawn, but saw nobody that might be Jason. The afternoon light darkened with storm clouds that filled the sky.

"Hell of a storm," a voice said in her ear.

She spun around to see his familiar blue eyes and blonde goatee. He smiled, but she gasped and threw her arms around his neck.

"Whoa," he said and almost fell back, but she felt his arms move around her as well.

"Oh my gosh," she said. "You're okay."

The trembling shook her slender frame as he wrapped his arms around her. "Of course I am. Why wouldn't I be?"

She pulled away from him and became aware that she had just thrown herself at him. "I—I had a dream that something bad happened to you."

"Must have been quite a dream," he said and touched her face. "Are you okay? You look like you've seen a ghost."

Nikka clenched her fists to hide the shaking in her fingers, but she was afraid to look up at him. There was no way she could tell him what troubled her mind now.

"Here," he said and pulled a chair up to her. "Sit down. Chillax."

She settled into the chair and put her elbows on the table as she covered her face with her hands. The tears threatened to flood her eyes again, but she couldn't allow that, not in front of Jason.

"Something tells me this is about more than just a dream," he whispered and leaned over her. She could feel his hair brush against her cheek. "What happened to you last night?"

"I can't—" she started, but felt her throat tighten.

"It's okay," he said and pulled her close to him. She rested her head on his chest. "It wasn't your brother, was it? Did he hurt you?"

"No," she said. "I just can't talk about it."

"Okay. No prob. We'll just hang here and talk library stuff, 'cause that's so much fun," he said with a sarcastic smile.

She laughed a little and felt her throat loosen and the tears fade. She had no plans to research her books today. The library had become her haven away from Gideon's world, and now she shared it only with Jason. That was how she planned on keeping it.

The sky began to clear, chasing the rain into the mountains. A chill remained as the sun began to set, and the clock ticked onward. The six o'clock hour approached, and she glared at the clock with contempt. Her time spent here with Jason was too short, and the thought of going back into Gideon's world sickened her. If she saw Gideon again right now she knew she would have thoughts of the woman she had killed. Even now, she felt the sour taste of it in her mouth.

"Looks like you gotta go soon," Jason muttered beside her where they rested back against the wall of the library with his hand behind her shoulders.

"No," she said and sat up, pulling her phone from her jeans. "I can't go back there."

He sat straighter and looked at her with a concern she had never seen before. "Are you sure he didn't do anything to you?"

If she had said yes, Nikka was sure that Jason would be ready to hunt Gideon to the ends of the earth. That thought made her skin tingle a little. And she was pretty sure what Jason was really asking; he was fishing for information on abuse. It almost seemed ridiculous, especially since she knew Gideon. But Jason knew nothing about him.

"He didn't. I just don't want to be around him right now," she said and selected Gideon's number on her quick dial.

Gideon answered, the timbre of his voice laced with worry.

"Don't bother picking me up. I'll come home later," she said as she turned away from Jason.

"Nikka, no," Gideon said firmly.

"This is not negotiable tonight," she said. "I'll find a way home later."

"Please do not do this," he said just as she ended the call with a finger swipe across the glass screen.

She turned to face Jason again and slid the phone into her pocket, but he watched her with worry.

"Are you sure about this?" he said.

"Yeah," she said. "Let's get out of here."

He stood and helped her from her place on the floor. "Okay. I've got a great idea. It will totally cheer you up, I know it."

Whatever he wanted to do, she would be ready and willing to do it. There had to be some change in her life right now, because if she continued down this path, she wasn't sure she was going to be able to make it.

CHAPTER 23

JASON HAD GIVEN HER HIS black leather jacket before they climbed onto his motorcycle. She was more than happy to sit behind him and just feel him against her as they rode. She didn't care where they went, but her mood brightened when she saw the lights and activity beyond the parking lot where they stopped.

The fall carnival.

People milled around the entrance to the old fairgrounds that transformed into a brightly lit amusement park every October. The smell of caramel and popcorn filled the air, reminding her of the days when she was a child and her father took her to the festival. She recalled being terrified of all the carnival workers dressed in scary costumes as they juggled or swallowed fire along the boardwalks.

Jason took her hand after they climbed off the bike and led her to the entry, where he paid for their tickets. It was like entering another world, like Alice jumping through the looking glass. Beyond the gates stood a brightly colored and flamboyant world that was so different from the one she had been living in. The flashing lights of the merry-go-round before them twinkled with the laughter of children and the sound of carnival games at the periphery of the fairgrounds.

He pulled her close enough that she could smell the cologne on his neck again. He wrapped his arms around her and gazed down at her. "Will this do for tonight?"

She smiled. "This is going to be the best night ever."

"I hope so," he said. For a moment he hesitated. She could almost read his thoughts through his eyes. She lifted herself on her tiptoes just as he leaned down and their lips met. The sounds of the carnival drowned out in a rush of noise as he kissed her, sending her worries into a fading void.

He pulled away from her. "Was that okay? I wasn't sure . . ."

"It was great," she stopped him before he could say any more.

"All right, then," he smiled, and she could see his dimples. "Let's go win you some horribly oversized stuffed animal. That's what guys do for their girls at this place, isn't it?"

"Sounds good to me," she said as he took her hand and lead her down the fairway. "I've never had a horribly oversized stuffed animal before."

He bought her a fluff of blue cotton candy just before he tried his hand at throwing a ring over empty bottles, which was obviously rigged since he couldn't win a single thing. The next game, or the game after that, didn't fare any better. But it didn't matter, because he laughed every time he lost. It was okay: his reward would be a dab of sticky cotton candy each time.

After rides on the Ferris Wheel and then the Tilt-a-Whirl, her stomach churned and she insisted that they rest for a moment. They found a long bench where she could rest her head on his lap while she breathed in the cool air to settle her stomach and just look up at him. The merry-go-round spun in a whorl of sparkling lights across the fairway from them, its music playing in the background to the chatter of people and children's laughter.

"Where do you see yourself in ten years?" she said as he bit into the caramel apple that he had bought before they sat down.

"I don't know," he said and intertwined his fingers with her. "Hopefully I have finished college and have moved on."

"To where?"

"I know it sounds stupid, but I want to get an engineering degree," he said as his face flushed.

"It's not stupid," she said and sat up to face him. "Don't say stuff like that."

"I want to design and build motorcycles," he said and handed her the apple.

"I'm not surprised," she said. "I think you would be a great designer."

"What about you?" he said.

She averted her gaze and felt her smile slip as she sat upright. "I wanted to be an artist once. Like for comic books."

"That's awesome," he said and squeezed her hand. "But you don't sound persuaded to do it anymore."

"My future is not my own," she said. "I have no say in what happens to me anymore."

A look of concern crossed his face as he turned toward her and held both of her hands. "Is this about your brother?"

"He means well," she said and looked up at him. "But he wants me to be something that I am not. I can't do what he wants me to do anymore, but I have no one else to help me."

Jason placed a hand on her cheek. "Whatever it is that he did to you that you're not telling me, there is a way out."

"I know you think he's some kind of creeper that touches little girls or something. It's not like that. He's just really overprotective," she said.

"I can't tell you how many times I've heard that in my life," he said. "Let me help you."

She pulled his hand away from her face and shook her head. "Nobody can help me."

He leaned toward her and kissed her again. He tasted like caramel as he pressed against her and then pulled away, resting his forehead against hers. "There is always a way."

Whatever he believed, she was not sure that she had the luxury to believe it too. Jason's view of the world was limited to his human existence and was not the vast horror that hers had become. There was so much she couldn't tell him. He would never understand her responsibility. How could he help her if he never comprehended the magnitude of her burden?

But there was something of herself she could share, a bit of the truth that she didn't want to hide anymore.

"I need to tell you something," she said and met his deep blue gaze.

"Okay," he said with a tinge of worry.

"About a year ago," she started, "I was diagnosed with cancer."

He raised his eyebrows in disbelief. "Nikka, I—I had no idea."

"After chemo and radiation, the doctors said I was going to die. This," she said as she ran her fingers through her hair, "is not my real hair. I lost all of it."

He touched a strand of her hair. "It's okay. With or without it, you're still beautiful."

She smiled. "It's not the hair that I cared about. It's my . . . brother. He saved me, and I owe him so much."

Jason nodded. "I understand. But he can't control you forever. You're alive and you're here. He has to understand that you need to be your own person now."

Maybe Jason was right about that. Gideon had given her a second life, but that didn't mean she had no control over it anymore. She was still Nikka, the same girl that once had a family and friends and the prom and college entrance exams. There was more to her existence than the narrow niche Gideon had created for her. She was not born to be a demon-killing machine without a soul.

As he smiled at her, she knew that she couldn't be with Gideon the rest of her life, however short that would be. She rested against him with his arm around her as they watched the lights of the carnival. The world felt a whole lot brighter when she was with him, just like the carnival in the darkness of a cold October night.

But as much as she wanted to stay there, she knew her time with him would be cut short eventually. The lights of the carnival had to die and she would have to return to the monastery, where Gideon waited for her. He would probably be angry, but she didn't care. Every second she spent with Jason was worth it.

The late hour turned into the extremely early hours of the morning by the time she rode with Jason up the hill. Just as she had instructed, he stopped at the base of the main road to the monastery. At least she would respect Gideon's wishes and keep their sanctuary a secret.

As the motorcycle rumbled, he pulled her closer and kissed her one more time. "Are you sure you want me to drop you off here? I can take you all the way to your place."

"I'll be okay," she said. "I'll see you tomorrow."

"Yeah. You promise?"

"Promise," she said and crossed her fingers over her heart.

"All right, then," he said as she backed away from him.

Jason revved the engine, and just before he started it back down the hill, she felt the tickle of uncertainty begin to rise in her gut. She would have to tell Gideon about him now, but she had to do one more thing to settle his mind. He would definitely have his suspicions about Jason.

Nikka let the power into her vision just for a moment as Jason looked back at her. She focused on him, searching his soul. There was no black creature there, no fire in his eyes. There was only Jason and his dimpled smile as he turned down the road and into the dark of the woods.

The faint taste of his caramel-laced kiss lingered on her lips as she turned toward the winding road that would lead her to the monastery. The problems she would face with Gideon were far from her mind as she re-membered Jason's kiss. She hugged her arms around her torso and realized that she still wore his jacket. A smile spread across her lips as she grasped the lapel of the jacket and took in his scent.

She entered the monastery doors and made her way up to the main room. She knew that Gideon would be in there, fuming. She opened the doors to the room and found him with his computer on his lap as he worked on the sofa. He glanced at her once when she entered the room.

"I have worried for many hours," he said with an even tone.

"Sorry," she said. "I just needed to be out."

"Who is he?" Gideon said as he placed the computer on the table.

"Who?" she said and tried to sound innocent. How did he already know about Jason?

"The man you were with. I can smell him on you," he said.

She looked down to the floor. "Just some guy I met at the library, and the smell-thing is a little creepy."

"Have you not heard anything that I have told you?" he said, his voice growing louder.

"I'm not doing this right now," she said and stepped out into the hall. But he followed her as she stormed up the stairs.

"You must be careful," he said. "You have no idea who he is."

"No, you don't," she shouted and slammed the door to her room shut. She walked to the window and looked out over the city that lit up the distance of the horizon below the tree line. "You can't keep me here forever," she yelled back over her shoulder.

Although there was only silence beyond her door, she knew that he was still there.

Then, he spoke. "If you involve a human, it is just one more thing that the demon can use against you. You will put him in danger."

The floor seemed to fall beneath her as she felt her knees weaken. This was an aspect of her situation that she had not expected, but Gideon had never needed to share before. The echoes of her dream flooded back to her as she saw Jason's face and heard his plea: don't let me die. Of course she wanted to protect him, but could Gideon be right?

She walked to her bed and slipped the jacket from her shoulders. It was all she had of him right now, but even this she couldn't give up. There was no way she could let him go, not yet. He was the only thing in the real world that she could still grasp; he was something that made her feel that the world was not falling into the fires of Hell.

Chapter 24

THE MONASTERY NOW FELT EMPTY, cold and harsh, like a prison meant to keep her from the world. Gideon was her warden and she was the princess locked in the tower.

She couldn't stay in her room forever; she was reminded of that when her stomach growled. The smell of lunch in the main hall was too tempting, but there was no way that she wanted to talk to Gideon today. He would just be full of grouchy doom, and she didn't want to hear any more of it.

Nikka walked into the dining hall to find a plate of biscuits and a side of butter and jam. But Gideon was not there. Her shoulders relaxed when she realized she didn't have to confront him right now. She started on a couple of biscuits and slid into the chair at the table. In place of her usual setting, though, was a sticky note with Gideon's handwriting.

Training today

Ugh, she thought. But she supposed it would only be a matter of time before she had to talk to him. She swallowed down the two biscuits with a gulp of water and then made her way to the gym. Before she opened the door, she took in a few even breaths and then turned the doorknob.

Daylight flooded through the windows that looked down onto the mat and equipment. Gideon stood at the punching bag, his hands wrapped and without a shirt. She had never seen him half-dressed before and was taken aback by how muscular he was. It certainly fit the Marine impression she had of him when they first met. The muscles in his shoulders rippled with each strike he gave to the bag. His mocha skin glistened with droplets of sweat.

She cleared her throat to get his attention, and he stopped to glance back at her.

"You are late," he said.

"Yeah," she said with a little raise of her eyebrows. Whatever.

"Let's start with your bow staff," he said, as though nothing had happened last night.

Fine, she thought. *Let's not talk about it. Ever.*

She grabbed the staff just as he took one of his own. As soon as she had her grip on the weapon, he lunged at her with a strike, which she blocked. Her feet moved, anticipating each maneuver. His anger-tinged eyes watched her from under his heavy brow. He swiped at her legs, but she jumped and rolled into a block as he brought his staff down at her head. If she didn't know better, she would have thought he might be trying to kill her.

Their staffs met with a sharp clack. She took the opportunity to spin her weapon and disarm him. His staff clattered against the wall, almost shattering with the force of her blow, as he lost his grip. Then, she swiped her staff toward him and stopped it inches from his throat.

"Finish him," she said, recalling her days playing *Mortal Kombat* with her childhood friends.

But the quip was lost on Gideon as he stood and glared at her. She stepped away from him and drew the staff to her side.

"I'm sorry that I had to leave yesterday," she said. "I just had to get out."

"What's his name?" he grumbled to her and averted his gaze.

His question took her by surprise. Something in his tone made her stop and watch him, especially the way he slumped his shoulders and stalked away from her like a furious ogre with his staff.

She put her hand on her hip and stared at him. "Is that why you're mad at me? Because I was out with someone else?"

He turned away from her and signaled to the balance beam. "Time for your forms."

"No," she said and tossed the staff to the side. "You're going to talk to me." She folded her arms across her chest. "Are you jealous?"

"Your forms," he said more forcefully.

Stubborn ass, she thought, and turned away from him. She mounted the balance beam and went through her routine as usual. Each backflip was flawless, and she never missed her footing. She finished with her full layout and landed on the mat at the end of the beam.

Then she turned to him again. "I need you to talk to me."

The anger almost rippled off of him like heat. She had never seen him like this before.

"His name is Jason," she said. "He listens to me and doesn't expect anything. I'm sorry I didn't tell you about him."

Gideon walked away from her and worked at replacing the staffs in their proper places along the rack. It was obvious that he was trying to keep himself busy with menial tasks rather than to talk to her or even look at her.

"I needed something else besides all this," she said, opening her hands to the room. "I don't think I can handle this anymore. After that woman, I—"

"I understand," he muttered from where he stood. Then he turned to face her, the anger melting from his face. "Do you not think that I know? I have witnessed hundreds of your kind, but you are the first woman. Your kindness, your innocence is new to me. But I do know your anguish. Your isolation."

She felt the tears form in her eyes. Though she tried to blink them away, she could not stop them.

"I did not call you to this position. Angels chose you because they knew you could do it. In fact, they knew you were the only one that could," he said and stepped toward her. "Without you, all may be lost."

She shook her head. "I can't do it. You don't know what it's like, when you kill someone like I did—"

"You know nothing of me," he whispered and averted his gaze.

"Because you won't tell me. You won't tell me anything meaningful. You just give me hints of where in history you've been." She approached him, but he turned away from her again. "What are you, Gideon?"

"I am a sinner," he said. "This is my penance: to watch over you, to keep you alive the best way I know how. This is the only thing I have to offer."

"I don't understand what any of that means."

"You were never meant to," he said and stepped toward the door. "I only ask that you think hard about those you love. If you love this man, you must let him go. Holding onto him could kill him." He exited the gym and left her standing in the shafts of daylight pouring from the windows.

There was nothing left of him there except the profound sadness that he placed upon her. She knew it was selfish of her to want something more; after all, Gideon had given her back her life, but took her world in exchange. Her life was no longer her own; it was now property of a higher power.

Everything that she had learned from him and from the books in the library had taken her to one conclusion: the drones were mere insects compared to the higher ranking demons, and these inhabited human bodies that she would have to kill.

She just couldn't do that again. She did not have the stomach to see another person taken down by her sword for the good of a war.

She ran after him and found him in the dining hall, where he sat on the sofa with his head back and his eyes closed.

"Why does it have to be this way?" she asked. "Why can't I take the demon out of them like I can the drones?"

He opened his eyes and fixed his gaze upon her. "A seraph does not have the power."

"But why? The angels gave me the power that I have," she started, her voice rising in frustration. "Why make me kill an innocent just to eliminate the demon?"

"Because the power it requires is too great for a human to handle," he spoke. "Even an angel could be destroyed by the power."

He stood and walked to the hearth where the orange blaze of the fire illuminated the skin of his bare chest. "I have only ever seen it happen once."

"So it is possible," she said and stepped closer to him. For the first time in hours she felt a glimmer of hope ignite in her chest.

"Only once did an angel pull a high rank demon from its host, and both demon and human lived," he muttered as if talking to the fire, his mind enthralled by a memory he would not share.

"How?"

"I will not talk about this anymore," he said.

The sadness in his voice startled her and she dared not press him anymore. Something about it hit a nerve with him, but it also ignited her curiosity. Perhaps this question would be the answer to her future. There had to be a way to save the human. It had been done once before. Maybe, if she could learn the true story, then she could figure out a way to save them.

"I need to study," she said.

"Very well," he said. "I will take you to the library."

His voice remained sad and withdrawn, which was something she had not expected. Gideon almost looked broken, a shell of who he once was.

CHAPTER 25

JASON WAS WAITING FOR HER when she arrived at the library. He was supposed to work, but he re-shelved his books in between his talks with her while she waited at her usual table. When his coworkers were no longer glancing up at him, he slid back to Nikka's corner table.

"Everything okay?" he whispered to her.

Her mind had been distracted ever since her discussion with Gideon this morning.

"I don't know," she said. "I'm not sure what to do anymore."

"What can I do?" he said and grasped her hand.

She wasn't sure. Everything had gotten so confused. She wanted to tell Jason everything, but she knew that would never be possible. Following Gideon's plan was suicide. She was lost.

The only person she ever shared her deepest concerns with was her mother, and that had been taken away from her as well. There had once been a time when she could cry on her shoulder about anything from boys to college applications. In this struggle to come to terms with this new existence, she had tried to forget about her family, but now she needed it more than ever. No matter how hard she tried to suppress the need to see her parents, it continued to swell within her.

"Maybe there's one thing you could do for me," she said.

She couldn't tell him anything more than she just needed to go somewhere, a place that Gideon would never have allowed her to see. Although the air had grown colder, the ride on the motorcycle brought her fresh air that she desperately needed right now.

She guided him through the streets and to the northern suburbs, along rows of homes built around the 1920's but kept in beautiful condition. The neighborhood had grown with the oak and maple trees that lined the streets and the church on Franklin Avenue had been added to the National Registry of Historic Places. She remembered everything about this beautiful place, from the centralized park to the smell of lilacs in the spring.

The motorcycle stopped where she had directed him and asked him to wait for her for a few minutes. She planned on walking the two blocks down from there because she couldn't have him see her do this. He just wouldn't understand.

Gold and red leaves rained down from nearly bare branches. Her boots crunched over them as she stepped across the sidewalks. Every house she passed reminded her of the time she would run through these streets or ride her bicycle on a warm summer day. With her hands in the pockets of the hoodie, she looked out over the neighborhood, knowing that the house was just around the corner from the crooked maple tree at the end of the street.

She felt the swirl of nerves begin in her stomach and her pace slowed against her will. The breeze blew strands of hair in her eyes as she looked out to the house with white vinyl fencing along the sidewalk. The two-story home looked just as it had the day the ambulance took her from its front door.

That day was as fresh to her now as when it had happened. She remembered getting dizzy and then coughing. The next thing she knew, she was on the floor with sputters of blood and foam coming from her mouth with each cough. Her hair had fallen out long before that and she thought the coughing was just another side effect of chemo. No. Pulmonary edema. That's what they called it. Something much worse.

That was the last day she had seen the wraparound porch with white trim. When EMT's had taken her out on their gurney, she remembered glancing up at the baskets of bleeding hearts blooming from their hooks in the trim of the porch. Those flowers had long since frozen and crumbled into blackened stems within their baskets that still swung in the autumn wind.

Nikka watched the porch and the door at the front of the house, but she wasn't sure what she was expecting to see. She stepped onto the sidewalk from the street and waited as the breeze chilled her arms through the long sleeves.

Then the door opened, and Nikka felt the tears flood her eyes. Her mother stepped through the door carrying a jack-o-lantern in her hands. She moved out onto the porch and stooped down to place it on the first step. Her slender fingers wiped the edges of the cutout eyes and mouth as if adding her finishing touches, those same fingers that had caressed her cheek when Nikka had been dying in the hospital.

She wanted to call out to her, to wrap her arms around her and tell her she loved her and that she was okay. She knew that what Gideon had told her was true: they had to be protected. There was a reason for it.

And she hated that reason.

This place was her home, her real home. Not that fortress that she now shared with Gideon. This place held all she ever knew about life and family.

Tears flowed down her cheeks as she watched her mother stand and turn toward the door. It took everything in her power to not run toward the house and shut herself in there with her family.

The woman stopped as the wind blew through her honey blonde hair and she wrapped her arms around her torso to ward away the chill. But she stopped as Nikka looked at her. Her mother slowly turned and her eyes moved toward Nikka as though she knew that someone was watching her.

She looked at Nikka with curiosity as though she recognized her but just couldn't place her. She stepped out further onto the porch.

"Can I help you?" she said.

Her voice sounded like an angel. Nikka had to swallow the lump that had formed in her throat. "I just wanted—" She couldn't get the words out.

"Are you okay?" the woman said as she stepped out onto the sidewalk and placed a hand on Nikka's shoulder.

The touch sent ripples through her body. "I just wanted to see my family, but they don't live here anymore. I thought—I thought they lived here, but I was wrong."

"Oh, honey," she said and it sounded though she wanted to cry with her. She embraced Nikka just like she had when she would fall and skin her knee. "Maybe I can help you. What is your family name?"

Nikka moved her trembling fingers around her mother and held her as long as she could, but she pulled away from her and looked into her eyes. Then, she had to think of something, anything, that could prolong this moment. "Uh, Smith."

Her mother sighed. "Sorry. I don't know any Smiths in this neighborhood."

"It's okay," Nikka said and wiped her cheek with the back of her hand.

"Would you like to come inside, have a cup of coffee or something? Maybe I can make some calls for you," she said and signaled her to come through the front door.

As much as she wanted to, Nikka knew that it would only break her heart even more to see the cherry wood banister that led up to her room or smell the pumpkin seeds carved out of the jack-o-lantern on the porch. Her mother had embraced her, but the woman had no idea she had a daughter. This could never be her home anymore. This brief moment would be the only thing that she could have. All that was left here was a façade, just the illusion of home, but there was no substance for her anymore.

"No, thank you," she said, the words sticking in her throat as she spoke them. "I can't stay."

"Oh, I'm sorry I couldn't be of more help," she said. "But you are welcome any time."

Nikka smiled even though she knew this would be the last time she would ever see her mother. She could never come to this place again.

"I would like that," she said and turned away.

The tears had wet her cheeks and chilled her skin against the breeze that drifted through the neighborhood. The sound of the door closing behind her echoed in her brain, and she knew she would remember that sound for a long time to come. She clenched her fists within her pockets and dug her nails into the skin of her palms. Hopefully the pain would dull the torment of walking away from her home forever.

She walked around the block, not wanting Jason to see her this way. The long walk would give her time to get some air and wipe her eyes dry.

The wind whistled through the trees that surrounded the park, now empty of the dozen or so children that would frequent it in the summer. At one time, she was among those children. The swings blew in the breeze on squeaky rusted chains. The monkey bars that rose far above the swings now dropped chips of blue and green paint.

This was all that was left of her home.

She took in a deep breath and walked around the block until she saw Jason leaning against his motorcycle. The look he gave her showed her that he understood the importance of coming here, even though he truly had no idea why. He opened his arms when she approached and took her in.

"You okay?" he whispered in her ear.

"I will be," she said.

He asked her nothing else about why she had come here. Her intentions were her own and he knew that. She just needed to go and never look back.

CHAPTER 26

THE FIRST TIME SHE HAD SEEN GIDEON in the hospital, he had promised her life, but he had never said anything about the deaths he would bring her as well.

But he had told her things would change.

Well, she had to change things for herself. She couldn't play this game anymore, if that's what this was. He may have cured her cancer and pulled her out of that hospital, but he did not give her life like he had said. This was no life.

When she dialed Jason's number, she was relieved when he picked up on the first ring.

"How ya doing?" he asked.

"Things have got to change," she said.

"Let me help you," he said, and she could tell that he was leaning into his phone, trying not to let anyone else hear his conversation. "I can get you away from your brother."

"How would you do that? I don't want you to get in any trouble because of me."

"I don't care," he said. "I was meant to be with you. Maybe I was meant to save you too."

She smiled. That was something she hadn't thought of before. "Maybe."

"I can take you away, to someplace that he can't do this to you anymore," he said. "Tomorrow. Let's just go."

"Where would we go?" she said and curled her knees up to her chest as she leaned back against the wall of her bedroom.

"I don't know, but we could just hit the road," he said. "I have money. I've saved some working at the university. We could just get on my bike and go."

"That sounds awfully romantic, and unrealistic," she said. "I didn't think you could leave with your probation and everything."

"I don't care," he whispered. "I'd do it for you."

"I know you would," she said. "I'm sorry I got you involved in this."

"I'm not."

She sighed and closed her eyes. Then he spoke again. "I can pick up and leave tomorrow. Let's just drive north. Hell, we might even make it to Canada. Wanna be Canadian for a little while, eh?"

She stifled a giggle. "You mean it?" she whispered.

"Of course I do."

It felt good to laugh again, especially with Jason.

For a moment, neither of them said anything. He offered a change in this life, one that she could command. They could go somewhere that didn't bring back so many painful memories, with someone that would respect her wishes. She could start fresh and be anybody. Hell, maybe they would even get married or something.

"I'll be waiting for you at the Promenade Fountains on Willow Street tomorrow at dusk. If you decide you want to leave, meet me there. If you don't come before sundown, then I'll understand," he said.

"Okay," she said and ended the call. But she watched the phone for several minutes, even though the screen had gone black.

The idea of leaving with him gave her jitters that she couldn't control. It was a big decision and it was one that she knew she couldn't take lightly. If she left, she would plan on leaving everything, with no plans to ever use her power again. The world had gone on without her for a long time and could do just fine without her now.

She reached behind her and withdrew her sword. Her dark room now glowed with a ghostly blue hue as she gazed at the blade before her. She ran her fingers along the sword as blue flames licked at her fingertips. In all its beauty, it had dealt such a deadly blow, something that she could never again take back.

She placed the sword on the floor and it lost its blue glow as soon as she lost contact with it. She rested her head back against her pillow and gazed at the silver blade in the moonlight. If she chose to leave, she would leave it behind as well. It was a part of that heartbreaking side of her existence that she now wished to abandon.

As her eyes swam in tears again, she fell asleep hoping that with whatever she decided, it would be the best thing for her.

CHAPTER 27

THE NOTE SHE PLACED ON THE BED was simple.

I have to leave. I'm sorry.

She rested it atop the sword that she placed with care on top of her bed. She stepped into the bathroom and packed a bar of soap and her toothbrush and toothpaste into her pack. As she closed the medicine cabinet, she caught sight of her reflection in the mirror. The wig on her head balanced her eyes and narrowed her face, but she knew it was a lie. When she met Jason tonight, she would show him the truth.

The pack slipped easily over her shoulder, but her feet wouldn't move at first. This was harder than she thought it would be. She looked at the note on the bed and hoped that Gideon would someday understand.

The afternoon sun began to crawl across the sky when she crept down the stairs and beyond the main hall. She heard Gideon, typing away on his laptop. He would never hear her move down the steps and out the door as she pressed it shut. As she walked down the drive, the monastery loomed over the tips of the surrounding trees. She glanced back at the crumbling exterior of her last remaining home. The place had never seemed as solemn as it did now.

She turned away and began her walk to the city. Everything in her heart wanted Gideon to see her, to stop her and say that everything would be okay, but she knew that would never happen. It would just be another lie. With each step she took, the monastery disappeared among the trees.

The light began to slip to the tips of the mountains, leaving a gold-pink hue across the city by the time she had walked the distance into the heart of the business district. The center of town was dotted with water fountains which were decorated with various marble and bronze statues, but she knew exactly where Jason would be waiting for her.

The promenade had a series of stairs around all four corners of the main fountain that spread over nearly a city block. The water sprayed in dancing arcs through a series of lights that appeared so beautiful at night. People could watch the display from the many benches and trellises that lined the periphery of the fountain and along the walkways that plunged into the trees of the greenbelt and surrounding parks.

Nikka pulled her hood down as she walked through town and wound her way to Willow Street. The late afternoon had driven most of the people from the businesses and left the promenade mostly deserted. As she walked past the shops, she glanced into the windows and saw that each shop had been adorned with black cats, witches and skeletons. A couple stepped out of a shop in front of her holding hands. They pardoned themselves, but she couldn't help but notice that they were dressed as campy vampires, red-velvet lined cape and all.

It must be Halloween.

She clutched at the straps of her pack over her shoulders and moved on despite the odd feeling that crept into her bones. It had to be just the realization of the holiday, but why did she have to pick that day to be the one to leave forever? It could only be worse if she had chosen Friday the 13th.

The gold of the sky began to give way to darker lights of pink and gray as the sun settled behind the mountains. The light faded just as she turned onto the promenade. From the base of the marble steps she could see Jason standing against a trellis. As soon as he saw her, he smiled and stood straighter.

Nikka ran up the steps, and he embraced her as soon as she reached him.

"I was starting to worry," he said.

"No way I was going to miss out on this," she said and kissed him.

As he held her, she knew that she was making the right choice despite the uneasy feeling that gnawed at her.

He grasped her hand. "My bike's over here."

"Wait," she stopped him. "I need to show you something before we go." She said and glanced around the promenade.

The place was empty, but it felt so open, so exposed. She pulled him back to the trees of the greenbelt, hiding in the shadows behind the line of trellises. This would be perfect cover to help keep her secret.

"What is it?" he asked with a laugh.

She turned and grasped both of his hands. "I want to tell you everything, and that means showing you everything. Before we ride off into the sunset, I need to know that you'll be okay with everything."

"Okay," he said with a hint of unease.

"I told you that I had had cancer," she started.

"I remember, and I don't care that you lost your hair. I told you that," he said and placed a hand on her cheek.

"I know," she said and pulled back her hood. "So, I need to know that you really will be okay if I look like this." Her fingers pulled back the wig, exposing her head to the cold October air. She unzipped her jacket and pulled it from her shoulders. Even in the faint light under the trees, she could see the marks across her pale skin.

But he didn't flinch or grimace at her hairless head and tattoos across her skin. "You're beautiful," he said and placed both hands on her cheeks. He leaned in and kissed her.

The warmth of his hands on her skin sent shivers down her spine. He pulled her close and she could feel his breath on her neck as his lips brushed her ear.

"I always suspected it was you," he whispered in her ear.

At first she wasn't sure that she heard him right. She moved to pull away from him, but his fingers grasped at her arms, digging painfully into the muscles.

"I knew that if I waited long enough that you would reveal yourself," he said and released her arms.

She stepped back as the uneasy feeling erupted into a violent storm of terror in her gut. Her knees trembled, and she felt as though she were falling from the top of a roller coaster. Through the shadows of the trees, she saw his face, his eyes trained on her with a smile on his face, but it wasn't the dimpled smile she loved. It was twisted and cruel.

From the shadows, his eyes lit up into two circles of fire around his dark pupils.

Nikka stumbled back as her tattoos began to sparkle. The power surged into her hands and up her arms.

"It can't be—" she stammered as she stumbled backwards.

"Oh, yes it can," he said and stepped toward her. "I don't think we've met. I am Abaddon." He bowed to her, but never averted his eyes.

She continued to back away from him. The ground seemed to tremble as the clear sky soon darkened into tumultuous clouds that flashed with lightning. She backed into a park bench and caught herself.

"That was so much easier than I thought it would be," he said with a wicked laugh.

Panic pulsed through her veins with every beat of her heart. Her entire world came crashing down on her as she looked into his flaming eyes.

Movement caught her eye from around the promenade. She glanced around to see other people coming out of the shadows and around the buildings surrounding the business district. They all looked at her, some with flaming eyes, and on others, she could see the mask of the black demon within the human host. With a singular mind, they stepped toward her from all directions, moving with silent ease.

She was surrounded, and her mind swam with confusion and terror. The power surged just under her skin, but she was too distraught to focus it. Her hand reached back to her shoulder, something that she had gotten so used to doing, but then the grim reality hit her that her sword was no longer with her.

"Ah," he said and leaned a little to his side with his arms opened outward. "No weapon. You're all alone. What are you gonna do now?"

She stepped back onto the promenade as the sound of the fountain sprayed behind her. There was nothing left for her to do. Her instincts pushed her into overdrive. She turned and ran through the fountain and jumped into the bank of shrubs that bordered the alleyway. From behind her, she heard his laughter echo among the buildings. She jumped into the street, her feet pounding the pavement as she ran as hard as she could.

Blood pounded in her head, and her lungs ached for air, but she couldn't stop. She heard him shout to the others just as she rounded the back of a building.

"I want her alive," he called out to them.

She felt each step on the pavement pound through her knees and hips. The breath rushed in and out, mostly out of panic. She couldn't think how this had gone so terribly wrong; she could only search the darkening city for an escape.

The clouds overhead rumbled and the first signs of rain started to coat the street. Soon, thick ribbons of water poured along the shoulders of the road and drain into the rain gutters. It ran down her bare head and into her eyes as she dodged into another alley and glanced back down the street as she hid. Several demons had begun to follow her on his orders. She sprinted down the alley and scrambled up the side of a chain link fence. She jumped to the other side just as a horde started into the alley.

She lunged into another back alley as the demons worked on the fence. The alley opened into a narrow street lined with old brick townhouses and other buildings, most of which looked like they were under construction. Utility trucks and other construction vehicles had been parked along the road at the next block, but the site appeared empty for the evening. She raced to the trucks and hunched down in the front of a dumpster that sat before the lot of an old building.

There were too many of them coming for her. She couldn't just fight them off, especially if she didn't have her sword. There was only one thing she could do, and as hard as it would be, if she didn't do it then she could be dead within the hour.

She reached into her pocket and with shaking fingers, she withdrew her cell phone and hit her quick dial.

Gideon answered on the first ring. "Nikka! Where are you?"

"They found me," she panted and glanced back down the street. She could not see anybody coming, but that didn't mean they weren't still following her. "I can't get out. I'm at a construction site behind Willow."

"Okay," he said, frantic. "I will come now."

"Hurry," she said before she ended the call and slid the phone in her pocket.

The site around her was surrounded by orange cones and warning tape. It all built up around an abandoned apartment building. The city was full of renovators that could flip a house or an apartment. This crew was probably doing the same thing to the building. It could be a good place to hide until she saw Gideon.

She sprinted to the front door and peeled open the boarded blockade. The interior of the building was coated in construction dust and littered with boards and masonry. She tripped over the pile of debris and ran to a rear stairwell up to the upper floors. She emerged onto the third floor which appeared to have been torn apart by the construction crew. The windows had all been removed and any interior walls were torn down. A tall wall of bricks was stacked in front of an old fireplace, ready to brick and mortar a new one. A debris chute rested against the far wall behind the stack of bricks, where the crew could toss their trash down to a dumpster on the ground outside the building.

Nikka moved around a stack of drywall and to the far end of the room when a figure emerged from the darkened corner. She stopped, a woman standing before her, her red hair falling in curls over her black leather jacket. Her eyes burned orange as she smiled and stepped toward Nikka.

"A seraph," she said through cherry gloss lips. "The Destroyer said that he could find it, and he was right. I never should have doubted him."

Nikka backed away from her, but stepped hard into another force. Powerful arms grabbed her from behind and turned her around. She looked at the man, handsome and dressed in a business suit. His eyes blazed as he gazed down on her.

"This is too much fun," he said. "Do we have to give her back so soon?"

The woman laughed. "Abaddon would be so upset if we got her dirty."

The man shoved her back into the woman, who grabbed her and then threw her against the wall. Nikka's face smacked into the brick, the pain exploding into a thousand shards of white light in her eye. She fell to the floor and felt a trickle of blood flow down her cheek. The woman stepped toward her, and before Nikka could stand, kicked her in the face with her leather boots adorned with spike heels.

Nikka crashed back. Her neck arched painfully, and her head hit the ground. The sound of the woman's heels came at her again. The power surged in her fingertips at that moment and she concentrated it as fast as she could. She collected the light at her fingertips, willed it into form, and threw it at the woman.

The light whistled through the air, but the woman dodged it at the last second. The power zoomed past her, catching her hair just before it collided into the back wall. Although it didn't hit her, it provided Nikka enough of an opportunity to distract them so she could get on her feet and run for the stairway.

As she caught her balance and started to move, the man came from behind and caught her. She kicked at him, but his grip was too strong, and he lifted her off her feet. The woman came around, facing her as she reached out to grab her arm. Nikka kicked her legs out and caught her in the gut, sending her against the pile of drywall in a heap of white dust. Nikka was able to twist just enough to free her arm and slide free of the man's grasp.

She landed on her feet and found her balance. As she started to run, his arm whipped around her neck. He pulled her, and she felt the hot blade of a knife plunge into her back. At first she only felt the pain and didn't know what it was. Then he twisted it, the metal slicing into her flesh. She gasped, unable to scream against the pain and the grip he had on her neck. Then he pulled away from her and jerked the knife free as he shoved her forward. The woman stood before her, eyes on fire, as she caught Nikka.

The pain rippled like aftershocks through her body. A warm liquid poured down her hip and she glanced down to see that the knife had pierced through to her abdomen, and blood streamed down her jeans.

The woman smiled and grabbed the sides of her jacket. She lifted Nikka from her feet and threw her as though she weighed nothing. Her body crashed into the stack of bricks, colliding into a jagged bed of masonry. The impact knocked the breath from her lungs and wracked her back with pain. The remainder of the stack collapsed onto her, leaving the room in a cloud of dust and chaos. The bricks fell on her outstretched arms, pummeling her face.

There was silence right after she landed. She wasn't sure if she just couldn't hear anything or if the room had gone completely quiet. The only thing she was sure of was that she very well could be bleeding to death, and the two demons in the room were stalking her like lions. She opened her eyes and the first thing she saw was the opening of the chute through the window. The bricks still fell in chunks around her, but she could hear the two demons walking around the room, trying to get to the other side of the brick pile through the cloud of masonry dust.

Every breath hurt, and her bones ached. She tried to get up, but the wound in her side fought back against her. But if she didn't move she knew she would die. She bit her lip and forced herself to rise. She pulled her body up to her knees and reached through the window. Her hand caught the edge of the chute. Her fingers trembled as she pulled herself to her feet. The pain in her side shot into her back like lightning, and she stifled a cry as she heaved herself into the chute.

The stability of the room disappeared as her feet left the floor and she hurtled down the yellow tunnel into some unknown destination. Within seconds, she landed in a soggy pile of broken drywall and chunks of cement mixed with insulation. Rain poured down on her as she caught her breath and reoriented herself to her surroundings. The building loomed over her from where she lay in a dumpster.

She did not have the luxury to stop and rest. She pulled herself up and over the lip of the dumpster and landed on the hard cement. Thunder shook the ground as she moved to her feet and stumbled into an alleyway. The rain came down in torrents, sleeking over her eyelids and soaking her jacket. She fought through the rain and plunged into another rim of shrubs.

The city opened onto a busier street, with cabs whizzing by despite the rainfall. She staggered into the street with car horns honking at her as she moved. The pain in her side pulsed in stabbing waves with each step. When she got to the far sidewalk, she stumbled into a side alley, but her legs wouldn't move any longer. She fell to her knees and collapsed against the side of a building that appeared to house a grocery store.

She removed her shaking hand from the wound to see her fingers coated in bright red blood. The rain washed it down her arms, and the pool of water stained dark red on the cement. Her ears began to ring and her fingers went numb as she tried to stand again. She had no energy left, and she collapsed onto the pavement.

In the echoes of the alley, a man shouted for help. He rushed to her side and placed a hand on her damp cheek. He spoke so fast she couldn't understand him. His hands felt at her side and touched the painful stab wound in her abdomen.

A car screeched to a halt just behind her, and soon she saw Gideon's face, like an angel surrounded in a halo of light. He scooped her into his arms despite the other man's argument to keep her still. His voice sounded so distant, like he was at the far end of a tunnel. Gideon shoved her into the back of his sedan and wiped the rain from her face with his soft hand.

"Nikka, stay awake," he said, his voice edged in panic.

She wanted to speak, to tell him she was sorry that she doubted him, but the words wouldn't come.

"Please," he said, but his voice grew further and further away.

The light around her, as dim as it was, darkened into a pale circle and then disappeared. She plunged into shadow where she could no longer feel her power. She was alone, and not even Gideon could find her there.

PART II

Hell is empty, and all the devils are here.

William Shakespeare, *The Tempest*

CHAPTER 28

THE PAIN IN HER SIDE BURNED LIKE MOLTEN LAVA, piercing her abdomen. She heard screaming, but didn't realize it came from her own throat until she tasted the blood in her mouth.

She only had brief moments that she could remember: Gideon lifting her out of the car and carrying her into the monastery, candlelight dancing in his eyes as he looked down at her, the cloying aroma of blood and rubbing alcohol mixing together making her cringe. Then she felt his hands on her side just before he poured a cold liquid on her skin. That was when the pain exploded into fire.

It cleared her head enough to open her eyes, although her right eyelid failed to lift as well as her left. The room was dark, and she wasn't in her bedroom. She saw a bank of patio windows and a door with billowing white curtains that had drifted away from the glass to reveal the moonlight. Gideon knelt at the edge of the bed where she lay and held her onto her right side. She could feel the warmth of his hands as he examined her wounds.

Tears flowed from her eyes with each movement he inflicted upon her. But the pain was only secondary to her memories. How could things have gone so wrong? She cried when she thought of the sudden change that had overcome Jason. The two circles of fire in his eyes still blazed in the back of her mind and burned into her soul every time she closed her eyes. And just like everything else, he had been taken away from her.

Stabbing pain started again at the wound in her side. She bit her lip to try and stop her cries, but it was too much.

"I am sorry," Gideon spoke, his voice full of torment. "I must stitch the edges."

Her fingers clutched at the bed linens with each pierce of the needle.

"I should have listened to you," she said, her throat hot and dry from her cries.

"Do not think on these things," he said. Another stitch and another.

She couldn't control the shaking in her body no matter how hard she tried. It was a mix of adrenaline and fatigue, but she also knew that she was terrified now.

He cut the thread and moved to examine the front of her abdomen. He knelt down before her, his fingers touching the skin of her exposed torso. "The wound went straight through, but it does not appear to have struck anything serious. I must close this one as well."

She nodded and grasped the sheet tighter as he started stitching the edges. She felt every single pull of the strand. When he had finished, he dressed her wound with gauze and tape and then pulled the edge of her shirt down to cover her abdomen. He helped her lie on her back and then leaned over her.

The hazel of his eyes looked green in the moonlight as he looked across her face. He placed a gentle finger around her swollen eye and down her cheekbone.

"It looks broken," he said. "But it will heal quickly."

He withdrew his hand, but she grasped it. "I'm sorry," she said as tears flowed from her eyes.

"There is no need," he whispered. "You were right to question all of this."

Gideon moved to stand, but she held his hand tighter. "Please don't go."

"I will not be far," he said. "You need more clean dressings. I will return shortly."

He released her grip and stood. She watched him leave the room, but he kept the door open. Without him there to distract her thoughts, she could feel the pain of every bruise and laceration.

She glanced at the spacious room with a bare wood floor and the bed in the center of the room. This must be Gideon's room, a place she had never even considered before. He didn't keep any lights here, but illuminated the room with only candles set at the base of the bed and on a table beside the door like some medieval study. The light failed to illuminate the shadows in the corners of the room, leaving those spaces in absolute darkness where anything could hide.

Gideon stepped into the room with his arms filled with towels and bandages. Then she could see the sword tucked under his arm. He set everything on the table, but brought her sword to her.

"I thought you may want to see this again," he said and knelt down with the katana held out before him.

Her shaking fingers reached out to touch the blade. As soon as she made contact, the blade illuminated in its familiar blue fire that undulated down the length of the sword. The light chased away the shadows in the room.

When she withdrew her hand, he placed the sword on the floor beside the bed and looked into her eyes. She grasped his hand.

"I don't want to be alone," she said.

"I know. I will not go anywhere," he whispered.

He moved a simple wooden chair up to the side of the bed and sat there as he held her hand. She watched him lean his elbows against his knees as he looked at her. It was the last thing she remembered as her eyes drifted closed and she fell asleep. As long as he remained there, she could rest without seeing fire-lit eyes in the dark, watching everything from the shadows. They knew she was there and waited for her to come out to them.

When she opened her eyes again, the morning light had passed and risen high above the monastery. She glanced to the side of the bed, although moving her head awakened the pain in her face again. Gideon was gone from her side, his chair remained at the bedside, but it was empty.

She took a deep breath and felt a sharp ache in her chest. The only way she felt she could get air was to sit upright. She forced herself to her side and slid her legs out over the side of the bed, pushing up to a sitting position. The effort was tiring, and she held her side as the stitches pulled with every motion.

Gideon walked into the room with a tray in his arms. "Careful," he said and put the tray on the table before he hurried to her side. "You have some broken ribs. Just take it slowly."

Nikka squinted against the light that poured through the windows. "How long have I been sleeping?"

"Almost two days," he said as he carried the tray to the bedside.

No wonder she felt so stiff. She would not have guessed that she had been there that long, though. The swelling had gone down in her eye enough for her to open her eyelids better and she blinked her vision clear.

"I have brought soup," he said. "I thought you might be hungry."

She nodded her head and accepted the bowl as he placed it in her hands. "Thank you."

He busied himself with things in the room. He carried a stack of shirts and pants to her bed. "I have brought up some of your clothes. You can stay in here as long as you need. It may be easier than going up the stairs every night."

She sipped some of the warm broth, and it slipped down her dry throat. Nothing had ever tasted so good. Then, she looked up at him as he moved about the room.

"It was him. Abaddon," she said.

Gideon stopped and gazed out the window. "I know."

"He knows who I am now."

"Yes," he said.

"What do we do?" she asked

He hesitated for a moment and then turned to her. "We take the fight to them."

"I can't beat him. He's too strong," she said.

"Yes, you can because you are stronger," Gideon said with a smile.

"I'm glad you are so confident, but that doesn't really help," she said and looked down at her bowl. It wasn't just Abaddon. It was the fact that it was a high general demon in Jason's body. How could she look at him while fighting to the death?

"I believe in you, even if you do not. I always have," he said and stepped out of the room.

He had left her in silence, but her thoughts were anything but quiet.

The next few days went on much the same way, but each day brought more relief from the pain. Gideon never pressured her to train while she recovered.

One evening, she stood outside on the patio that overlooked the woods from his room. The air had grown colder since Halloween and had left the trees barren. The scent of burning fireplaces from cabins around the hills drifted into the room. She hugged her arms around her to ward off the chill, but she still felt it against her bare head. The white curtains billowed out and tickled against her ankles as she stood against the stone railing.

Beyond the monastery, the city sparkled in the night. Abaddon was somewhere out there waiting for her. It had been over a week since he revealed himself, but he had not forgotten her. Deep in the recesses of her memories, she longed to feel Jason's touch again, but she knew that would never happen. He was lost to her now.

CHAPTER 29

THE NIGHT HAD GIVEN WAY to the light of a waning moon. Trees among the woods surrounding the monastery whispered secrets in the faint November breeze, clicking against the stone walls in rhythmic tapping. Nikka walked back into the room from the patio, and was surprised to see Gideon standing in the room. When she turned to see him, he averted his gaze.

"Were you there long?" she said and moved her fingers up her arm covered in a thin white cover-up that kept the chill from her underwear.

"No," he said. "It is time to remove your stitches."

"Oh," she said. "Thank heavens. They are starting to itch something fierce."

He produced a pair of small scissors and graspers from his table.

She stood behind him, but was unsure of where he wanted her to be for the procedure. When he turned to look at her, there was something awkward about the way he acted now.

"Uh," he stammered. "Maybe, just lie on your side," he said and signaled to the bed.

She nodded and stretched out on the bed and lifted her cover-up just to her ribs, revealing her black underwear. The bruising around her wound had improved since the last time she dared to look at it. She wished the hematoma around her face had done the same. At least the swelling had gone away, but there were still ugly purple marks edged in a sickly yellow that curled around her right eye like a mask.

He kneeled with his tools in hand and leaned over her to work at the stitches on her back. She could feel the threads slide out after he clipped each one. It was uncomfortable, but nothing like when he put them into her. Then he moved to begin taking out the stitches from her abdomen.

The shaking in his hands was unlike him. Gideon was usually so matter-of-fact, and nothing ever seemed to faze him, but he was clearly nervous and she was sure it was not the stitches that made him this way.

He clipped the last stitch and Nikka grabbed his forearm before he could pull away from her.

"What's up with you?" she said and sat upright to face him.

He didn't look at her and placed his tools on the ground. "I do not wish to speak of it."

"Gideon," she said and placed her hands on his shoulders. She turned him, and he finally looked at her. "It's me. What is going on? Did you find out something about Abaddon?"

The fading light illuminated his eyes. She had never seen that look in his face before. It wasn't scary or intimidating in any way. It was something else.

"Oh my gosh," she said with almost a whisper. Her hands lifted from his shoulders as he looked away from her as though she would make things so much worse by touching him right now. "Why haven't you said anything?"

His shoulders slumped and he stood, trying to back away from her. "There is nothing to say. It is forbidden."

"But it's true, isn't it?" she said and stood. "Do you . . . like me?"

He turned to look at her again and his face had softened. "No, Nikkola." He had never said her full name since the first day they met. He straightened his shoulders. "I think . . . I think I love you."

He actually said it. She wasn't sure that he would. The shame was evident was evident in the hang of his head and the way he glanced toward the furthest corners of the room, anything to not look at her right now.

"It's okay," she said and placed a hand on his shoulder, but he quickly shoved away from her.

"No, it is not," he growled. "It is my punishment."

How could he say that? She knew it wasn't meant as an insult, but she couldn't help but feel a little angry at how he was responding right now.

"Is that what I am? A punishment?" she said.

Anguish filled his eyes. His fists clenched tight, and he put them over his eyes as he grimaced. "No. You are light and joy and everything that is good about this place. I do not know what to do."

His torment pained her far worse than did her wound. As he stood there, wracked with guilt, she saw him as she first did in the hospital. He was someone with hope and purpose. He pulled her from the grip of death and gave her this life, whatever it was. Gideon never abandoned her like she did him. He always believed in her.

Now he stood there, and she knew that he had never told another person what he had just said to her. He had always taken care of her, and she should have known something was going on with him. The way he had reacted when he first learned about Jason was something more than just being upset about her attentions being elsewhere. He really had been jealous then. And maybe there were things before then, too. Every time he worried that she was late to meet him. Making her dinner every night. He knew everything about her, and still seemed to love her anyway. She had no secrets from him anymore.

And she had probably begun to like him too, especially his quirky mannerisms that reminded her of someone who had stepped out of the Renaissance period. Or maybe it was the way he talked and his total innocence, despite the fact the he had taught her how to kill demons. She had never really thought of him as more than just a mentor and friend, but she certainly couldn't deny that she had affection for him after spending this many weeks together with him.

She stepped up to him and grasped his wrists, pulling them away from his face. He looked at her with sadness and regret.

"There is nothing to be ashamed of," she whispered and placed a hand on his face.

Maybe there was something she could do that would ease his fear. He seemed so fragile at this moment, and it was endearing at the same time. It was no trick on his part. He was so afraid to look at her because of how he felt, and whatever he was, this feeling was new to him and he had no idea how to handle it.

What if she could help *him* now? The butterflies started in her gut again when she thought about it, but she knew that she wanted to do this. After all the time she had spent with him, maybe she had become as fond of him. Ever since Jason . . . Abaddon . . . had betrayed her, she longed to be touched again the way he had touched her, even if it was all a lie. Gideon would never betray her like that.

She leaned in, feeling his torso against her. He closed his eyes and touched her arms. Just as her lips were about to meet his, he grasped her arms and pulled her away.

"I cannot do this," he spoke and shoved away from her. He turned and raced out the door.

"Gideon, don't go," she said, but it was too late.

Nikka stood in disbelief. She had been so close that her lips still tingled. Her hands felt empty and cold now. All she wanted was to touch him again and tell him it was okay, that maybe she felt the same way. But he had left her alone in the room, denying everything he wanted to feel.

She stepped back and felt the cold wood floor beneath her bare feet. Confused, she turned to face the patio door and gazed out upon the lights of the city.

Then, his voice sounded behind her. "I will tell you everything, and then I will know if you still look at me the same way."

She turned and met him as he came toward her, his face set and resolute. He looked desperate, not sad and simple like he often did. Each step was firm and quick. He wrapped his arms around her, pulling her to him, much to her surprise. He must have come to terms with his feelings after he ran out of the room, because he leaned in and kissed her before she knew what was happening. The way he held her against him was so much stronger than Jason had, and now she knew the difference. Jason, Abaddon, had been playing her. Gideon really cared.

The taste of him, the smell of him was enough to make her kiss him in return. Her hand moved to the small of his back, and that was when she felt the first buzz in her fingertips.

Her power erupted into her arms and shot through her heart, faster than it ever had before. It raced out of her control through her limbs. Nikka gasped as she felt the surge, and she pushed away from him. Something formidable had triggered her power, just like it had as soon as Abaddon made himself known or when she had stumbled upon the portal. It had sensed something equally as strong, an evil so great that her energy shuddered like an earthquake at the edge of a fault line.

The tattoos began to light up all over her body, illuminating under her cover-up. Gideon watched her, but he didn't look surprised. He closed his eyes, lowered his head and fell onto his knees before her like a man ready to face his punishment.

The power burned through her veins. What was happening? She couldn't control the power as it took over her soul, wanting to destroy Gideon.

He turned his head up to her, and her heart nearly stopped when he opened his eyes. Two circles of fire surrounded his pupils, blazing in the dark of the room.

She cried out in horror and staggered backward, clambering for her sword the muscle-memory of the action occurring before she knew what was happening. Her fingers felt the hilt and the weapon blazed into blue fire. She spun around and held the katana with both hands, pointing the tip at him.

He opened his arms, his face painted in grief behind his eyes of fire. "Destroy me now."

"What is this?" she shouted, fighting back the urge to strike him down where he knelt.

"My true nature," he said. "This is what I am."

The power filled her limbs, stronger than she had ever felt. It threatened to control her mind, her actions. Every drop of the light told her to kill him . . . *now*. He was a demon, hidden from her for all this time. The power needed him dead or it would kill her itself if she didn't let it take over her body.

But she looked at him where he knelt. He had never tried to kill her. He was more honest with her than Jason ever was. What was his ploy? Why tell her like this?

The power flooded into her thoughts. She must destroy him. She was the Seraph. That was what she did best.

The sword shook in her hands as she fought against the power. She screamed, forcing the energy into her core. It released her hands for a moment, long enough for her to lower the sword. When she felt control of her legs, she bolted from the room. The power would not hold still for long. Like a powder keg, it wanted to explode in all directions and it needed an outlet. Until she knew what was going on, she didn't want Gideon caught at ground zero.

She ran down the stairs and bolted out the front door just in time for the power to break free. The light erupted from her body like a burst of lightning. It rose into the sky with a single charge as she screamed from the rush of energy that coursed through her veins. Within seconds, the light disappeared and she collapsed to the cold ground. The sword clattered into the gravel. Her weakened fingers couldn't hold it any longer.

The aftershocks throbbed through her muscles in little twitches until everything died down to a quiet calm. She could barely open her eyes or lift her head from the ground. Everything had drained from her. When the last vestiges of the power sparked into her muscles, she was able to pull herself to her feet and stagger back up the stairs into the entryway of the monastery.

That was the most powerful jolt of energy she had ever felt, and she had produced it herself.

And the demon inside Gideon had triggered it.

She glanced at the doors behind her. He was still in there somewhere, and now she knew what he was. But everything about him was wrong. How could he be on holy ground? That's why they were in the monastery to begin with. Demons could not walk on sacred earth, unless that was a lie to keep her complacent. What else had he lied about?

CHAPTER 30

NIKKA FORCED HERSELF TO HER FEET and used the walls for support as she walked through the entry. The atrium was dark, but she could see candlelight at the end of the hall. She had never ventured into that portion of the monastery before. In the daylight, it appeared just as a crumbling room that seemed too dangerous to explore. But now, a golden light shone through one of the doorways.

She walked down the corridor, stepping around fallen bricks and remnants of old wooden tables scattered across the floor. As she neared the light, she saw that it came from an open door to the left of the hall. She peered around the door and saw the light that came from a series of candles set upon a broken table.

It was a chapel, the roof partially fallen in and the frescoes faded and chipped. Rows of wooden pews stood with layers of dust and cobwebs. Upon the dais, monks had left statues of Jesus and saints, although many were broken and looked like monsters in a horror movie with their hollow eyes and fractured hands. The candlelight on the table illuminated their pale, empty faces as though they were ghosts watching over the remains of the old church.

Gideon sat on the front pew, his head bowed and his back to her.

What was he doing?

Nikka was so confused now. Her body still shuddered with the remnants of the blast she had released outside, and it felt just like the way her body quaked after a round of fierce chemotherapy that would often leave her used and wasted. But this power had come from deep inside her soul because of Gideon. No, not Gideon, but what was inside of him.

She stepped through the threshold of the chapel and between the rows of pews. Cold wind whistled through the gaps in the crumbling walls and made the candlelight dance. The whole time she walked into the church, she watched him, waiting for him to strike like all the other demons had, but he didn't move. She stepped to the front row across the main aisle and sat down on the wooden bench. At first she dared not look at him or even breathe. Whatever he was could attack her at any moment, and she had to be ready, even if it appeared to be Gideon. She looked at him, his eyes closed and his face twisted with an internal agony.

"Everything that I have ever told you was truth," he said, his voice echoing in the empty chapel.

"Not everything," she said.

"Yes. I told you that I was a sinner," he said and lifted his eyes. He looked upon the broken statue of Jesus before him and his eyes were now their familiar hazel color. "I sinned against my God. I did something that I knew was wrong, but I wanted to see what the others saw, so I followed them, all the other angels that fell from Heaven. I followed Lucifer blindly for so long. I did horrible things. I commanded legions. They called me Pazuzu, and I was a high general once."

Pazuzu. She recalled that name from her readings. She had read that the demon Pazuzu controlled the armies of demons that likely corrupted the cities of Sodom and Gomorrah.

And he had just revealed his name, something that a demon did not do lightly.

"But then I looked on humanity and saw what I had done. I felt guilt," he said, and she saw tears streaming down his face. "An archangel took pity on me. He pulled me from my host and gave me a second chance. My atonement would be that I must create the Seraphim to fight the demon hordes, that I must train them and teach them."

Nikka could see his anguish as he told her his story. The pain of it reached her from where she sat. She stood, stepped to where he sat and settled down next to him. It wasn't as frightening as she had thought it would be.

"The angel told me that my days would be uncounted, and that I would live as a human, feeling everything that a human could feel. When I was in the dark of Hell, I could not feel anything until the angel came. Then, I felt guilt. Now, I am tortured by anger, hate, envy—"

"And love," Nikka said. The word echoed around them.

He turned to her as he took her hand. "And love."

"They gave you a soul," she said. "It was the only thing you never had as a demon."

"And every day has been a torment since. It has taken over a thousand years to control my guilt. Human emotions are not to be taken lightly."

Nikka smiled. "That's the truth."

She felt him squeeze her hand. "I had no idea how hard it would be, but I managed . . . until now."

"You have never loved before," she muttered.

He shook his head. "Never. And it is so much harder than guilt or anger or hate."

"You want it, but you don't want it at the same time," she said.

Gideon looked at her with curious eyes. "Exactly."

"It messes with your head and screws up your judgment."

"Yes," he said. "You have loved before?"

She pointed to the bruises on her face. "Do you see my face? Question asked and answered. Like I said, it screws up your judgment."

"You loved him?" he asked as his brows knit together.

"I thought I did, but as the song goes, love hurts."

"It should not be that way," he said and hung his head. "I do not want to hurt you."

"Then don't," she said and placed a hand under his chin. She pulled his head up to look at her.

For only a moment she thought of his kiss, when he held her so quickly and desperately, knowing the consequences of his actions. She realized that he knew the power would try to destroy him, but he did it anyway because he needed it. And that kiss was a powerful thing.

She leaned toward him and their lips met, carefully at first. If her power threatened to erupt again, she didn't know what she would do. He was so tentative, as was she, as she continued to feel for any signs of the surge within her.

But it never came this time.

Nikka pulled away from him, feeling the warmth of him still on her lips.

"So," he said and cleared his throat nervously. "What do we do now?"

Nikka turned to him and smiled, feeling the fireworks of her power bubbling inside her chest as she contained them deeper in her soul.. That was one little victory in control of such a strong force. This could work after all.

"We do what we do best. Let's kick some demon ass together."

CHAPTER 31

WHEN THE SUN CAME UP the next morning, Nikka was already an hour into her training. Now, she had more purpose than ever before. Abaddon was out there waiting for her, and she needed to be ready.

But she had to admit to herself that a little of her motivation was driven by revenge for what he did to her.

Gideon never arrived at the gym, although he knew she was ready to fight. She understood it. He was still coming to terms with his feelings and that could be a little tough to deal with, especially when it was just the two of them living in the old church. But, he was always reliable for breakfast, and she found him in the dining hall when she followed the scent of bacon.

He sat at the table with his laptop open, finishing his breakfast when she arrived.

"Hey there," she said as she entered the room.

He didn't look at her, but she saw him turn his computer away from her just a little bit.

"I said hello," she said as she sat down at the table.

"Good morning," he said and continued with his work, his eyes straining a little too hard on the laptop.

She crunched into a piece of bacon. "You know, this doesn't have to be weird between us unless you make it weird." She reached across the table and touched her fingers to the top of his hand where he typed on the keyboard. He stopped and glanced down to her hand.

"I am sorry," he said. "I will try to do better."

"No, stop saying 'sorry' all the time." She scooted her chair closer to him and forced his shoulders around until he looked at her. "There's nothing to be sorry about."

"That is not what I meant," he said, but still had trouble looking into her eyes.

She could tell he was troubled with something. His voice lowered to a whisper as though he was afraid someone else in the room would hear him. "I keep having thoughts since last night."

She scrunched her nose, confused. "Thoughts? What do you mean?"

He shook his head as he fought to say the words that he wanted to say. "Inappropriate thoughts. About you."

Inappropriate? When she took a second to think about it, she smiled. "You mean thoughts of me with maybe . . . fewer clothes?" She sat back and cocked her head to the side and arched her back in her best impression of a swimsuit cover model as she looked at him. "Maybe doing things that might make you blush?"

He turned away from her again. "Yes," he said.

Nikka laughed. "It's okay. That's what guys do. All us girls know that. That's just you being human."

He glanced back at her, confused. "It is?"

"Of course," she said and tipped her head up to his computer. "You've been looking at things on your computer, too?"

"What?" he said and glanced back to the screen, where he had pulled up a newspaper article. "I was working, if that is what you mean."

She almost choked when she laughed. "No, but that's okay. What have you got?"

He turned to his computer. "I was going through the files that you collected, and found some things that I wanted to show you." His fingers moved over the keys with ease, and Nikka found herself impressed with what he had learned in the short time that she showed him how to use the internet more effectively.

"One file held a collection of businesses around town. Some were linked with security footage, some with ID photos." He pulled up a compilation of several photos, some in black and white, of various men and women. "I cross referenced them, and most of these people are influential in the city or state. Either they own a business or have high level access to some major companies. There are defense contractors and major computer firms in here. But there are also smaller industries, things that I just do not understand why they would have an interest in—"

"Wait," she said as he scrolled through several pages of photographs. "Go back." As he rolled his mouse back through the pictures, she saw the one that piqued her interest. "Stop there."

She looked at the photo, examining every detail of the woman who stood in the security footage. "That's her."

"Who?"

"She's the bitch that sucker punched me," she said as she looked at her familiar red hair and tight leather outfit. Her name was typed at the bottom of the picture: Cherry Simms.

"And that guy is the one that stabbed me." She pointed to a picture of a man who looked like he was posing for a full page ad in the business section of the paper. "Are they lieutenants?"

Gideon clicked his mouse on the woman's picture and nodded. "Yes. It says that she runs a nightclub downtown. The Snake Pit. And he works at Smith and Cline, a law firm on Willow Street."

"I've heard of The Pit," Nikka said, glaring at the club's home page. "It's supposed to be a pretty nasty place. I bet they find some of their potential clients there, the ones that have that high level access you're talking about."

"So it is a dirty place?" he said, confused.

"Uh, sort of," she said with a smirk. "You know those inappropriate thoughts? Well, that's a whole club full of it, and I bet their thoughts are much worse."

He nodded his head, but Nikka knew that there was no way he could completely grasp what she meant.

"Well, whatever this establishment is," he said, "we know that at least one demon would be there, and she is working directly with Abaddon. Perhaps you could get her to give us his location."

"I would love to pay her back for this," she said pointing at her cheek that still held onto the last vestiges of bruising.

"We will go tonight," he said and stood. "But there is something that I would like you to see first."

He walked out of the main hall, and she followed him. Her curiosity was rising as he took her up the stairs to the top level of the building. He led her to a room that she had never visited and opened the door to a smaller space than the rooms they had chosen to sleep in. Standing in the center of the room was a tailor's dummy adorned with unusual clothing.

Gideon walked into the room and stood beside the dummy.

"What is this?" she asked.

"It is something I have been working on ever since you showed me those movies," he said and ran his finger along the coat. It was shaped in pliable, dark leather and moved down the floor like a long duster, but it remained sleeveless. The edges of the coat were stamped in marks very similar to the ones that marked her arms and legs. The designs curved up along the lapel and over the edge of a hood made of the same dark leather.

"Every superhero had their defining article of clothing, something practical yet useful," he said. "I made this for you. The leather will protect you, but it is very functional for what you need. The marks are an additional layer of protection."

Nikka walked up to the coat and ran her fingers along the stitching. "This is amazing. I had no idea you knew how to do something like this."

"Well, after hundreds of years, I have picked up a few tricks," he said with a smile. "Will this work for you?"

"Are you kidding? I love it," she said as she touched the broad belt that cinched the coat at the waist.

He released a nervous breath. "Excellent. Maybe you should do some of your forms wearing it before we take down the night club tonight. I would not want you to just go in there with something new that you had never tried."

"Good idea, Q," she said and punched him lightly on the shoulder.

"I do not understand," he said.

"Yeah, I'm not surprised," she said and worked at getting the coat off the dummy.

CHAPTER 32

THE AIR HAD GROWN COLD with a hint of frost as Nikka walked across the street. Music with a heavy beat and a guitar thrummed along the ground from the doors of the nightclub in front of her. The streets glistened with a wet sheen from the light rain that had ended an hour ago. The tangy scent of fresh rain still hung in the air.

Nobody could see her coming. The line of young men and women anxious to get into the club would never know that she could simply slip past the bouncer. Her presence was just another breeze in the cold night. Her illusion of invisibility was flawless and made stronger with the sigils that lined the hem of her duster..

Her black boots never made a sound as she stepped across the threshold of The Snake Pit. A gust of warm air filled her lungs along with the smell of liquor and sweat. The music pounded against her bare arms, her tattoos black and extending down to her wrists. The hood rested over her head just enough that she could scan the club.

The place was filled with people standing around tables with glasses of liquor. Smoke filled the air, some from cigarettes and some from the smoke machines that blasted from the base of the stage that curved around the entire club. Dancers stood around the edges of the stage in black leather and chains, mostly women entertaining the men that clambered around them.

She looked around the place with her unique sight. In some of the corners she could see bouncers standing guard and their faces masked the black, slithering creatures inside of them. Drones. Most of the clubbers were human, but she noticed an occasional drone within the crowd. These she could handle, but she needed to find the woman.

Nikka stepped through the crowd and looked at each face. Young women dragged to this hell hole by their boyfriends who just wanted to gawk at the dancers. Men who came to prey on these women when they left their boyfriends.

Then she saw a group walking past the main entrance and into a pair of doors to the left of the bar. The entourage moved with purpose and authority. Several drones filled the pack and they surrounded a single person: a woman. Nikka pushed through the crowd and watched the group just before they disappeared through the doors. It was definitely the redhead, and she still wore her tight leathers and spiked heels like a dominatrix.

The entourage went through the doors and two bouncers stepped into the doorway, blocking it. She moved to the bar where she could watch the doors and the men guarding it. Patience was everything now.

The coat fit firmly around her chest, the neckline plunging into a V and then closed with gold buttons. It opened just above her navel, revealing the tattoos over her abdomen.

Wait until she gets a load of me, Nikka thought as she felt her anger boil into her chest. They had taken her by surprise last time. Now it was her turn.

She willed the power into her chest and down her limbs. It filled her strength and clarified her eyesight. With her illusion still in place she stepped to the doors as she eyed both bouncers. She pushed the power into her fingertips and threw the energy at both men. The power struck them directly in the chest and pulled the demons out at the same time. The effect was subtle enough that nobody around them noticed, but the loud music and darkness in the room helped as well. The demons screamed as they squirmed from where they were pinned to the wall. She removed their heads with her katana and stepped through the doors before they even hit the ground.

The music muffled a little as the doors closed. She entered into a dimly lit hallway painted in blood red and covered with a red carpet. Single spotlights lit the corridor every few feet, but did little to brighten her path. She let the illusion fall as she gripped her sword. There would be no need for it from now on.

Her fingers curled tightly around the hilt. A surge of power floated just under her skin, making her tattoos glow with a faint white light. Closed doors along the hallway concealed things that she could hear, things she did not want to see. The debauchery in those rooms did not concern her. She came for only one thing.

She rounded a corner and saw another set of double doors. Two men stood on either side of it and reacted as soon as they noticed her. The two drones, who appeared as bouncers except for their white eyes and black liquid oozing from their mouths, snarled at her as she approached.

"Hello, boys," she said and held her position in the corridor. "Guess who?"

They ran at her at the same time. The smell of sulfur and decay preceded them. The man to first reach her lunged out at her. She ran at them as well, but just as he reached for her, she fell to her knees and slid across the floor and arched backward. The drone missed her and collided into the far wall. She jumped to her feet and sheathed her sword. The second man growled and pounced.

He landed on her, and they crashed against the cosed doors. Her fingers curled around the front of his shirt. She kicked her leg against the wall and forced him up against the pillars across the hallway. Before he could counter her maneuver, she called the power into an instant light into her hand. She reached through his chest and found the demon that spawned inside of him. When her fingers had latched onto the creature's spine, she ripped it out of him as he screamed. The demon lashed out at her with black oil dripping from its thrashing teeth. Then she pulled her sword and decapitated the monster.

The other drone moved at her, his feet sliding across the floor as an unseen force carried him toward her. It was on her before she could turn, its fingers at her throat. Her fingers slipped from the hilt, and her sword clanked to the ground.

He growled at her through clenched, rotten teeth. He threw her against the wall while her hands grasped at his claws. The creature laughed and threw her against the adjoining wall, leaving a break in the drywall. Its white blank eyes glared at her with hatred.

The pain of his grip threatened to break her confidence, but this was just another drone. She had to remember that, despite the fear that now crept into her thoughts, she had to react fast.

She willed the power into her fingertips and formed the light in her palm before the creature knew what she was doing. He squeezed tighter on her throat, but she let the light erupt from her hand. It struck him with such force that he crashed into the wall behind him. The light pierced through him and took the demon with it. Nikka pulled herself from the collapsing wall behind her and picked up her sword. The beast wailed from where the light pinned it to the wall. She swung the blade and cut off its head and ended the horrible noise that came from its rotting throat.

Nikka sheathed her sword and turned to face the double doors that had once been guarded by the two drones. There was something, or someone, very important behind those doors and she knew who it would be.

She took a deep breath and gathered her strength, controlling the power that flowed through her tattoos. This kind of power needed to be recharged, especially if she was going to face a lieutenant in the next room.

She placed her hands on the doors and opened them together. The rush of air from inside the room came at her, smelling of smoke and decay. The edges of her duster brushed against her black boots as she stepped into the room and faced the group that had collected in there like a hive of bees.

The walls and floor were the same red as the corridor. Red velvet chairs and drapes decorated the room like some gothic vampire romance novel, including a sparkling crystal chandelier and sconces on the walls. The red haired woman sat in the chair at the center of the room like a queen. The others, men infected with drones, stood around the room and collected her things as she had ordered. When Nikka entered the room, the place went silent as all eyes turned toward her.

"My, my," the woman said through her blood red lip gloss. "Look who has come to play." She stood, her leather pants creaking as she did so, and looked at Nikka with a wicked grin. Her eyes blazed into two fiery rings.

"I just thought I would come finish what you started," Nikka said.

"Bring it on," the she-demon said.

With a snap of the demon's fingers, the lights cut out as the drones moved into action. Nikka could hear movement all around and feel the shift in the air. A chill drifted over her, and she dodged just as an arm swung toward her. The drone shifted, but she caught his arm and pulled the demon from the body as quickly as he had come at her.

Another bounded at her and hit her in the side. She rolled and kicked his legs out from under him. As he fell, she was on top of him and pulled the creature from his chest. But more came at her from the dark, and her hands lost the demons she held. There was nothing she could do to hold onto them.

More hands came at her from the dark, and she struck them down as fast as they could come at her. When they would come, she never lost sight of the woman's orange-red eyes. She still waited for her to attack. The army of drones would slow her down, and then the woman in leather would come at her eventually.

Nikka fought her way through the last drone and the orange eyes blinked out. Something skittered in the dark like a cockroach moving along the walls.

Enough of this, she thought.

She drew her sword and the blue fire illuminated the room into a ghostly hue. The woman crawled up the wall toward the ceiling with unnatural insectoid twitching as she moved. Her eyes blazed into fire again and she hissed with rows of sharp and dripping teeth. The creature moved so fast that Nikka didn't have time to step back. It skittered across the ceiling and jumped at her from above.

Nikka fell with the thing on top of her, snapping its jaws at her face. She held it back with all the strength that she had left and turned her head to the side. The creature's hot, fetid breath brushed against her neck. Its claws raked at her chest, but caught against the leather bodice. The demon lost its focus for just a second, but that was long enough for Nikka to lodge her foot in the demon's abdomen and kick it away. It screamed and crashed into the back of the sofa. The furniture tumbled over with it.

Nikka jumped to her feet with the sword held out in front of her. The light reached to the chair but could not show her the dark recesses of the room. The sofa had tipped, and she thought the demon might be hiding behind it.

A deep-throated laugh resounded through the room. She heard the skittering again, but now it sounded as though it was coming from every corner, in every shadow. Nikka turned at each sound, shining the blue light into the dark of the room.

"You think you can defeat us?" a voice said from the north corner. It sounded like a mix of the woman and a hyena speaking through the red head's throat. "We are legion."

"You are nothing," Nikka said, trying to follow the voice.

"I don't see what the big deal is," it continued. "What does Abaddon want you for? A silly girl with her knife."

That dismayed her for a moment. Abaddon wants her; and then she remembered his voice across the promenade as she ran from him. He wanted them to take her alive.

"Oh," the woman said with a laugh. "You didn't know that. Well, we all have our little secrets, don't we."

"Where is Abaddon?" Nikka shouted.

"Do not fret, my dear," the voice said.

The creature appeared from the upper corner of the room and landed on her. They fell to the ground as the woman's red hair fell over her face that had now contorted into a gruesome black skull with fire red eyes and a gaping jaw full of teeth.

"He will find you," it said as it grasped at her arms.

Nikka twisted fast enough to knock the creature from her body. Its claws raked at her and wrapped around her wrist. It threatened to pull her into its rotting form, but she planted her boot into the carpet. She was able to free her right hand, and she turned to see her sword on the ground. Her fingers moved quickly and grasped the hilt.

The blue flame erupted just as she swung it down on the demon's arm, severing it from the creature's body. Nikka fell backwards, free from the demon, but its hands still grasped at her wrist. The beast screamed and writhed on the floor as it coddled its bleeding stump. The black oil poured from its veins and pooled around it.

The woman's red eyes turned up to her, angry and full of hatred. It screeched and scrambled onto its three other limbs. Nikka crawled backward as the beast raced at her, its rotting breath assaulting her senses. It screamed and descended on her in a blur of shadows and fire. Nikka swung the sword again, and the blade sliced through its neck.

The head flew from the body of the demon in a whirl of long red hair. The body twitched, its good hand reaching blindly at the neck stump. Then it collapsed into a twitching pool of black ooze.

Nikka watched this from her place against the toppled sofa. She held the sword in her hands, ready for anything else that this monster had for her. The body twitched one final time, and then its twisted limbs morphed into pale and limp human flesh.

This time, her hands didn't shake. She held the sword steady, feeling the black oil drip from her hands and face where the demon had sprayed her.

She felt vindicated at last. One down. One more to go. And then she would kill Abaddon at last.

CHAPTER 33

GIDEON MET HER at the door when she returned. She had never noticed him look so worried, but he grabbed her and held her in a tight embrace when she entered the threshold. She must have smelled awful, and the black goo that had dampened her skin was not appealing in any way, but he didn't seem to care.

"Are you all right?" he asked.

"I'm fine," she said and pulled away from him. "She's dead, along with a lot of drones. But I couldn't get any info on Abaddon. She was too pissed, trying to kill me and all."

He walked with her to the main hall. "But you are really okay?"

"Of course," she said and left him in the hall while she called back to him. "I just need a shower."

She walked up the stairs to her room and let her clothes fall to the floor as she walked to the shower. The water washed away the demon blood, and for once, she was grateful that she didn't have hair. That stuff would have never come out. As she reveled in the hot water, she examined all her new bruises. There were a few scratches here and there as well, but nothing that wouldn't heal in a day. The duster Gideon had made really did make a difference. It protected her from the final onslaught from the lieutenant.

She wrapped herself in a towel and stepped into her room. Gideon had already taken her clothes, probably to clean them. The smell was awful and she would forgive him for sneaking into her room if it was to take those horrible things away. She dressed in fresh clothes and stepped to the door when she heard something in the corner of her room.

The sound was muffled at first, but it grew more distinct as she neared the source. Her pack sat in the corner beside the table. The sound came again and she recognized it as the buzzing of her cell phone.

Only one other person besides Gideon had her cell phone number. She had almost forgotten it after her last meeting with Jason. The buzz came again, and she felt her blood chill.

Nikka stooped and reached her hand into the front pocket for her phone. She glanced at the screen and saw his number. The device vibrated in her hand, but she wasn't sure if the shaking was coming from the phone or her hands. Her mouth went dry as she looked at the screen.

With a trembling finger, she swiped her finger across the screen and placed the phone to her ear.

At first there was nothing, but then she could hear his breath.

"How's my girl?" his smoky voice spoke through the phone. "You make it home okay?"

Nikka tried to hold the phone steady but it was difficult with her hands shaking as they were.

"I've been thinking about you," he said. She could hear the smile in his voice. "I was trying to be nice. Wanted to give you your space. But then you go and do a thing like this."

The room around him echoed into the phone and she heard his footsteps. "I really liked Cherry. Hated the name she picked, but I really liked her. And then you had to go and chop her head off."

"That bitch deserved it," Nikka said. She knew that she should never have said anything. He was only calling to rattle her nerves, but she couldn't help it.

"You're probably right. She hit my girl and I really didn't like that."

"What do you care?" she said. Her voice began to break.

"I care a lot," he said. "You know, it took a lot for me to find you. You certainly didn't make it easy. And you've got a killer ass. Couldn't really say that about any other seraph."

She cringed and felt nauseated.

"In fact, if it had turned out that you weren't the seraph, I was gonna take you out on that little road trip. We would have stopped at the rest area at exit 262. Nobody would be there, nobody would hear you scream as I took you right there. Of course, I would have left your body in the woods; maybe some coyotes could have enjoyed it, but not as much as I would have."

The tears flooded her eyes with the horrible things that came from his mouth. How could she have been so blind to what he truly was?

"What do you want?" She had to say something to shut him up.

"Just you, sweetie," he said. "I know you're looking for me. Don't worry. I will lead you right to me in due time."

"And then I'll kill you," she said as she felt her jaw tighten.

"You first," he said and the line went dead.

The phone clicked against her ear as she held it for a moment. It almost slipped from her trembling fingers. Anger swelled from deep in her gut. It felt almost like the power beginning to rise, but it was different. It made her bones ache and her head hurt.

With the phone in her hand, she shouted into the air and threw it across the room, shattering it against the wall. The small gesture wouldn't do much, but for now it made her feel just a little better, even if her phone was broken.

Gideon appeared in the door and rushed to her side. "What is wrong?"

The words wouldn't come out right away. She could still hear him as though he was in the room. She could almost feel Abaddon's breath on her neck.

Gideon wrapped his arms around her, and she shook against his strong frame. "He called me."

Gideon looked down at her and held her face in his hands. "Abaddon? Why?"

"He's just trying to rattle me," she said. "But he did say that he was going to let us find him. Why would he do that?"

"He is just trying to trick you to come out into the open. He knows he cannot come here if it is sacred ground."

"There's something else," she said. "The other day, he wanted me alive. On the phone, he said he wants me. Why does he need me? Why not just let his minions kill me?"

Gideon remained silent for a moment and Nikka could see the trouble in his eyes.

"What do you know?" she asked.

"The symbol on the floor that you saw," he said. "I said it was a portal, but it can only be opened once and I am sure they opened it to let Abaddon through. But with the blood of a seraph, they could keep the portal open and allow any number of beasts to come through it."

"You mean a sacrifice."

He nodded.

"Okay," she said, feeling the nausea again. "Let's say that he is success-ful—"

"I will not let him get to you."

"Gideon," she interrupted him. "If he manages to open that thing, how can you close it?"

He shook his head. He probably didn't want to think of the possibilities any more than she did. "By killing the demon that opened it."

"Can you kill him if I die?" she asked.

The terror in his eyes pierced her soul. "I am not sure. Maybe."

CHAPTER 34

NIKKA SAT IN FRONT OF THE FIRE, her knees drawn to her chest. The warmth hardly seemed to soothe her aching muscles and joints tonight. The snapping of small air pockets in the wood startled her as she watched the warm glow. In the dancing flames, she could sometimes see his face: Abaddon. The fire quivered and shimmered in his eyes as he looked out at her, as though he knew how to find her.

Gideon sat beside her and took her hand, as if he knew what she was thinking. Somehow, his touch was warmer than the flames. It drew her attention from the face in the fire, and she leaned against his shoulder.

The fire consumed the logs as they toppled into a heap. Embers spurted from the wood and drifted up into the chimney. The neat stack they had made together now crumbled into a heap of fire.

Everything was going up in flames.

Everything.

Her tattoos tingled just a little and sparkled just under her skin. She glanced down at them and gazed at the twinkling like starlight on her flesh.

"What is wrong?" he said as he glanced down at the marks.

The wood crumbled in the fireplace again. Embers glowed orange at the base of the fireplace.

Something terrible is going to happen.

Her power knew it. It practically screamed at her now, but there was no way of knowing what it wanted to tell her.

She turned and looked at Gideon, the lights dancing in his eyes. The fire-light mixed with her own light and played across his skin in a savage fight. The longer he touched her skin, she knew the truth.

Everything that they had been through since he came to her that day in the hospital flashed across her mind in a volley of images. And then she saw only fire.

When he had told her that he loved her, she thought that she might love him as well, but the thought of losing him pierced through her heart. If he was gone, she didn't know how she could go on.

She realized she loved him too. She had for a long time now.

"Don't go," she whispered and held him close.

"I will not be going anywhere," he whispered in her ear.

"Just promise that you will stay."

"I promise."

She kissed him, which took him by surprise at first, but then he held her closer.

Something terrible was going to happen, and she was going to stop it. It had to be done, no matter what the cost.

The evening moonlight poured like liquid silver through the white curtains, spilling over the ground but never touching the bed. Nikka lay on her back and watched the shadows in the silence of the room. Gideon slept beside her, his arm draped over her bare torso. The warmth of his body next to her made the sheet unnecessary, but it covered the rest of her body against the chill of the room. She had always been suspicious in the back of her mind that he never slept, but he did now. His breathing remained steady and relaxed.

Everything that had happened tonight was so unexpected, but she would never wish it to be any different. She had never been with anyone but him, and she knew it to be true for him as well. In a thousand years or more, he had walked this earth with no purpose but to teach a seraph. And now that he loved one, he loved with all his power. She knew that when he touched her and kissed her, and when he made love to her. If this was their first experience, why did it feel so much like it would be their last?

Even a month ago she would not have thought she would be here with him now, and she would not want it any other way. If it were just for this night, at least they didn't have to think about all the horrible things waiting for them outside the walls of their sanctuary.

She kept her hand over his where he touched her. The memory of the flames and the terrible feeling still plagued her, and it nearly made her cry when she was with him, but she never told him what she suspected. She closed her eyes and concentrated on his even breathing, his legs intertwined with hers.

I won't let anything happen to you. Ever.

His fingers moved, curling around hers. She opened her eyes, but felt her muscles stiffen and her veins become ice when she saw him, and it wasn't Gideon. She could no longer breathe when she saw Jason's face next to her.

Haunting blue eyes looked at her as his blond hair fell around the pillow. She gasped and tried to get away from him, but he pulled her back and pinned her to the bed. His strength was too much, and she couldn't get her hand free to fight back.

"I told you truth," he said. "Remember that."

"I don't care." She cried out, but nobody could hear her in the dark room.

"Don't let me die," he said and looked down on her, his face a twisted picture of desperation.

She stopped struggling and saw his face and the blue of his eyes. There was no fire there. He appeared just as she had remembered him on the day he saw her in the library for the first time. Innocent. Beautiful.

Nikka awoke with a start, catching the cold air of the room in her lungs. There was nobody on top of her, holding her down. She looked beside her and saw Gideon's still form as he slept in silence, his hand still on her torso.

The echoes of the dream tortured her. She slid out from under the sheet and let his hand down to the bed as she stepped across the room. The cold air quickly chilled her naked body and she slipped into the bathroom.

She faced herself in the mirror and saw the last remnants of bruising around her cheek from the fracture she had endured. As she looked, she remembered another mirror somewhere in the recesses of her mind. But it wasn't real. That had been a dream too, but Jason had been there at that time as well. He had said the same thing to her then as he did now.

Don't let me die.

She turned the faucet and splashed cold water on her face. The dreams slipped away with the zip of cold against her flesh.

What was she supposed to do? She had to kill Abaddon, there was no other way to end this. If he didn't die, then he would kill her. Without his death, the hordes could destroy everything, and that was why she was here. To end them.

The look in his eyes continued to flicker in her thoughts, though. His pleading words, things that he nearly cried to her with such panic, played over and over again. For the first time since she saw his transformation on the promenade, she wanted to save Jason.

Something out there was telling her that she had to find another way.

She clasped her hands together and rested them on the sink. Her forehead touched her thumbs and she felt tears filling her eyes.

She had never done this before. *How do you start doing this?*

The words first came out in a whisper. "God, please help me."

The cold mixed with the water on her hands and arms made her shiver.

"I know I don't usually do this, but I need your help now. Help me save them both. I can't do this alone."

Bright lights and loud noises. That was what she had initially expected, but there was nothing. Only darkness and cold. Emptiness everywhere. She clasped her fingers tighter, hoping to keep them from freezing. She lifted her head and gazed into the mirror again. There was nothing different about her.

Perhaps she had to do this alone after all.

CHAPTER 35

SHE WASN'T SURE when she had fallen asleep, but when she opened her eyes, the morning light appeared gray and overcast. Her eyes squinted against the light. But there was something wrong. She glanced to the side of the bed and found herself alone. Gideon was gone and his place among the sheets had grown cold.

Panic took over her senses as she jumped out of the bed and put her clothes on. She raced down the stairs and into the gym. She rushed through the doors, but the place was empty. Only the gray morning light lit up the floor in broad rectangles.

"Gideon," she shouted and moved among the equipment just in case he was there.

But she was alone in the room.

She turned down the stairs and rushed into the main dining hall. At this time in the morning he usually had cooked something and added enough seasonings that you could smell it out in the hall, but today it was empty. She called his name again and again, searching through rooms and even closets. She rushed down to the collapsing chapel, but found it abandoned.

Tears clouded her vision and she felt a pain in her chest. He was gone, disappeared from right under her watch. Her fingers grasped at her chest to ease the pain, but it only grew. The air in her lungs burned like fire.

A rumbling sound came from beyond the walls of the monastery and then faded away. Nikka held her breath for a moment and listened. There was only silence for a few seconds and then another sound rebounded through the crumbling chapel.

A car.

She bolted for the main door and rushed out into the cold morning. When she saw the familiar sedan, she felt that she could breathe again.

Gideon moved away from the car with two grocery bags in his arms. He looked up at her and smiled at first, but then saw the look on her face.

She ran down the steps and met him at the chain link fence. He put the bags down and pushed his way through the breech in the fence to meet her. Her arms wrapped around him as he held her.

"What is it?" he asked. "Are you injured?"

At first she couldn't speak. "You were gone. I—"

"Everything is okay," he said. "We needed more eggs. And milk."

She pulled away from him and held his face in her hands, examining him to make sure that he was indeed all right.

"Really, I am okay," he said. "Let me get the bags and I will come inside with you."

It was hard to release him, but he was right. He looked okay and uninjured. She walked into the building with him and to the main hall, where she sat down and covered her eyes with her hands. She had to get control of her shaking, now that she had been jolted from bed with terror.

"What is really going on?" he asked as he knelt before her and touched her knee.

She removed her hands and looked down at him. "Something awful is coming. I can feel it. I don't want something bad to happen to you."

"Nothing will happen," he said. He leaned into her and touched his forehead to hers. "I promise."

"Famous last words. Don't make promises you can't keep," she said.

"I never do," he said and kissed her.

She kissed him in return and felt his hands around her back. When she felt the heat of him through her thin nightshirt, the shaking eased a little. They stayed this way for a minute before she felt his fingers moved under the hem of her shirt and against her skin.

She grasped his wrists. "All right, lover boy." She backed away from him, feeling the air grow lighter around them. "We need breakfast before any of that."

"Breakfast can wait," he said and came in again with a kiss on her neck.

She slipped away from the couch and stood. "Not when I'm this hungry."

He laughed and hung his head. "You are killing me."

She turned to face him with a smile. "Did Gideon just make a joke? See, you can act human like the rest of us." She stepped into the kitchen and left him in the hall.

As she worked on scrambling eggs, he prepared some toast. She would laugh every time he would look at her. His thoughts couldn't have been louder had they been broadcast on the radio. She shook her head and carried a plate to the table.

That was when she stopped, startled by a figure in the doorway. She immediately recognized his dark suit and white collar. It was Father Beyers.

Gideon almost ran into her when he followed her to the dining area. When he saw the priest, he lost his smile and stepped away from Nikka as though the priest could sense his thoughts as well.

"Father Beyers," he said after he cleared his throat.

"I'm sorry," the priest spoke and looked at them with a stern glare. "Am I interrupting something?"

Nikka narrowed her eyes at him. What was he doing here? She didn't trust this man who had been following her from the day that she met him. "Yeah. Breakfast. Why are you interrupting?"

"My apologies," he said and nodded to her. "I should have called first, I know."

"Yeah, you should have," Nikka said. She meant it to sound as rude as it did.

Gideon nudged her arm and invited the priest to sit with them.

"I'm sorry, but I have no time. I really need to speak to you, Gideon," the priest said with a sense of urgency.

"Whatever you have to say, you can say it in front of my . . . my apprentice," Gideon said.

"Very well," he said and sat at the table. "I need your help again. Last night, several churches around town were destroyed. Most were literally burned to the ground. Horrible things have been happening the last few days, and I suspect we are dealing with something very unnatural. Something demonic."

Gideon glanced at Nikka. "Yes, we are aware."

"Does this have anything to do with you following me?" Nikka said and crossed her arms over her chest.

The priest looked at her with guilt. "I was worried for you. When you left the house that day, I sensed that you may be in terrible danger. I never meant to scare you. But I continued to have that feeling for days, and I saw you with that . . . that man at the college. Something was not right."

She unfolded her arms and felt her shoulders soften. The priest had more insight about Jason than she did. If only he could have warned her sooner.

He turned back to Gideon. "I believe my church is next."

"Why do you think this?" Nikka asked.

"When I arrived yesterday, all the crosses in the chapel had been turned upside down."

Gideon straightened in his chair, and it felt as though the room had grown colder.

Nikka looked at both of them, confused. "What does that mean?"

"An upside-down cross is an offense to the Heavens. It defiles the space in which it lies and makes holy ground tainted. It would no longer be sacred, and a demon can then enter," Gideon explained.

Nikka thought about that for a moment. Someone had purposely tainted the holy ground, but a demon could not have done that. It had to be some-one that could have crossed the threshold to begin with.

"I believe that these are the signs of Armageddon," the priest spoke. "They are eliminating holy spaces. There will soon be nothing left to stop them."

"Not if we can help it," Nikka said.

"You said you needed my help," Gideon said. "What can I do?"

The priest glanced at him. "If we can sanctify the area tonight, we can stop them. It may be a small gesture, but it is something that can keep others safe. You're the only one that has the ability to do it in such a short amount of time."

"What is he talking about?" Nikka asked.

"I carry something very special, a liquid that with one drop can heal the earth on which it falls," Gideon said.

She remembered seeing Gideon with a bottle of fluid the day she took out her first demon. Was this the same stuff?

"It's the blood of martyred saints," the priest muttered.

Nikka felt her eyebrows rise with curiosity. "What? Like, Joan of Arc and stuff?" She looked at him. "Holy hell, Gideon. Why is this the first time I am hearing about this?"

Gideon shrugged. "I had no need to tell you. I use it to sanctify homes that have been invaded by demons. I have used it many times to strengthen the power of churches and graveyards." He turned to the priest. "I can bring this to your chapel and protect it tonight."

"Wait a second," she said. "He can just take it, do his thing, and then bring it back to you."

Gideon shook his head. "It does not work that way. It was bestowed upon me and only me. I am the only one that can carry it. If anyone else were to use it, nothing would work. Only I can sanctify his land."

She wanted to say more, but she didn't know where to start. The priest stood and Gideon rose with him.

"Wait," she said and pulled Gideon aside. "Don't go."

"I must do this. I cannot leave their sanctuary unprotected. They know I have been helping him exorcise demons for a long time now. They will kill him if he is left vulnerable," he said. "I will be back as soon as I can."

"Do you remember what I said? Something awful is coming," she said. "Don't go out there today."

He grasped her hand. "This is my duty. I must go and help him." He reached into his pocket and removed his phone, placing it in the palm of her hand. It was identical to the one she had broken last night. "Keep this with you. I will let you know what is going on out there and when I will be back. Do not leave the monastery until I return."

Nikka closed her eyes as he squeezed her hand. "I will be back before nightfall."

He stepped away from her and she watched him walk away with the priest. Father Beyers glanced back at her one more time as they left and she could see the look of desperation in his eyes. Then he turned around and they were out of sight. She clutched the phone to her chest, but she couldn't shake that horrible feeling that had crept into her gut again.

She finished her breakfast and cleaned the hall, mostly just to keep her hands busy, but it didn't keep her mind from wandering back to him and the look on the priest's face. When she found herself pacing, she sat down on the couch and opened Gideon's computer. She scrolled through the several documents that he had compiled. The page with the photos of individuals opened and she scanned through until she found the man's face, the one who had stabbed her and nearly killed her.

The smug look on his face made her sick, with his all-American smile and pretty-boy blonde hair styled to perfection. It took a lot for her to remember that the one who stabbed her was the demon, not the man, but she just couldn't stand to look at his face. She clicked on his picture and that linked her to the website of his firm. Mark Taylor, a partner at Smith and Cline.

The building had been situated on the adjoining street that ran in front of the security firm. She scrolled through other files that Gideon had deemed urgent: a very large bank, The Snake Pit, the Main Street subway tunnel entryway, and a real estate agency.

Five locations. Five points.

She opened the next page to see that Gideon had plotted out the points on a map of the city and then he had drawn over them. The places formed a perfect inverted pentagram, with the security firm in the center.

Somehow, that didn't surprise her.

She opened more pages that Gideon had compiled, but found nothing more in relation to the pentagram or what else it could mean besides the fact that Abaddon was a really horrible demon and was working very hard to possess the entire city, maybe the entire coast. Her eyes moved along the screen, but then stopped at the time signature at the bottom right corner of the screen.

Several hours had gone by since Gideon left, yet the phone never rang. She placed the computer on the table and paced to the windows. The overcast gray sky had grown darker as though a thunderstorm was moving over the mountains.

The feeling grew stronger in her gut, moving into her chest and tickling at the pain in her heart again.

"Where are you, Gideon?" she whispered to herself.

She turned away from the window and left the room, rushing up the stairs to her bedroom. The coat, her boots and her black cargo pants were lying neatly folded on her bed, a gift from Gideon. Her fingers ran over the symbols on the edging of the coat. The tingle began in her fingertips as she did this.

Something's wrong, she thought.

It didn't take long to change her clothes. As soon as she had tightened the belt of her duster, she rushed out of the room and down the stairs. She emerged into the bottom floor that now grew darker with the impending storm. Thunder rumbled under her feet, and a flash of lightning blinked through the spaces in the boarded windows.

The lightning flashed again followed by a sharp crack of thunder. The light was bright enough for her to see across the room and to the door. Something had changed. Something that she had never noticed before.

She walked up to the door. The smell of rain flooded into the room. As the sky grew darker, the lightning became as bright as road flares. Then her legs felt as though they would collapse under her.

Someone had placed a cross on the door, only it was upside down. There had never been a cross there until today.

Whoever had done this now defiled the monastery and she was no longer safe. That had been the plan all along. Only a person could have done this, because a demon could never have walked into the monastery.

Father Beyers did this.

He had convinced Gideon to go with him, leaving Nikka alone and unprotected, in a sanctuary that he had left defiled.

And he had Gideon now.

CHAPTER 36

THE LIGHTNING CONTINUED TO FLASH, and after the thunder crack, she was startled when the cell phone beeped. It took her a moment to realize what the sound was, but she found it in her pocket and looked at the screen. Gideon had placed Father Beyers in his quick dial, and that was the name she read on the face of the phone. It stated there was a new text message from the priest.

The phone vibrated in her hand as another beep came from the phone. She touched the screen and the text message field appeared, followed by a black screen as it prepared to play a video sent from Father Beyers' phone.

"Greetings," a voice said, and a man recorded himself as he talked into the phone. She recognized his well-coifed hair and neat suit. Mark Taylor, the demon who had stabbed her. The camera was shaky in his hands as he moved while he talked. "I just thought I would send you a little message. I have somebody here that would just love to talk to you."

The camera swung in a dizzying arc to the center of the room. Nikka felt as though the floor had collapsed underneath her. The camera focused on Gideon, tied to a hook by a rope at his wrists. His shirt had been removed and streaks of blood dripped down his torso from several lacerations on his chest and arms.

"Well," Mark said as he placed the camera down on something and stepped in front of it. "He doesn't appear to be in a talking mood."

As the demon stepped away from the camera and toward Gideon, he produced a knife from his suit jacket. The silver blade glinted in the harsh lighting.

"Hey, I've got a great idea." He smiled as though he were hosting a game show. "Why don't you come down and join us, Nikka? I'm sure Gideon and the gang here would love to have you over. Right Gideon?"

Gideon's head moved as he looked at Mark. Sweat glistened on his skin. His eyelids fluttered with fatigue, and Nikka could see his ribs with every troubled breath.

"See," Mark said. "I would suggest you hurry, Nikka." As he glanced away from the camera, the knife flashed as he sliced it down the length of Gideon's arm. He screamed out as fresh blood flowed down his arm and dripped onto the floor.

The video cut out and the phone closed its media player. Nikka fell to her knees. She couldn't breathe, and the pain started in her chest again.

It was happening; everything that she could feel coming had started and Gideon was going to die.

She gripped the phone as she remembered the smirk on Mark Taylor's face when he cut Gideon. She was sure that he had done the majority of the abuse to him. If she went to the law firm, she knew it would be a trap, but she couldn't leave Gideon there to die.

The shaking in her hands was no longer fear. It was anger. Her fingers clenched tightly until her knuckles turned white.

The demon wanted her to come to him, so that's exactly what she was going to do.

She stood, pocketed her phone and stepped out the front door. The storm began to rage through the trees with fierce wind and rain. She walked across the lot and to Gideon's car, her thick-soled boots crunching against the gravel under her feet. The car started right up and she rushed down the darkened hillside road. Her mind was a whorl of hate, fueled by the look on Gideon's face as he hung from that hook.

The streets of the city had become bare. Most people now sought shelter from the oncoming storm. The clouds began to swirl overhead. She had never seen a tornado before, but she had to imagine that it must look and feel something like this.

She stopped the car along a curb and gazed out at the dark clouds. Rain spattered over the windshield and looked like a chaos of sparkling light when the lightning flashed. The storm whorled over the downtown district, right above the center of the pentagram that she had seen on the map, and the upper right point of that pentagram was one block away at the Smith and

Cline law firm just down the street from the office building that she had infiltrated and killed her first lieutenant.

A bank of lights shone on the third floor, northeast corner. The remainder of the building appeared closed down. She knew that the lights were a beacon lit just for her. They wanted her to find them.

She stepped out of the car and walked down the center of the street. The wind blowing between the empty buildings with the rumble of thunder along the hills reminded her of a post-apocalyptic future, one that she hoped to avoid. The sky grew darker as she moved closer to the building.

The front lobby was dark and empty. She thought that there might have been somebody to meet her there, but it was silent without a trace of human or demon. They probably thought they could just track her with security cameras and motion detectors.

They would be wrong.

She pulled her power into full strength and started her invisibility illusion. She didn't care how much energy it would take from her. She needed it long enough to get to Gideon and then she would fight their way out.

Nikka walked through the front doors and met the silence in the lobby. It appeared to be the normal décor of a typical law firm, but under the well-upholstered chairs and drapes, she could smell the faint scent of decay. Demons had infiltrated this place long ago. There was probably not a single human left working in this place during the day.

She entered an elevator and the door slid closed, but she didn't push a single button. They had likely detected motion in the lobby and at the elevator, but that would be all they would know. She couldn't risk riding up in the elevator. She dislodged the upper elevator access panel and crawled to the top of the elevator.

The elevator shaft was dark and cold, with a chilling draft of air that swirled at every level. She ascended along the elevator cables, inching her way up past the first two elevator bay doors, where the air grew colder. She focused on each hand hold while keeping the illusion in place. She couldn't afford to let it drop even in the elevator shaft. Security cameras could be installed anywhere.

She climbed to the third level and swung herself over to the elevator doors. Her fingers slid between the doors and pried them open. The hallway beyond the elevator bank remained dark, lit only by the lamps from the street. The place flashed in bright light with the lightning, and then plunged into murky darkness. She stepped into the corridor and glanced down both ends of the hall. There was nobody on this level either.

They're making this very easy, she thought. *What's the catch?*

She pressed back against the north wall and stepped down the corridor until it opened into a larger atrium and waiting area dotted with sofas and chairs. Beyond the area was a set of double doors that appeared to open into a large room. Two men stood at the doors and watched the space before them.

That had to be where they were keeping Gideon.

Her suspicions were validated when she heard him scream from behind those doors. It was the same sound he had made when Mark had cut him and recorded the whole thing. She stopped and closed her eyes. The sound was heartbreaking and it threatened to shatter her concentration.

Mark's laugh resounded from the room , followed by the sound of something hitting Gideon. She cringed and dug her fingernails into the palms of her hands when she heard him cry out again.

Do what you are here to do, she thought. *You are the Seraph. Destroy them.*

She opened her eyes and tried to not hear his cries beyond the door. Her vision focused through the dark and found the two men who guarded the doors. They scanned the floor and that was when she saw their eyes.

These were not drones. They were lieutenants.

So they were getting serious about her. They wanted to make sure that she was stopped.

Well, not tonight. Even if she had to kill them. Human and demon.

She bolstered the illusion and stepped toward them with singular purpose. She drew her sword, its light invisible to the demons that stood guard. She would not allow them to stop her.

They must have sensed movement. Their shoulders tensed as they looked through the dark, but they saw nothing. In a flash of blue light, Nikka dropped the illusion when she stepped between them. She swung the sword in a single continuous round and decapitated both of them with one strike. The bodies fell to the floor and she stood before the doors as she caught her breath.

They could see her now; she knew it. But Gideon was on the other side of those doors and she was not about to run and hide now. She wanted them to see her. She wanted them to fear her.

With all the power that she formed at her core, she kicked the doors open. The air from the room rushed at her as she stepped inside to see a board room with a long table in the center. Gideon's cries came again and she glanced around the space, but there wasn't a single person there. Along the far wall, a pull-down screen displayed video images, and she now realized where the sounds of Gideon were coming from.

He appeared on the screen, displayed from a digital projector set on the center of the table. Like a horror movie, the scenes of Gideon's torture continued to play before her.

The lights of the board room illuminated, and Mark walked in from the double doors.

"I have to say," he said with a toothy smile, "You got here faster than I thought."

"Where is he?" she shouted.

The recording continued on the screen as she turned and faced him.

"Oh, he's close. Just not here. I never said he was here."

"What do you want from me?" she said, feeling the warmth of the hilt in her hand. Her fingers gripped it tight, ready to take him down.

"It's not me, sugar lips," he said and laughed. "It's my boss. You see, he's a little infatuated with you and he just wants me to deliver."

A gun appeared in his hand and, before she knew what he was doing, he fired. She flinched and waited for the pain, but she felt a sting in her thigh. She glanced down to see the end of a red dart in her leg, the tip piercing through her trousers.

A tranquilizer dart.

She had not expected that, or any of this for that matter. In her fury, she had not planned for this contingency. How could she have been so stupid? She knew it was a trap all along, just not this kind of a trap.

The sedative in the dart worked quickly. The sounds of the room faded as though she stood in a hollow tube. Her vision blurred, and she stumbled.

"Oh, watch out," he said and caught her before she fell against the table. "Wouldn't want you to crack your head open."

Before everything went dark and silent, she heard Gideon again in the background, but she knew it was only the projection of him. Mark lifted her up and hoisted her over his shoulder.

"All right," he said, the sound cold and distant. "Abaddon is waiting for you. Sweet dreams, kiddo."

CHAPTER 37

EACH STEP ECHOED in a long tunnel when she forced her eyes open. Her lids were heavy, and everything in her vision was a swirl of colors at first. A wave of nausea washed over her. She closed her eyes and listened.

She felt herself being carried. It must be Mark. They neared an opening in the tunnel; she could tell from the change in the sounds around them. And there were many more people in the opening, but they were possessed by demons of all ranks. The smell of decay grew stronger as they neared the opening.

Hands grabbed at her arms and torso, lifting her off of Mark's shoulder. They pulled her to the ground and then dropped her against the concrete. She caught her breath and lifted herself to her hands and knees.

The candlelight around her glistened in her vision. She tried to blink away the haze left behind by the tranquilizer. When she opened her eyes again, she saw Gideon hanging by his wrists, hung from a frame further down the corridor. This sent a surge of adrenaline into her bloodstream that cleared her head.

She scrambled to her feet and ran toward him, but an arm clasped around her throat and held her back. He pinned her against his chest as she looked at Gideon across the room. His hazel eyes opened and saw her, but they were vacant. Lost.

"I told them all you would come," Jason's voice echoed from somewhere further behind her.

The man holding her turned her around to face Jason, who stood in the center of the expansive room. It was a place she recognized, but now the red circles etched with symbols on the ground were surrounded by people infected with demons. There had to be at least fifty men and women standing in the sub-basement, each with a lit candle on the ground before them. Among them stood Father Beyers, his face cast in shame as he looked away from her. In that shame, she knew he was still himself and unpossessed.

"How could you do this?" she said with a grimace toward him.

"Oh," Abaddon said and glanced between the two of them. "It's not his fault, sweetie. He did what I told him to do to make you come to me."

He stepped between them and broke her line of sight.

"There were some doubters," he continued. "But I had faith in you." He stepped from the circle, his silver chain dangling from his belt and over dark jeans.

Abaddon approached her with a smile. He placed a hand under her chin, but his touch felt like poison. She tried to jerk away from him, but he held her in place.

"What? Not happy to see me?" he said and stepped around them to face Gideon. "And you," he said, pointing to Gideon as his voice rose in anger, "What the hell happened to you? You were the Great Pazuzu. You taught me everything I know, and now I find you tapping a seraph."

Abaddon swung his fist and hit him in the gut. Gideon coughed, spitting blood from his lip and then hung his head, groaning.

Nikka cried out and struggled against the man that held her. She felt the power tickle at her insides. It wanted to erupt, and she was ready to allow it. She let it grow and rush into her arms. The power burned in her veins and she screamed. It shot from her fingers in a surge of bright light.

The demon that held her fell to the ground as it struck him. Two demons standing beside Gideon fell back against the wall, but Abaddon stood his ground.

The energy left her fingertips and quickly ebbed away from her reach. Abaddon glared and rushed toward her. Before she could react, he swung his hand and the back of his hand caught her cheek. She felt her head whip to the side, and she fell hard to the ground.

"Hey," he said and kneeled down beside her.

The taste of blood filled her mouth. Pain exploded in her cheek where she felt a bruise forming. He grabbed her arm and turned her on her back. The ache in her cheek throbbed as she moved.

"Did I say you could do that?" he said to her and pulled her to her feet.

The motion made her dizzy. She stumbled as he pulled her closer to Gideon, so close that she could smell the blood on him.

"Now, you know what I want. Look at him and tell me that I won't kill him if you say 'no.'"

Gideon opened his eyes again and looked at her. "Don't do it," he muttered just as Abaddon pulled her away.

He dragged her through the crowd of people, their eyes ablaze in fire. They emerged into the circles painted on the cement. Abaddon pulled her around to face him as he held fast to her wrists.

"You know," he said, his eyes the blue and innocent hue that had lied to her, "I thought we had something, you and I. But I guess you just wanted something a little more. And you can have that. I just want a little blood to open the portal, and I will let the two of you go to live out the rest of your lives."

"You're a liar," she said, but her voice broke.

He laughed. "Who am I kidding? You know . . . you're right. But if you don't do it, I will kill the both of you now and get the blood I need anyway. So—" he said, shrugging his shoulders.

He shoved her back where someone caught her from behind, wrapping arms around her. Abaddon stepped up to her and pulled her left hand free. Mark stepped up to his side and handed him the silver knife. In a quick motion, he sliced across her palm. The incision welled with blood and ached up her arm. Blood filled her hand and dripped down her fingertips as he pulled her into the center of the circle.

The people, the possessed, gathered around the circle and lifted their hands open to their sides. As she glanced at them, their eyes blazed brighter. Her blood flowed from her fingertips and dripped onto the blackened concrete at their feet. Abaddon continued to hold her arm with a tight grip.

A rumble started just below their feet, like a low growl that rose from an invisible throat. The ground began to tremble and shake as each drop fell to the ground. Debris rained down around them from the cement supports overhead.

Abaddon smiled and began to speak in a language that she didn't understand, shouting over the sound of the rumbling. His grip loosened on her arm.

Nikka pulled away from him, but he seemed to not notice. He was too entranced with the earthquake that had started below their feet. She stumbled back through the crowd and ran toward Gideon. She reached for her sword as she ran.

The blade flashed blue, and she swung it at the ropes that held him. He collapsed as she caught him and lowered him. The ground shook again and a chunk of cement crashed to the floor behind them. Gideon pushed himself to his knees, but still leaned over, trying to catch his breath. She placed a shaking hand on his face and wiped a trickle of blood from around his eye.

He grasped her hand and looked up at her. "You have to go now."

The ground rumbled and a tearing sound echoed through the basement. A large crack emerged within the cement, ripping from one end of the room to the other. Then, the sound of an explosion erupted into the room. Nikka glanced back to see the center of the circle had burst open, rocks and cement falling everywhere. A billow of smoke and fire rose from a hole that had punctured deep within the earth like the mouth of a volcano.

A roar, like the sound of a freight train, rose from the gash in the earth. As though the volcano had erupted, a horde of black creatures poured through the mouth, climbing onto the walls. Fire and stone followed with them, breaking through the center of the building above them. More beasts emerged, smaller, insectoid creatures like the drones, and others that were much larger and more sinister. They all climbed out of the hole and into the earthly plain.

"I have to stop him," Gideon said.

She turned back to him, and she didn't like the look on his face.

"It's the only way to close the portal."

"No," she said. "I can do it."

"There are too many. You will die. You must run, now."

"Come with me," she pleaded and placed both of her hands on his face.

"I cannot. I was sent here to protect you, to save you," he said, and his eyes sparkled with tears. "There is no other reason an angel would have had mercy on me. This is what I was meant to do. I was once a demon and I know where that portal starts."

"Please," she said. She could barely see through her tears. "Don't leave me."

"I must go," he said. "You need to survive to destroy the rest of them. But now, you need to run. Get as far away from here as you can."

He rose to his feet and held her hand as he leaned down to kiss her. Her fingers curled around his, not wanting to let him go. He touched his forehead to hers one last time.

His hazel eyes turned to Abaddon, who had his back turned, reveling in the beasts that emerged. "Get out now!"

He released her hands, and she backed away from him. Gideon broke into a rapid run toward Abaddon. Nikka turned away from him when she found the stairway that would lead her up to the parking garage. She hurried up the steps, taking them two at a time. Her hand grasped the railing but almost slipped from the coating of blood that soaked her palm.

She stopped for only a moment and glanced back. Gideon ran into the circle and tackled Abaddon at the edge of the portal. From her vantage point, she could see into the gaping hole and the turbulent fires that roiled below the level of the cement flooring. Abaddon staggered forward as Gideon landed on him, but he twisted and threw him off. Gideon slipped to the lip of the portal.

Nikka wanted to run back down and help him, but she also knew that Gideon was right. There was no way to win a fight down here with so many of them. Taking on one lieutenant was hard enough. To battle fifty of them plus the high general would be suicide. She could only watch from the stairs as Gideon crawled over to Abaddon and grasped his leg.

Abaddon kicked him, but then Gideon pulled and Abaddon fell to his side. The silver knife slipped from his hand, clattering to the portal edge and then falling into the hole.

Beasts began to crawl like spiders over the walls and reached the base of the stairs. She felt the railing shake as a creature as large as a grizzly bear, but with more teeth ,pounded its foot on the first step. Its orange-red eyes saw her and it growled, its hot breath drifting up to her.

She looked back down at the portal as Abaddon tried to kick Gideon away from him. Gideon scrambled to his knees and brought his hands down on Abaddon's neck. Gideon's eyes blazed into a bright orange fire as he shouted into the air, his hands clamping down tighter.

Abaddon swung his arms down and hit Gideon, breaking the hold he had on his neck. He twisted around, catching Gideon in the side. Gideon lost his balance, but not before grabbing Abaddon. Their feet slipped over the edge of the portal.

And then they fell into the hole.

Nikka felt the air rush from her lungs in a scream. The stairs rattled again and she glanced down to see the beast bounding up the stairs. Although she felt her heart disappearing, leaving only a hollow space, she ran up the stairs and pushed through the door into the dark parking lot.

The building trembled in a violent roar of crashing metal and brick. That was the moment she knew it was going to collapse. She ran hard and felt a burst of heat explode behind her. The door she had come through flew over her head and crashed into the wall before her. Her feet pounded against the pavement as she neared the garage exit.

She broke free into the cold night, but she knew she wasn't safe yet. The explosions continued to come, one after another. A burst of heat and light erupted behind her and knocked her off her feet. She hit the pavement and covered her head. Heat seared over her, burning against the flesh of her arms and hands. The building roared like a monster, wounded and bleeding. In a cloud of dust and smoke, the building that had housed the security firm collapsed downward.

She got to her feet and ran hard across the block as the dust enveloped her. Another explosion threatened to drop her again, but she held her balance and ran to the car. Once inside, she rested her forehead against the steering wheel and let her tears fall.

No matter how hard she had tried to prevent it, she had lost him. He had taken down the entire coven of demons. He had collapsed the portal. And now he was gone.

CHAPTER 38

THE GROUND CONTINUED TO SHAKE as though the center of the city was about to be swallowed into the earth. The car trembled and a fire hydrant ruptured along the curb beside her, showering the car in a burst of water. She looked up to the plume of smoke that billowed from the collapsed building.

The sound of sirens wailing in the distance caught her attention. If the city's fire and police departments were now getting involved, she had to get out of there fast. She started the car and spun the tires until the tread finally took hold and she rushed away from the scene. The car's wipers cleared away the water and debris from the windshield, but her vision was still clouded from the tears in her eyes.

Fire trucks and ambulances raced past her as she maneuvered from the site of the fireball. She couldn't look back. She had to keep going, to get out of the city. There were things at the monastery she needed to collect, things that belonged to Gideon. They were the only things she had left.

She moved the car through the dark of the woods, up the road that wound to the access into the monastery. The forest was quiet, a protection from the pandemonium happening in the city. It was ignorant to the event that would be talked about for years afterward: the deadly explosion that downed a skyscraper in the center of town.

The car turned down the dark access road, kicking up a cloud of dust behind it. She neared the chain link fence. The headlights fell across the fence and just trickled against the entryway of the monastery.

She gazed out into the beams of light and felt her heart race. The swarm of bees started in her gut as a wave of panic raced through her muscles.

A web of black vines had taken over the fencing, curling like an octopus through the links. They snaked across the open grounds surrounding the church. As she moved her eyes up the sides of the monastery, she thought the walls were moving in a water-like undulation. When her vision adjusted, she realized that black, slithering creatures crawled over the walls as though they were creating a cocoon.

Hell beasts had taken over her home. The home she had shared with Gideon.

The ground shuddered in a violent uproar. The front of the car heaved upward as the ground tore open in a deep gash that split into the woods. It slipped backwards, ready to be engulfed in the chasm that formed in the earth.

She opened the door and jumped from the car just as it fell back and crashed into the trench. The ground trembled once more and then became still. Whatever had just happened now managed to trap her within the confines of the infested monastery.

Serpentine creatures moved around her, surrounding her on all sides. Eyes ablaze in fire looked at her, their tails curling around her arms and pulling her to her feet. The creatures salivated along sharp glass-like teeth, looking at her hungrily but not daring to have a taste. They pulled her forward and she began to see that they encouraged her to enter the monastery. She wasn't sure she wanted to find out what would happen if she turned and ran the other way.

When she began to walk on her own toward the entry, the creatures released her but flanked her like an army. She walked to the front steps and stopped as she looked at the front atrium. The black vines had invaded through the door, tearing it from its hinges and crushing the pillars that opened into the bottom floor.

A beast shoved her from behind and she stepped into the monastery. The chittering of monsters and spidery feet echoed in the dark. The inner walls moved with the bodies of the creatures that climbed up and onto the ceiling. Red eyes turned her way in interest as she walked to the stairs.

She took each step carefully, hoping to avoid the slithering black vines that moved along the stairs and through the banister. The beasts slipped in front of her as if to lead her to where she was supposed to go. She stepped into the hall and glanced at the main dining hall. The windows had all been broken. Vines had penetrated the windows and now covered the floor and tables. They had defiled everything in that room.

A whip-like tail curled around her wrist and pulled her forward with the rest of her demonic entourage. It cut into her flesh as it wound tighter with each step. It hissed through its glass teeth, a threat that if she did not keep moving it would make her move. It pulled her along and it soon became clear that they were headed to the gym.

They approached the double doors into the gym, but the doors were no longer there. The entryway had been invaded just like everything else.

She walked into the large gym, but everything had changed. The far wall had collapsed and now the floor was broken open into a large trench within the earth below it. The beasts that had surrounded her now skittered away into the room and took their places among the other creatures that sprawled throughout the place and watched her.

The sky seemed to clear the moment she entered and a shaft of silver moonlight spilled into the space that was once her gym. It shone like a spotlight down on the remnants of the far wall, and to the figure that stood on the chunks of masonry that remained.

Abaddon.

He had survived the pit and the fireball that consumed the building. Everything Gideon did was for nothing.

"Miss me yet?" he said and jumped off the stones. He sauntered across the room, glancing down into the trench. "I thought I would do a little redecorating."

"How are you here?" she spoke as she looked at him.

"Easy," he said with a smile and his hands held out before him. "I am all powerful. You can't stop me. But you know something, we really don't need to be at odds with one another. I know you used to like me. I think we can make it work."

"Go to Hell," she said and backed away from him.

"Been there, done that," he said and lost his smile. "Not interested. Now, you don't have to die here tonight. I'm a reasonable guy."

He walked in and out of the shadows. In the darkness, his eyes glowed orange, but in the light they were Jason's blue. He stepped around her and she turned to watch him.

"What are you saying?" she asked.

"A truce. I don't kill you, and you promise to stay at my side. You give me your sword, you give up your power. You be my slave, and I will protect you. Nobody will ever harm you. I can make sure of that. And I'll be the most popular guy in Hell with a Seraph on his arm."

"Hmm," she said and then glared at him. "Tempting, but I think I'll pass."

His eyes turned angry and viscous. "Don't be so hasty to dismiss my generous offer. I will only offer it this once."

She glanced back to the trench and the jagged edges that had broken down the first few feet of the gap like shelves along the abyss. She stepped away from the edge and backed to the door.

"Final offer," he said with a growl.

"No way, you bastard," she said and drew her sword. The blue light lit the small corner where she stood. She stepped back and held the katana in a steady grasp before her, daring him to come at her.

He snarled with anger and she could have sworn that his eyes blazed brighter. Like a predator stalking his prey, he moved around her and dipped into the shadows. His eyes disappeared and his form blended into the dark recesses of the gym.

Everything fell silent. His footsteps vanished along with his silhouette. She could only hear her own breathing that came out in little white wisps in the cold air. The light of her sword spread down her arms and over her chest, but she could not see much beyond that.

The shadows morphed to her side and she turned just in time to see him coming at her. At first it appeared as Jason's body, but as it moved toward her, his skin darkened and stretched, bulging over thick muscle and bone that grew from within his body. The demon bounded for her, its legs becoming sinewy haunches that ran with the force of a train. It stretched its arms for her and black claws flashed in the moonlight. She lunged and brought her sword through the center of its gravity. Abaddon dodged back as its form continued to change, its muscles rolling around its back until the creature stood over ten feet tall. The demon recoiled and forced its hulking arm around to catch her in the face. She fell to the ground, her vision spinning.

Abaddon rushed at her again, and she rolled off to her side as he neared her. Nikka jumped to her feet and dodged to the left as the full weight of the demon bowled down toward her. It's enormous hands smashed against the stone where she had just been lying, sending shards of rock shooting in all directions. The dust cleared and Abaddon glanced up to where she now crouched. The beast rose on its haunches again.

She saw him step back and swung her sword, ready to catch his neck, but he leaned back enough to miss the tip. He grasped her wrist that held the sword and yanked her into the shadows with him. She fell to the ground as Abaddon twisted her arm above her head and pinned her to the ground.

With his other hand, he raked his thick, black claw down across her shoulder, stabbing into her flesh. She screamed as the talon pierced through her coat and entered just under her collarbone.

"Why won't you accept my offer?" The demon's voice rumbled in the darkness, no longer any hint of Jason within this creature.

Her fingernails clawed at his arm. "I would rather die."

"But you would rather be with Gideon? With Pazuzu? If you only knew the things he had done."

She felt the shudder of pain erupt from the wound in her shoulder. "You know nothing about him."

"No. You don't." He yanked his claw from her shoulder.

The pain of it leaving her flesh was almost as awful as when he stabbed her. He still held fast to her arm that held the sword, and with a crushing blow he pounded her wrist into the concrete. The sword slipped from her fingers when she could no longer feel them.

The blue light of her sword died out when she lost it. Then, he grabbed her and lifted her off her feet.

"I've killed better Seraphs than you." He growled at her, a sound that thundered against the stones surrounding the trench.

Then his body morphed again, the thick muscles around the demon's bones twisted and rolled until she could see Jason's face. His powerful arms still held her above the ground, his face grinning below eyes that still burned orange. She knew that this was it. He wanted her to see him one last time before he killed her. He wanted her to know that she could do nothing to him, no matter what form he took.

He threw her back toward the chasm. She hit the rocks with her hip first and tumbled backwards into the trench. At first she only saw the black gaping hole. The sky spun around in a dizzying whorl of stars and deep blackness. Her hand caught a jagged rock as her legs fell over the edge. The pain in her shoulder and hip nearly took her consciousness, but her hand held tight to the rock. It was the only thing that felt real to her right now.

The abyss seemed to breathe its stench of decay all over her. Her fingers slipped a little and she could envision the pluming flames of the portal as Gideon had fallen over the side. She now knew why he had done this.

Gideon couldn't have killed Abaddon or closed the portal. He had known that all along. Only the Seraph could do something like that.

He had to kill the rest of the horde that surrounded them. He needed to get Abaddon alone with her, because she could kill him if he didn't have his reinforcements. And these slimy Hell beasts that infested her former home were an improvisation on Abaddon's part. He had nothing else to grasp onto. He was alone now and desperate to take control.

She felt the strength return to her arm, and then she saw the light sparkle under her skin along the tattoos. The power was like a living thing: it knew when it was needed. She pulled herself onto the small shelf of rock and swung her legs over the side. With the power surging through her veins, she didn't need to catch her breath like she normally would. Instead, she stood on the ledge and faced him.

Abaddon had his back to her, but he must have sensed her ascension onto the edge of the trench. He held onto her sword, but it failed to come to life with fire in his hands.

"Back for more?" he said with a twisted laugh.

The power raced into every cell, every vessel, and every muscle in her body. It grew, feeding on itself, until it was ready to explode. The last time she felt this she wasn't able to control it and it burst from her like a bolt of lightning. But now, she wanted it. She needed it.

Then a sound came from the darkest shadows of the woods. At first it was a subtle hum, something that you might dismiss as a ringing in your ears. It fluctuated and warped into a whistle; it became so loud that it almost pierced her eardrums. The sound rose in pitch and frequency at the same time as the light burst from her just as it had the other day. It became a strong, steady beam that held her in place.

Abaddon fell backwards and shielded his eyes from the light that surrounded her.

She looked up into the shaft of light that emerged from the center of her body. There was only light there. The sound had stopped, leaving her in silence and peace. In this space of light, she felt no pain. Within the folds of it, she thought she saw a figure moving in and out, but it was something that wanted to see her. It meant her no harm, but it wanted to help her. She saw its hand coming to her and placed its fingers in the center of her chest. A warm ripple expanded from its touch, erasing her anger and her despair, replacing it with hope.

A sudden searing pain moved along the skin of her chest. She remembered the pain from a moment in her past, something that she had tried to keep in the furthest corners of her memories. It was the same pain that had tortured her in the light before she awoke as the Seraph. She looked down and saw a new mark etched into her skin in the center of her chest. It glowed like moonlight and then faded to a black tattoo, curving and beautiful, just like the other sigils on her body..

The light surrounding her ebbed away and she found herself in the shadows of the broken monastery. Abaddon took his hand away from his eyes and gazed at her with blazing red eyes.

"What did you do?" he shouted at her.

When she looked at him, she knew what she was meant to do. Whether it was from the new mark etched into her chest or not, everything became calm and clear. In his face, for only a second, she saw Jason and heard his voice, even if it had come in a dream.

Don't let me die.

Abaddon rose to his feet, his tall and muscular frame standing a good foot above her. Nikka strode with confidence to him, fear no longer a part of her. He lunged at her, but she swiped away his hand. In that moment, the power rushed into her fingers. The light shone through her eyes and her tattoos glimmered. The mark in the center of her chest glowed in a blue light as her hand plunged into his chest.

Abaddon wailed and froze. Her fingers found the monster inside him, writhing and fighting to stay inside its host. A monstrous sound rose from his throat where she had grasped him. She pulled it out and it began to tear away. The creature emerged with its blackened claws and black scaled skin, muscles rippling over its frame. The creature's face emerged from Jason's face, yellow jaundiced eyes staring at her as its jaws snapped at her neck. The beast had been so large and hulking before and it fought against the grip she had on its throat. But it could not defeat the power that she had now, a gift given to her from some higher source.

It ripped free from the human, and the body that was Jason fell unconscious to the ground. The fiend in her hand struggled and fought. It was much stronger than the drones that she had removed in the past. She reached to the sword on the ground. The demon screeched and screamed in anger. The blue flame glowed against its skin.

She dropped the creature and swung the blade. Before its body even hit the ground, she had severed its head. The beast burst into sparks like a faulty firework and then puffed into a cloud of yellow smoke.

The air cleared and she felt the chill of it against her skin again. The night had grown silent. The distant wail of sirens hardly broke the peace of the forest around the monastery grounds. Even the church had grown still. The creatures that had infested it had disappeared with their master. The vines withered and turned to ash.

A groan sounded at her feet and she glanced down to see Jason lying on the broken stones. She crouched and her fingers touched his neck. His pulse was present and strong.

He opened his eyes and she could see the ocean blue in the moonlight. He appeared to be human again and looked the way she had remembered him from the moment she first met him in the library.

"I know you," he spoke, his voice weak and raspy.

She smiled and helped him sit upright. He watched her as he rose like he could not get enough of her. "You're real."

"Yeah," she nodded.

He grasped her hand with shaking fingers. "I remember you. I saw you in the library."

Had he been there, seeing what Abaddon was doing the whole time?

"I tried to warn you," he said. "But you couldn't hear me."

But she knew that his message had come through. He would never believe it, but she had seen him in her dreams. She knew that they were real visions now.

"And I think . . . I was in love with you," he said while he looked into her eyes.

All the raw beauty and allure that had caught her attention now came flooding back. This was the true man that she had first seen. Abaddon may have possessed him, but he was still there and fought back.

And she didn't let him die.

There must have been a reason for it.

She grasped his hand and embraced him. His strong arms wrapped around her like a familiar friend. She felt the same strength and warmth in his torso as she did the first time she had touched him, riding on the back of

232

the motorcycle. He buried his head in her neck, his breath brushing against her skin.

The city was empty for her now. With her communication in the light she knew there were other places that needed her. The portal had opened its fetid mouth and spewed out a host of creatures that had escaped into the world. Abaddon might be gone, but those that had escaped needed to be found and destroyed. That's why she had been saved by Gideon, and that was why he had given her the knowledge that he had.

And with him in her arms, she knew Jason would follow her anywhere. He was now just as much a part of this.

CHAPTER 39

AS THE SONG GOES, let me please introduce myself.

But you probably already know who I am. Hell, anybody with a Black Sabbath album should know who I am.

I've had to come up here and address the problem of a certain woman that decimated my legion. How she managed it, I don't really know, but I have my suspicions.

That doesn't matter anymore. What matters is that I have had to come to this garbage dump and straighten out a few things. I've never really liked coming to Las Vegas, but it is what it is. This place is hardly worth my concern. These people are already on the proverbial highway to Hell. There is very little that I have left to do here.

No. What matters is where did the girl go? And why was the Seraph a woman this time? That single change in the rules ruined everything, took away my High General and now she disappeared.

I could think of these things until this world burned to the ground, but I don't have that kind of time.

This limousine. This suit. A man of wealth and taste, right? These things are nothing, but they seem to evoke the proper response that I expect when coming to a cesspool like this. Even this face, which I am told is one of the most popular right now in theaters all over the world, seems to get the ladies right out of their clothes. I can't say that I don't love it when the women here fawn over me and would do anything to sleep with me. I have taken my share of souls that way.

But taking that kind of soul is just child's play. It's too easy. Too pedestrian.

The fall of a Seraph, though. Now that's what I'm talking about. I would love to see that, and maybe there is a way now that the Seraph is a woman. Just got to hit the right nerve.

I can see the hotel coming up. The driver is doing his best to get around the crowds of tourists that have thronged along the sidewalks. When I walk in they will take their pictures and videos, but they don't really know who I am. They only think they know. The chauffeur opens the door and I step out into the hot desert air.

I hate this place.

I walk into the hotel, or rather the gaudy representation of Paris, although it is more of an embarrassment compared to the real thing. My servants greet me and take me to the one who can tell me how the Seraph killed Abaddon the way she did. That kind of shit is not supposed to happen.

More importantly, I desire to know how it is that Pazuzu has walked back into my fold. I've missed him, in any way that a master could miss his servant. I'm sure that he will have much to tell me about this Seraph and where he has been this long while. It shouldn't be long now that I can have him back in my ranks and step into the position that Abaddon held these many centuries. Something tells me that Pazuzu is the key to the Seraph, and you damn sure better bank on me using that to my advantage.

So I am eager to speak to him, even if I must step among the mortals as though I was one of them. My time on this plain is hopefully very short-lived. I can't stand the sounds or the smells of it, but that is no matter. In due time, it will fall just like the walls of Jericho.

I walk past the throng of women and into the hotel elevators. The car rises as I patiently bide my time on the way to the suite at the top of the building where I will discover the truths that await me.

And just like the song, I am pleased to meet you and I hope that you guessed my name.

About the Author

 When she isn't delivering babies, Carrie Merrill is a prolific writer who has been putting pen to paper since the age of 8, when she wrote her first story about a dragon that lived in a cave across the river from her house in Idaho. A day has not gone by since that time when she didn't have a story floating around in her head. She is currently a full-time OB/GYN in Montana with her six rescue cats when she isn't writing about the things that lurk in the dark.